A
WORLD
LIKE THIS

Helen Benedict

A World Like This

E. P. DUTTON   NEW YORK

Copyright © 1990 by Helen Benedict

All rights reserved. Printed in the U.S.A.

Publisher's Note: *Bullwood Hall is real, but all the characters and events in this book are fictitious. Any resemblance between them and actual events or persons, living or dead, is purely coincidental.*

No part of this publication may be reproduced or transmitted in any form or by any means, electronic or mechanical, including photocopy, recording, or any information storage and retrieval system now known or to be invented, without permission in writing from the publisher, except by a reviewer who wishes to quote brief passages in connection with a review written for inclusion in a magazine, newspaper, or broadcast.

*Published in the United States by E. P. Dutton,
a division of Penguin Books USA Inc.,
2 Park Avenue, New York, N.Y. 10016.*

*Published simultaneously in Canada
by Fitzhenry and Whiteside, Limited, Toronto.*

Library of Congress Cataloging-in-Publication Data

*Benedict, Helen.
A world like this / Helen Benedict.
p.   cm.
ISBN 0-525-24831-5
I. Title.
PS3552.E5397W67   1990*
813'.54—dc20   *89-34509*
                                                      CIP

1   3   5   7   9   10   8   6   4   2

First Edition

The first chapter of A World Like This *was published, in slightly different form, in* The Ontario Review, *Fall-Winter 1987–88.*

To Steve

ACKNOWLEDGMENTS

My thanks go to the MacDowell Colony and the Cummington Community of the Arts for time and peace; to Seán McConville, for interesting me in prisons in the first place; to the Slattery family, especially Mrs. Slattery for her hospitality, Jim for his enthusiasm, and Helen and Eamonn for their invaluable tour; to Elinor Nauen, Johnny Stanton, and the rest of the group for listening; to Marion and Burton Benedict, Peter Chapman, Rob Cohen, Charlotte Innes, Roberta Israeloff, and Joan Silber for their generous reading and comments; to my son, Simon, for listening with his (then) four-year-old wisdom and laughing in the right places; and finally, of course, to Stephen O'Connor, my companion in trouble and triumph, for his sensitive editing, patient readings, and tremendous faith.

AUTHOR'S NOTE

At the time this novel is set, 1975, Borstals were prisons in Britain for boys or girls aged between fifteen and twenty-one. Most Borstals were "open" and run much like reform schools in the United States—the inmates slept in dormitories and were allowed to roam quite freely—but a few, like Bullwood Hall, were "closed" and the inmates were locked in cells. The main difference between Borstals and prisons is that Borstal youths were given indeterminate sentences between six months and two years, rather than sentences of a set length. How much time they actually served depended more on their behavior inside than on their crime.

In the 1970s, many of the girls sentenced to Borstals had not committed one serious crime but a series of petty thieveries and misdemeanors, such as shoplifting, prostitution, passing bad checks, or using drugs. Most of them were products of broken or foster homes, orphanages or other institutions, and they usually had a history of running away from these places. A few of them had committed GBH (grievous bodily harm) and other violent crimes, but it was generally acknowledged that the courts put these girls in Borstal simply because they didn't know what else to do with them.

The girls ranged in age from fourteen to twenty-two, although legally they were not supposed to be in Borstal until fifteen, and tended to come from the poorer cities of northern England, Ireland, and Scotland—Birmingham, Manchester, Liverpool, Dublin, Glasgow. Seventy percent of them had been raped by relatives at home. At least 60 percent of them returned to Borstal, and later to prison, over and over again throughout their lives.

In an attempt to crack down on the "liberal" treatment of criminals, Margaret Thatcher's government did away with the Borstal system by the end of the 1970s, and youthful offenders are now given determinate sentences and sent to adult prisons. Bullwood Hall, a former Borstal in Essex, still exists, but is now a prison that holds both adolescent girls and adult women.

HELEN BENEDICT, 1990

. . . in the end you turn your back on reality and live in a contorted world of make-believe . . . there is no daylight in this world . . . and it is in this darkness that we find peace and the ability to live in a world of our own . . .

—a life prisoner quoted by Stanley Cohen and Laurie Taylor in *Psychological Survival, The Experience of Long-Term Imprisonment, 1972*

A
WORLD
LIKE THIS

1

Sometimes, when Reardon walked down the wing, she could see Brandy's fingers poking out of the spyhole. Each cell door had a hole with a flap on it that the prison officers could lift from the outside, and the holes were just big enough for three fingers to squeeze through and grab a cigarette. Brandy wiggled them at her, taunting—nail-bitten and nicotine-stained like the fingers of an old woman, ink-blotched and chubby like the fingers of a child.

Brandy knew how to torture Reardon with that hole. Oh, Reardon could open the flap and look in whenever she wanted, catch her on the toilet or feeling herself in bed, but that was nothing compared to what Brandy could do to her. Reardon was amazed at how much power a person could have when she was locked up, how much she could say with a one-inch hole and half an eye. Brandy leered at her or pushed a bit of mouth up and flapped her tongue, making the hole obscene. Reardon tried to punish her by holding back the cigarettes until she whimpered or by banging down the flap hard on her fingers, but Brandy wouldn't stop.

The girl had that kind of strength; Reardon recognized it straightaway. Even on Brandy's first evening in the wing, during free association, she was able to draw the other inmates to her, control them. It wasn't that she was pretty—her face was scarred with acne, her hair hung in greasy strings, and she was shaped like a sugar cube on legs (someone said she looked like the lead singer of The Animals, Eric Burdon)—but she had a stillness about her that was rare in Borstal girls. Most of them cowered in their cells on their first night, or swaggered around claiming old friends if they'd been in before. Not Brandy. She owned a little tin, the kind that cough drops come in, and spent the entire evening poring over its contents as if they were the Dead Sea Scrolls. She created an invisible wall around herself with that tin that acted as both a magnet and a defense. When the girls began to gravitate towards her, she gave them just enough of a peek to keep them curious but respectful; she even had Reardon craning over the heads to see. Brandy knew prison ways, all right. She was in for robbing an old woman, and this was her second time inside a Borstal. She knew how to give out just enough cigarettes and secrets to keep everyone under her spell.

Reardon had been working at Bullwood Hall for two years when Brandy came, and she considered herself one of the best warders in the place. When she'd taken the job everyone at home had said she was too good for it, but she knew they didn't understand. "Shouldn't a clever, strapping girl like you do something more suitable?" her mother had said. "Like what?" Reardon replied. "Be a factory girl all me life like you? That's not what I was made for. I'm not wasting me life at the end of a machine." Reardon believed that she was put on earth to help the unhappy people of this world, to give girls like Brandy a little Christian faith and self-respect. So when she arrived at Bullwood Hall she quickly made herself known as a reformer. She got an old drunk named Lindy fired after she caught her throwing away the girls' letters instead of censoring them, and another officer reprimanded for her habit of spying on the inmates as they bathed and threatening to take their knickers down. Reardon considered herself the only officer in the place who saw the girls as human.

Sometimes she tried to picture the way she must have appeared to Brandy when they first met, standing tall and strong in her uniform, keys jangling, head up. She knew she had no

2

looks, her father had made that clear with his jokes about pig eyes and ax jaws, but her hair was nice, thick and brown. She always kept it long and fastened on top of her head in a big shining pile, just to hint that there was more to her than people knew. She thought later that it was probably her hair, catching the light from the wing windows and glistening, that had first attracted Brandy, for in those early weeks she would often look up to find the girl staring at it. Then Brandy would blush and turn away. You don't see a lot of blushes in Borstal.

Perhaps it was the blush that set Reardon noticing Brandy at first, not the tin; Reardon didn't know. But she began to take special notice of the girl, hoping that this one was different, someone with a bit of heart for a change—the one she had been waiting for, the one she could save. She stood near Brandy whenever she could: by the cell while Brandy scrubbed the floor; in the workroom where the inmates had to fold boxes or put together Thermos flasks and Tinkertoys; during the meals the girls took along the vast portable table that stretched down the middle of the wing. Reardon tried not to let on that she was watching Brandy, of course, for she didn't want to be laughed at, but she couldn't keep away. At first she thought that she was only developing another of those one-sided obsessions that hit her once in a while like a bout of the flu, but gradually she noticed that Brandy was seeking her out, too. Soon the two of them had such a strong pull on each other that Reardon could feel it even with her eyes closed. If she just stood near Brandy, their skins crackled like sparklers.

One day, after a few weeks of this silent flirtation, Brandy came to breakfast looking different. She had been dressing in brown prison overalls up until then, with straps that fell down all the time and her shirt open past her bra, but that day she had put on a skirt and green socks. She'd even washed her hair and tied it up in a cheap ribbon. Of course her hair was still half-dyed like the others' and she had one of those new tattoos on her knuckles that spelled the word LOVE with the blood still drying, but Reardon was touched to see her at least trying to look pretty. She had seen so many girls come in and let themselves go, slipping into the disheveled, slutty look of the teenage con: mismatched clothes, undone buttons, and those ugly tattoos they all insisted on even though they were against the rules, scratching themselves with pins and rubbing in ink or makeup, writing FREEDOM on their foreheads or FUCK on their arms and not even squealing when the doctor cut it out. It made her ache to see Brandy trying to fight the Borstal look. Reardon knew that Brandy didn't have visitors—the girl was doing it for her, she was certain, and no one had done that in all her years of hoping.

Brandy caught Reardon studying her and smiled directly at her for the first time, right into her face, open and raw. She pinned Reardon to the wall with that gaze until Reardon felt as if a wire had reached out from Brandy's green and steady eyes and slit her open, spilling every secret she'd ever had onto the ground for all to see. Her uniform and her keys and her hair and her height didn't matter anymore. She only needed Brandy to stretch out and touch her.

When Brandy at last turned away, Reardon scurried into the staff room. She sat and pretended to go over the inmates' letters for a while—ostensibly to black out anything they said about the Borstal—but was unable to see a word. She could feel Brandy there on the other side of the wall; if she just stood up she would see her through the window. Reardon knew she could do whatever she wanted about Brandy, right then or later: call her into the staff room on a pretext; get her a job in the officers' quarters so they could meet in secret; visit her at night in her cell. Reardon had seen other warders do the same. Brandy couldn't avoid her if she wanted to.

As soon as it was lunchtime Reardon was able to leave. She walked across the bleak courtyard to the officers' quarters and went straight into her room and locked the door. All the officers had to live on the Borstal grounds, but instead of the giant brick block dotted with square windows that was the inmates' home, their building was low, bright and motel-like; it even had wall-to-wall carpets and white-painted rooms. The beds and tables were bolted down and the cupboards and refrigerator were padlocked, but there were no five-inch-thick doors with spyholes in them, no bars on their windows.

Reardon looked in the mirror to see if she'd changed, lay on the bed, got up, and lay back down. She had never been wanted before and she had to feel what it was doing to her. For most of her life she had fancied the girls, but had never let herself do anything about it; she'd been too ashamed. Now her shame was giving way to longing so easily that it shocked her. She looked at the blank walls of her room and tried to recall her life before Bullwood Hall, tried to resurrect a world that wasn't so small and hot and too tight to breathe. She tried to save herself.

Reardon had grown up in Liverpool, in council housing that

looked like the Borstal but was rougher and dirtier. The walls were like paper there, and sounds screamed around her all day long: the neighbors whacking their kids, her sisters squabbling over makeup, the boys who came to snog with them but who never looked at her, her dad shouting that she should work on a bus with him 'cause she looked like the back of one. Her mother had a job in a packing factory, putting jars of jam into boxes all day, and Reardon worked next to her for six years after she left school.

When Reardon wasn't in the factory, she was in church. The one she went to in her local parish was so stark and cold that her breath always surrounded her in a fog and her hands would stiffen until she could hardly curl them up. She spent hours there, praying, dreaming, staring at the altar waiting for the right idea to come that would prove she was different from her mother and her layabout sisters. The priest stopped even noticing her after a while, she was there so often. She never let him talk to her—she didn't like his smarmy ways and toffee-nosed accent—but she tried to act as holy as she could. It was stay there or go home, and that was even worse. Whenever Reardon thought of home, all she could feel was the cold. It was everywhere she went, from the house to the church to the factory, and it made her fingers so numb around the jam jars it seemed they'd stick to the glass and get stamped and packed and shipped off to some posh lady's kitchen, where the lady would spread them on toast and have them for tea.

Reardon opened her eyes. Outside, the girls were shouting in the courtyard, where they were having their after-lunch exercise. Some officers came into the building, slamming doors and grunting. Reardon had listened to these same sounds every day for two years, just as she had felt the same sensations circling around in slow numbness, with no change ever until that morning. She shut her eyes and thought of Brandy's look. She put her hands up to her face to feel what Brandy had seen, and touched it where it was still young, in the cheeks and the chin. She felt her hair and imagined what it might be like to have someone take it down and caress it, which had never happened in all her twenty-six years. She kept her eyes shut and moved her hands slowly over her lips as if someone were kissing them, feeling her lips with her fingertips to see what they might be like for that someone. She unbuttoned her blouse and ran her hands lightly over her breasts, trying to think what it would be like to have that happen, too, to feel them as soft and feminine, not just as stuff pushed into a uniform. She pulled her hands over her ribs, which that someone would still be able to feel even though she had been putting on weight from never leaving the Borstal. And she pushed her hands down under her skirt to the part of her no one else had ever touched. She tried to imagine that she had a man somewhere who would want to spread his body over hers and breathe her breath and hold her with a fervor she supposed was called love, but she couldn't. Her will had softened like a sleeping muscle.

At two it was her shift again so she got up, washed, and straightened her clothes. She hadn't eaten but didn't care. She walked back to the Borstal building, unlocking and locking gates as she went, feeling like Cinderella going to the ball, not Roanna Reardon going to a prison wing. She hardly noticed the graying, whitewashed walls or the deadened faces of the other officers for a change. Brandy was in the workroom at this time of day, earning her 40p credit a week, and it was Reardon's job to supervise the afternoon there. As she entered the room her legs turned weak.

She saw Brandy straightaway at a table near the far windows. The girl didn't look up when she came in and Reardon was afraid that she hadn't even noticed her. Brandy was more of a mess than she had been in the morning—the ribbon was slipping out of her hair and her face had settled into a glum frown. Reardon meant to walk in the opposite direction, to force Brandy to look around for her, but she felt pulled towards the girl like a fish on a line. She managed to stop and tell off a couple of the other inmates on the way, but she couldn't resist that pull. It was as if the line were dragging her straight across the room.

When she got to Brandy the girl pretended not to see her at first. Reardon could do nothing but stand in front of her anyway, terrified that she'd imagined the whole thing. Her body squirmed to get away in case someone noticed, in case Brandy mocked her, in case she was wrong, but she was rooted, helpless. She could have collapsed and begged. Brandy looked up at last, running her eyes over Reardon slowly.

"You're doing that wrong, y'know," Reardon said, taking a box from her and folding it.

"Nah, I'm not," Brandy objected, but she was laughing. She cocked her head to one side, chewing her gum loudly, and dropped her voice, a low Birmingham drawl that all by itself gave Reardon a thrill. "Show me again, then." Her tongue was very pink.

6

Reardon blushed. She picked up another box, folded and packed it, while Brandy crossed her arms, leaned against the wall, and watched. "See?" Reardon said, only just daring to lift her eyes. "You do it like that."

"All right, Officer." Brandy was being gently insolent, the way a girl flirts with a soldier. "Thanks a lot." She flipped her hair over her shoulder and caught Reardon's eyes again.

Reardon blushed deeper and looked down. Brandy's ribbon was lying on the floor. "Your ribbon's dropped," she said, pointing.

Brandy bent down and picked it up. "Here, miss, you have it. It'd look better in your hair." She held it out in front of her discreetly, so that no one else could see. Reardon caught a whiff of soap and sweat. She grabbed it and hid it in her palm.

"Thanks," she whispered, and hurried away.

You make things happen slowly in prison. Everyone knows that. It passes the time better, and passing the time is what it's all about. So Reardon didn't do anything more that day. She put the ribbon in her bra, where she could feel it scratch, and acted as if it were a day like any other. In the evening she sat far away from Brandy, talking to another officer and shouting occasionally at a couple of inmates necking in the TV room. Yet her eyes were filled with the girl. Brandy kept darting looks at her, or walking close and then away again. Once she began laughing with a group of girls, even putting her arm around one, which Reardon had never seen her do before, and Reardon would have been jealous except she saw Brandy glancing at her to make sure she'd seen. She felt Brandy controlling her with that wire again, pulling it tight until she was swiveling Reardon's eyes whichever way she wanted. Reardon began to think about Brandy's hands and how they'd feel. But she didn't want anything to happen yet. Maybe never.

For weeks the two of them went on like that. The days would have seemed the same to anyone else, but for Reardon it was as if the sun had burst through and lit up each moment. She lost weight because she was too excited to eat. Every minute on the wing was as exhilarating and terrifying as walking on the edge of a cliff. Brandy began to look bigger to her, and she felt shrunken. If Brandy smiled Reardon's heart would lift up to the light, if she turned away the ache would nearly bring Reardon to her knees. They played their prison game, so subtle that on some days Reardon was afraid it was all in her head. Five weeks of inside time

7

went by this way, with the inmates turning from fourteen to fifteen or seventeen to eighteen, losing their youth forever as the days inched along with every moment prescribed and inescapable. As Reardon had been losing her youth, too, until Brandy had sent time spinning.

At last the day came for Reardon to start the night shift again, when she had to patrol the wing and pass out cigarettes to the girls through the spyholes. All month she'd thought about it, trying to picture the scene. Sometimes she would imagine quietly unlocking Brandy's door, going inside, bowing her head while Brandy unpinned her hair. At other times she saw Brandy giving her an indifferent stare through the hole, turning her back. . . .

That night the courtyard was unusually quiet. Normally, once the girls were locked in, they would press their faces to the window bars and scream at one another for hours, their voices echoing over the valley. "All me love, Sarah!" "And mine!" "Susie, you owe me a packet of fags!" "I love you, I love you!" "I want to go home!" When Reardon first came those voices had given her the goose bumps, hoarse and sore and wild like pack animals in a trap. Some of the girls had almost no voices left they screamed so loud and so long. But that night only a few of them were shouting. Perhaps it was the full moon, Reardon didn't know, or the cold air. Her breath shot out in spurts, surrounding her and making her face wet. She shoved her hands into her pockets, hurrying her step and feeling her keys clank against her thigh. The chain-link fences around the Borstal loomed over her, tall and steel gray with giant rolls of barbed wire along the tops. Almost no one had ever escaped the place in the ten years or so it had been there. Reardon had never left, either, never gone farther than the village down the road, even on holidays. Most of the officers hadn't—they had nowhere to go. A cold feeling wormed through Reardon as she saw herself, a tall ugly woman in a uniform, striding into this prison she called a home, thinking she was in love with a sixteen-year-old con whom she knew was too sharp not to use her. This place is warped, Reardon thought.

But when she got inside, door after door, lock after lock, wall after wall, she forgot all that. She knew the feeling of every key, of every bar as she pulled open or pushed shut a gate. She knew the sound her feet would make in each hall and at each corner as the echo changed. She knew all the types of girls who came through there: the terrified first-timers; the Northerners like herself, undernourished and always looking for a fight; the West

Indians, as muscular and cocky as boys; the prostitutes, who never did up their buttons and slunk around like cats; the ones who always came back, too stupid or scared to make it out in the world. And she knew they'd all end up the same after a few weeks, sitting with their legs apart and their sleeves rolled up, holding their cigarettes like men between their thumbs and forefingers, eyeing each other greedily, wearing their love bites like necklaces. Knowing all that made her safe.

She got to the wing and saw the other officer out. During the day the Borstal was a screaming mayhem, not only because the girls had forgotten what a normal voice was, but because their noise was echoed and magnified by all the walls. But at night it was quiet inside, for even when the girls were still shouting out of their windows their voices didn't penetrate the thick cell doors. By the time Reardon got there, almost all the lights were out and the white walls glowed like piled bones. Under each door a beam of light filtered across the floor. It gave her chills even though she was used to it. She was feeling everything in a new way, as if her skin had been pulled off. She walked slowly around the bottom floor, lifting the spyhole covers, shoving two or three cigarettes in. "Ta, miss." "Ooh, lovely." "Just one more, please!" Then she went up to the top level where Brandy's cell was and did the rounds there. She left Brandy until last.

When she came to Brandy's door she stopped because she could hardly breathe. She'd been letting this moment fill her dreams for so long that she felt as if she were about to step onto a highwire. She tapped on the door and slowly opened the spyhole to look in. Brandy was right there, her eye pressed to the hole. She stared at Reardon for a long time. "Evenin', miss," she finally whispered, and drew back a little so that Reardon had to push her face closer. Brandy was still dressed and her hands were behind her back. "Could you help me, miss? Me zip's broken."

Reardon nodded, her guts in a twist. Quietly she unlocked the door, slipped into the cell, and rested the door against the jamb behind her, hiding herself and Brandy from the world. She held out a handful of cigarettes. Brandy took them without saying anything, cupping her hand under Reardon's so that they touched. She hid them inside her pillow, where the girls always hid things.

"Where's it broken?" Reardon stammered. They were still whispering. Brandy pulled her skirt around and pointed to the zip, halfway open. Reardon knelt, just the way she had in her

9

dreams, and pretended to work at it, feeling Brandy's heat so near her she could taste it. The zip wasn't jammed of course but they both kept pretending in order to prolong the moment as long as they could. She pulled the zip down while Brandy stood there, then Brandy put her hands on Reardon's hair.

"You've got beautiful hair, miss," she whispered. "How long is it?" Reardon felt her undoing the pins, releasing her hair so that it fell heavily, and she wanted to cry. She put her arms around Brandy and pressed her face into the girl's belly, hugging her yet afraid to move. Brandy stroked Reardon's hair, lifting it and dropping it in strands like a curtain of beads. Reardon held her tight, the first time she'd held anyone since she was a child.

"Let me get the light," Brandy said, and gently pushed off Reardon's arms. She stepped out of her skirt and walked across the room with Reardon kneeling there, watching. She turned off the light, got onto the bottom bunk, and smiled. "What's your name, miss?"

"Roanna." Reardon could barely whisper it, her mouth was so dry. She looked at Brandy from the middle of the floor, waiting to be told what to do.

For months Reardon visited Brandy whenever she had the chance. She stayed on night shift as long as she could without arousing suspicion, got Brandy the job of cleaning the officers' quarters, and, sometimes, was able to find her there during the day so that they could grab a kiss and a cuddle behind a door. They were careful, knowing the trouble it would cause both of them if they were found out. They kept apart in front of everyone else and Brandy deflected suspicion by talking about a boyfriend called Jeff, a letter from whom she kept in that tin of hers with a photograph of her sister, Liz. Reardon didn't like that Jeff business at first, but Brandy told her not to worry—he was in Borstal, too—so Reardon stopped thinking about it. It didn't matter much anyway, she told herself, because all that counted was the present, every moment, the most alive she had ever been. The days swung giddily from delight to pain, depending on whether Brandy looked at Reardon with a smile or laughed too long with another girl, whether she slipped her a note or took some chewing gum from her with indifference, whether she called her miss or whispered her name.

One night they were lying on Brandy's bed, Reardon so big she could hardly fit, their hands in each other's shirts, when

Brandy asked, "Whatever made you became a screw anyroad, Roanna?"

Reardon didn't reply at first, reluctant to reveal her missionary dreams even to Brandy. "I did it to help people," she said cautiously.

Brandy laughed. "Help people? What makes you think locking people up would help anyone?" She looked at Reardon, expecting her to laugh, too.

"No, I'm serious," Reardon said. "There's a lot of help needed in here, an' you know it."

"The only help that'd do any good 'round here is a bloody miracle, if you ask me. A bomb or summat—blow us all up to heaven and turn us into angels."

"No, Brandy, it's more'n that. God put me here to help you girls, I know it. I can feel it in me heart."

Brandy glanced at her. "You must be joking. You think God makes people into screws?" She began to laugh again, but the expression on Reardon's face stopped her.

"No, I mean it," Reardon said gruffly, and she flushed and shifted on the bed. She told Brandy about how she'd watched her sisters become cheap and her mother get so tired her black eyes seemed to drip down her face, about how she wanted to help the girls here so they wouldn't have to end up like them. "I want to give the girls here some love, y'see, so they can leave this place with their heads held high. I want to help them understand God so they can learn how to be good."

Brandy shook her head. "God doesn't teach people to be good," she said, turning serious herself. "That's not what He does with His time. Look, if He was that interested in us, the world wouldn't be like it is, would it? There's enough rot in this place to make the devil jump for joy."

Reardon smiled. No one had ever listened to her like this, no one had ever paid her this much attention. It gave her hope that Brandy might see the light after all, change and find a mission, the way she had. "Well," she said gently, "but the Bible does say He gives us all the hard times to test us, remember."

"Test us for what, I'd like to know? To see if we know the rules? Play the rules an' you're good, break 'em an' you're bad? Is that what you think?" Brandy snorted and wrapped a strand of Reardon's hair around her fingers. "I've never understood what rules have got to do with being good or bad. We know all about living with rules in this place, don't we? Get up at this time, scrub out at that. Walk to the right, walk to the left. Lock up then and now and bloody once again. No screwing in the open, though everyone knows we do it. And does that make us good, eh? Don't make me laugh. Rules are made for breaking, everyone knows that. Maybe that sorta stuff's written in the Bible, Roanna, but all I'm saying is if being good just means following some fucking rule, then good isn't worth much. It's got to be deep inside you if it's going to mean anything."

"Yeah," Reardon said, "that's true if you look at it like that, I s'pose. But y'know, Brandy, I think you learn about goodness through love. A lot of people believe that God is love, and I think . . ."

Brandy giggled. "I don't think they meant this sorta love." She gave Reardon's breast a tweak.

Annoyed, Reardon pushed her hand off. "I'm serious, Brandy. If you can love, if you are loved, it gives you a pure heart, and that's where the goodness comes from. So spreading love is like spreading faith, you see."

Brandy leaned against the wall. "Is that what you're doing to me, then, spreading faith?"

Reardon colored. "I don't mean that. But don't you feel happier than before? I mean, don't you see now that you can do more than this with your life?" She nodded at the cell, its gray walls that Brandy had covered with pictures of pop stars, the toilet in the corner, the thick door that blocked out her life.

"What're you trying to do?" Brandy said with a grin. "Turn me into a screw? Or d'you just want to marry me and save me reputation?" She laughed and reached over to trace Reardon's nipple with her finger.

"You're just pretending not to understand." Reardon sighed and closed her eyes, helpless as always under Brandy's hands. "You know I love you."

Months went by. Brandy turned seventeen, Reardon twenty-seven. The winter came and went. Brandy marked a year off on her calendar. On some days the two of them got on better than others, of course, and it did seem to Reardon that sometimes Brandy had her mind elsewhere, but Reardon told herself that was normal in love. Especially Borstal love. After all, Brandy's life was hard with the other girls pressuring her to be like them, the routine that never changed, the seasons passing without her. So Reardon wasn't even counting the months because it seemed that every moment with Brandy could last forever, slow and easy and beautiful the way time can be when you have nowhere to go and no say over your own life.

One evening, as Reardon was walking towards the officers' building for a break, she bumped into Brandy on her way back from her cleaning shift. "Hullo, love," she said gently, looking around to make sure no one could see. Taking Brandy by the sleeve, she pulled her behind a door. "Everything all right?" Brandy was looking feverish, as if a sort of glitter had stuck to her face.

"Yeah, more'n all right. Look at this." She handed Reardon a note on prison stationery. GOVERNMENT PROPERTY was stamped at the top of the page. The phrase was even printed on the toilet paper. "Read it, go on. I got it from the Assistant Governor today."

Reardon opened the note and looked. "To Amanda Botley. Congratulations on your quarterly report. The Board has reviewed your case and herewith informs you that you will be released to the halfway house at Hill Hall on the 15th of January, pending continued Good Behavior."

"Y'know what that means?" Brandy said, her hoarse voice cracking. "Only three months left! Then I'll be outta this hellhole. It feels fucking marvelous, I can tell you."

"Good," Reardon said quietly. "That's nice."

"Yeah." Brandy smiled. "Well, I better get going. You coming tomorrow night?"

Reardon nodded and stared after her as she scurried back to the wing.

For the first few minutes it didn't mean much, just a number floating about like all the other numbers in that place—number of inmates, number of cells, number of keys, number of visitors, number of letters, number of gates and locks and walls and meals and boxes packed in the factory, number of days that opened and closed one after another with no change ever except a warm wind or a cold one. But three was a small number, small enough to blink away, and Reardon realized that when Brandy left she'd still be there, with nowhere to go and no one to talk to and touch and feel and brush her hair over and warm her heart with day in and day out, even in her dreams.

She stumbled into the officers' building in a daze. The other officers were still out, so she wandered the silent halls by herself. The thought of living there without Brandy opened such a panic in her that she couldn't stay still. She found herself in the kitchen, which was opposite her room, and, seeking comfort, unlocked the refrigerator. Other people's food: a meat pasty, a plate of eggs, a bottle of milk, a half-eaten cake left over from an officer's birthday the day before. She reached for the cake, knowing she shouldn't, picked up the knife beside it, cut a sliver and stuck it in her mouth. The cake looked so comforting and childish, so pink and brown and bright in the stark kitchen. It reminded her of her sisters' birthdays and of the way a sweet could make the tears and misery from a hard day at school go away. She cut another sliver and another, letting her worries dissolve with the sugary crumbs. When she heard some officers coming in, she guiltily shut the refrigerator and went into her room to think.

She sat on the bed with her head in her hands. The panic was returning. She couldn't think how she would bear it, going back to the routine she'd had before, back to the old numbness she'd wrapped around herself so that she could get through the days. She began to dream of being someone else—the sort of person who could throw in the job and go live with Brandy. Dimly she became aware of a commotion in the kitchen but she didn't pay attention at first, too absorbed in her dreams of being brave. But when she heard an officer say "Someone left the lock off, look!" she lifted her head to listen. "Look, it's almost gone! What a nerve! Who works here Tuesday P.M.s anyway?" She recognized Murdock's voice, an old-timer who'd always had it in for her. In a second, they were knocking on her door. She got up and opened it.

"Yeah?"

"Did you go into the kitchen this afternoon?"

"No, I only just got back. Why?" Reardon blinked innocently, the way she'd seen the girls do.

"Someone left the fridge lock off and one of the girls has nicked half a cake."

"Oh." She saw them looking at her, eyes glittering, like a bunch of skinny ravens. "Are you sure?"

"Course we're sure!"

Reardon looked at Murdock. "Well, who did it, d'you think?" she said.

"It must have been the girl on the P.M. shift today. At least half the cake was there this morning, wasn't it?" Murdock turned to one of the other officers, who nodded, then focused back on Reardon. "Do you have the roster?"

"Hold on a minute." Reardon opened her desk drawer and

pulled out the list of cleaning girls and their shifts. She handed it to Murdock, who looked down the list to Tuesday afternoon. Reardon already knew what she'd find so she stared at the wall, a heaviness like sand shifting through her veins. "Ah, I thought so," Murdock crowed. "It's your girl, isn't it? That Botley." Reardon nodded, not daring to think what Murdock was hinting at. "It's her, then." Satisfied, Murdock turned to the others. Reardon wanted to say something, she was about to try, but then Murdock spoke up again. "I suppose we ought to tell the Governor."

The other women nodded, barely containing their glee. Reardon looked from one to the other, trying to tell if they were only excited at having some action in this deathly place, or if they were jealous.

"That's her parole gone, then," Murdock said. "Serves her right, smug little blighter. I've never seen a girl so full of herself. Let's go and tell the Governor. Coming?" She turned to Reardon.

"No thanks. There seems to be enough of you already." Her sarcasm fell limp. She stood silently while they marched down the hall.

Reardon turned off the lights and lay down on her bed. In a minute she'd get up and straighten things out, she promised herself. In a minute. Meanwhile, she watched the room slowly darken, first to a dusky pink, then to blue, then gray. She knew she had six months of Brandy's life in her hands—she squirmed and sweated at the thought—and she knew that each passing moment made it harder to tell the truth, but still she couldn't move. She lay there for an hour, listening to the clock ticking, until she heard the officers come back, clucking in satisfaction over how Brandy's privileges would be revoked, her sentence extended. "How can you punish a girl like that just for taking a few bites of cake?" Reardon wanted to shout, forgetting for a moment that Brandy hadn't taken the cake at all. For most of the night she lay there like that, listening for Brandy's voice screaming along with the other girls' and waiting for her sense of justice, for her belief in God, for her self respect to make her get up and confess. But all the while, through her guilt and through her faith, through everything that she thought she knew about herself, she knew perfectly well that underneath, in the sinful depths of her soul, she was really thinking, Now I've got her for nine more months.

They broke the news to Brandy the next morning. In Bullwood Hall, where the girls were already convicted criminals, no one got a hearing for anything but the most serious of crimes. Brandy was found guilty instantly and when she denied it, Murdock barked at her and ordered her locked up in solitary for three days. Reardon was there when it happened, standing in a corner like a broom. Brandy looked at her, tears streaming, and shouted, "You tell 'em, miss, you tell 'em I didn't do it! Don't let them take me parole away, please!" Reardon looked down at the floor.

Reardon went to visit Brandy in solitary. It was a bare cell with a pad to sleep on and nothing else. She peered through the spyhole and saw the girl slumped against the wall. "Brandy," she whispered.

Brandy glanced up, her face drained and old-looking. "What're you doing here?"

"Don't be angry at me, please," Reardon said. "I couldn't do anything."

"I didn't do it, Roanna, I didn't! When I find out who took that fucking cake, I'm going to cut her face to ribbons, fucking cunt, cunt, cunt!" Brandy sounded almost tired, her anger had worn so deep. She looked at the hole pleadingly. "You believe me, don't you?"

"Yeah, yeah," Reardon said, glad Brandy couldn't see her. "Course I do, love."

Brandy stood up and paced the tiny room, passing in and out of Reardon's vision. "Why'd they put me in here, Roanna?" she said. "I don't understand why they're doing this to me. I feel like a fucking rat!" She kicked the wall. "They shouldn't do this to people, they shouldn't! I've only got one life!" She began pacing again, and Reardon could just see the glimmer of tears on her cheeks. "Nobody should have the right to treat human beings like this. It should be against the law! I mean, humans aren't animals, are they?" She looked at Reardon's eye framed against the hole. "Why are they doing this to me, Roanna?"

Reardon stared back at her. She had no idea how to answer, how to help. Everything seemed to have floated beyond her, to have grown larger than she could grasp.

"I dunno," she said finally. "Look, I'll try to help, Brandy, I will." Even she could hear the whine in her voice.

Brandy glared at the hole for a moment. "You're pathetic," she spat. "You're fucking pathetic." And she turned away.

When Brandy was released from solitary Reardon was relieved. She had spent three miserable days wondering if she should confess to Brandy, knowing she wouldn't, thinking that at least she should tell Brandy the truth: that she did it for love; that if Brandy had more time with her, where it was safe, it would do her good, protect her from the world out there where she'd only get into trouble again. But Reardon knew that Brandy would never believe her if she said such things. Like all the other girls, Brandy thought she'd straighten out once she was released—she had these ideas that she'd marry her Jeff when he got out and settle down with him, then become a hairdresser like her sister. "Let them dream," Reardon always said. All the warders knew that the girls would go crooked again within a month; after Borstal they couldn't stand life outside, not knowing where the next meal or bed would come from, and half of them were in love with someone inside anyway. Brandy may have thought she was different, but Reardon knew better.

As soon as Brandy was in her cell again Reardon went to visit her. Brandy looked up when she arrived and Reardon's heart lifted, thinking things would get back to normal now, but all the girl did was curl her lip. "I'm fed up with you," she said, her voice cold. "You've got no guts."

"Don't say that," Reardon whispered, shocked, closing the door behind them. "I couldn't help it."

"Oh yes you fucking could. You could get me outta this stinking Borstal fast if you wanted and you know it. I'm dying in here and you don't even give a shit!"

"But . . . what about me?" It was all Reardon could say. She meant how could Brandy be dying when she had her love, but the hate in Brandy's voice prevented her from being able to say anything right.

"Fuck you, that's what about you!" Brandy swerved towards her, her face suddenly red. "Leave me alone if you can't help me, just sodding leave me alone. Piss off and go and find some bloke outside and stop screwing little girls!"

"Don't." Reardon didn't know if she moaned, but she knew she tried to stretch out to Brandy, to stop her words, to reach back to the tenderness they'd had before. "You don't mean it, please."

"Get the fuck out of here or I'll scream!"

Reardon looked around at the darkened cell and imagined officers bursting in, Brandy shouting accusations in front of them, exposing her, shaming her. She backed away from the girl's furious eyes and stumbled out of the door, pressing her face against it as she shut it, and automatically turned the key. For a long time she stood there, her face against the steel.

A week later Brandy asked for a cellmate, and soon the two of them were walking about with those love-bite necklaces and their arms around each other as if they'd been married in heaven. Reardon and Murdock separated them but Brandy quickly took up with another inmate. One night she attacked a girl during free association, accusing her of taking the cake during the lunchtime shift and screwing up her parole. They tore each other's faces like paper while Reardon looked the other way. Before long Brandy was behaving like all the other girls, screeching, fighting, acting up, and she began to defy and mock Reardon, to torture her with that spyhole. But even when Reardon thought she was dying of the pain, when she knew she would never love anyone else, when the disappointment and guilt seemed to be crushing her and she felt her precious faith slipping away, she never blamed Brandy. She knew how hard it was to be good in a world like this.

2

Brandy stood in the visiting room, the one place where outsiders and inmates were allowed to meet, waiting for her mother to come and take her home. The room was huge and echoing, filled with plastic tables and chairs that gave it the air of an unused cafeteria, and Brandy was alone in it except for the prison officer watching her. She clutched the small duffel bag crammed with all her possessions to her chest, her knuckles growing cold and white, and tried not to feel afraid.

At last the door opened and Murdock walked in, followed by a tall young woman with hair in a fantastic array of blond spikes. Long, clanking earrings hung to her shoulders and her mouth was a loud purple. Brandy stared.

"Liz!" she said. "What the fuck are you doing here?"

"I thought I'd give you a surprise." Liz patted her younger sister on the shoulder and stepped back to look at how she had turned out. Brandy was dressed in her best skirt, a pleated green, and her cleanest yellow blouse. Her hair, dark at the roots and blond at the tips, was washed and tied back, and her eyes glared under bright green eyeshadow. She looked like a plump daffodil. "You have grown up," Liz said, chuckling. "You look a right mess, though. What the hell is that?" She pointed to a row of purple love bites on Brandy's neck.

Brandy ignored her, too astonished to listen. She hadn't seen her sister for five years, and now, suddenly, here she was, standing in front of her as solid as a tree. Brandy blinked. "Fuck me, you've given me a shock," she finally managed to say. "I thought Mum'd come to get me."

Liz pulled a face. "You know Mum. She couldn't get a pit out of a peach. Anyway, I thought you'd rather come home with me."

"You're sodding right I would!" Brandy laughed, not knowing what to do with her pleasure.

Liz shifted her eyes away from her sister's bruised neck and turned to the officer. "Can we go now?"

Murdock led them to the door, her fat thighs swishing against each other, a sound that set Brandy's teeth on edge. When she opened the outside gate, the one that led to the real world, to freedom, she grinned at Brandy, revealing brown blotched teeth. "Bet you'll be back within a year," she said. "Don't do anything I wouldn't do!" The sisters heard her laughing as she closed the door behind them.

"Are they all like that?" Liz said.

"She's not so bad," Brandy replied. "There's some a lot worse, I can tell you." Brandy stepped out into the sun and stood for a moment, breathing. She felt dizzy, as if the ground beneath her feet were liable to tip her over, or suddenly melt away. This abrupt change to freedom, even the mere fact that she was standing there without an officer beside her, knowing that she could walk straight and keep on walking, right past the gate and over the hill and through five valleys if she wished, pressed on her head like too much wine. She tilted her eyes to the sun. "Fuck you all," she whispered, "fuck this whole sodding place." She strode out into the middle of the courtyard and turned around to face the rows of barred windows that lifted above her like a shadow. "Fuck you all!" she screamed. "I'm free!" And she burst into raucous laughter.

"Brandy." Liz stepped forward and laid a calming hand on her arm. "Shush." She looked at the chain-link fences towering above them, at the asphalt spreading around them like ink, and wondered how her sister had survived such a place.

On the train, once they were settled into the scratchy red seats, with a window and a compartment to themselves, Liz began to lecture. "Now look, Brandy," she said, "I want some things understood straight off. You can come and stay with us for one month, but no more. Ron wasn't too pleased to hear I had a sister in Borstal, I can tell you, and nor was I for that matter. So if I catch you nicking one thing, even an aspirin, you not only get out, you get out forever. I've got a good job now, things with Ron aren't bad, and I don't want you messing up. All right?"

Brandy nodded, her eyes fixed on the window. Trees whizzed by in a green fuzz, the grass was so bright it hurt, the sky was wide enough to swallow her up. Her eyes stung from it all, the brightness, the life, the speed. She clutched the seat under her legs.

"Are you listening?"

"Yeah, Liz, yeah." Brandy pulled her eyes from the fields to look at her sister again. "You sound different."

"What're you talking about?"

Brandy studied her, trying to align the Liz sitting there with her memories. Liz had been writing to her at the Borstal for the past three months, but that was just spidery marks on paper, or at the most an echo of a voice in Brandy's head—it hadn't made Liz real. Now her sister seemed drenched in color, like a sheet splattered with paint. Brandy had to squint just to look at her. "You sound like a bleeding Southerner."

Liz frowned but was secretly flattered. "You're a cheeky little sod, you are. That's not what I was talking about. I want you to find a job, fast."

"A job?" Brandy's voice caught, and she glanced around the speeding train. She'd never had a job. "Do I have to? Can't I wait a bit first, Liz? Just stay home an' look after the kid an' such? I mean . . . well, what would I do?"

Liz looked at her in surprise. "What're you scared of? You know I can't have you freeloading on me all the time. You bring in your dole and give it to me till you find some work. Who knows, if you behave yourself I might even get you something at the salon."

"Really?" Brandy sat forward. "You really think so, Liz? That's what I'd like the best, you know. I even practiced on the girls a bit inside. I couldn't do much 'cause they wouldn't let me have scissors, but . . ."

Liz laughed. "How can you cut hair without scissors, you git? Anyway, they'll only let you sweep up and stuff at first—the cutting comes later." She gave Brandy a good-natured pat on the knee, but then her face took on a curious, strained expression. "Brandy?" she said. "What was it like in there?"

Brandy slumped into her seat and turned back to the window. "Don't ask," she mumbled. The sounds of keys clanking, doors slamming, filled her head. Reardon's hand came towards her, big and flat.

Liz eyed the marks on Brandy's neck, the bandages over her knuckles, and pursed her lips. She didn't really want to know what Brandy had got up to in that place; it was too disgusting to think about.

Brandy and Liz had grown up together on a council estate in Birmingham, in one of those solitary high rises that clutter the outskirts of the city, every one blankly identical and already crumbling only a few years after it had been built. The girls had been close as children, drawn to each other by the desertion of their father when Brandy was five and their mother's subsequent night job, but once Liz turned fourteen, that changed. She grew tall and slim and spent her time doing her hair and nails after school instead of playing with Brandy, trying to imitate what she saw in magazines and shooing her sister away when she suggested their old games. She began going out with pimply boys who had brown fuzz over their lips, and she would come back late, mysterious and sullen. Brandy hung around at first, hoping to be included, but quickly grew bored and then disgusted. She didn't like those boys, the way their voices squeaked, the way they smelled of sweat and knocked into things. Above all she didn't like the airs Liz put on, waving her nails about and laughing like a grown-up.

One day, when Brandy was twelve and Liz sixteen, Brandy came home from school to find her sister packing a battered suitcase in their bedroom. "What're you doing?" Brandy said.

"Standing on me head. What does it look like?" Liz was meticulously folding a striped jumper and tucking it into a corner. She had a big wad of chewing gum in her mouth and was chomping on it loudly. Brandy could smell the peppermint from across the room.

"Come on, Liz, are you going somewhere?"

"Well, I'm not packing the laundry, am I? I'm leaving, that's what I'm doing. Me and Ron are getting married." Ron was a large, plump lad from the estate who had been hanging around Liz for months. Brandy had always thought he was a half-wit.

"Marry Ron? Are you joking?"

"No I'm bloody well not, and I'd thank you to keep your frigging remarks to yourself." Liz pushed past her, jerked open a bureau drawer, and began piling up her underwear in color-coordinated rows. "I've been dying to get out of here and you know it. I can't stand one more night of Mum blubbering over that bottle, or of your cheek, for that matter." She turned to Brandy and looked her over. Brandy's blouse was untucked, her round belly was showing above her skirt, and her hair was in a tangle of rat's tails. Liz wrinkled her nose. "You look a fright and you pong, as well. Don't you ever take a bath before you go to school?"

"Leave off," Brandy muttered.

Liz put her hands on her hips, a gesture exactly like their mother's. "Look, love," she said, "I'll send you me address so you can come visit, if you want, but you've got to promise not to tell Mum where I am, all right? If she comes sniveling 'round trying to ruin me life, I'll never speak to either of you again. Promise?"

"Cross me heart." Brandy drew an X on her chest and sat on the bed, watching Liz in silence. Liz was wearing her smartest outfit: a tight black miniskirt that looked like leather but was really plastic and a white skinny-ribbed pullover that showed off her tiny breasts. Her hair, cut across the front in a straight fringe, was bleached blond. "You look smashing," Brandy sighed.

Liz smiled. "Ta." She clicked the suitcase shut, picked up her cardigan and coat, and turned to Brandy. "I'm meeting Ron at the bus stop. When Mum gets home tell her I'm never coming back, all right? Tell her I'm getting married and I'm going to lead a decent life, no thanks to her, and I don't want her ever to come near me again. Got it?"

Brandy nodded, not trusting herself to speak. Take me with you, she wanted to say, but she didn't dare. Liz would only get angry.

"Right, then." Liz took a last look around the room she had shared with her sister for twelve years—the twin beds sagging with age, the peeling yellow wallpaper that she'd tried to salvage by pinning up pictures of Twiggy and Diana Rigg, the grimy window that stared out into endless gray skies. Her eyes moved back to Brandy, slumped on the bed. "You'll get rid of that puppy fat soon, you'll see. Soon as you turn thirteen, I bet. Then you'll find a bloke and you can move out, too." And with that Liz took out her gum, stuck it on the mirror, and swung her skinny hips out the door.

By the time the train reached Brighton station, it was four o'clock and both sisters were starved. Brandy stepped down onto the platform, shrinking from the sudden crowds and bustle around them, and clutched Liz's sleeve.

"Watch it! You're wrinkling me blouse."

"Sorry." But Brandy was afraid to let go. She'd had the same feeling the other time she'd gotten out of Borstal, and again an hour earlier when they'd changed trains in London: the chaos blaring in her ears, buffeting her about like a paper hat in the wind.

"Come on," Liz said, pulling her towards the British Rail cafeteria. "Fancy some tea?" Brandy's mouth watered at the promise of non-Borstal food and she followed Liz eagerly. She chose two cakes and a bar of chocolate.

"You can't eat all that muck!" Liz exclaimed. "No wonder you're such a pudge. And look at your face! You'll never get a job at a salon looking like that. Take a salad roll, go on."

"Ah, Liz, come on. I haven't had anything this good in years."

"Looks like that's all you've been eating to me. Who'd ever have thought you'd get so spotty? Go on then, take one cake. But that's it."

They sat together at a corner table littered with empty coffee cups and cigarette butts. Liz swept them aside, wiping the area in front of her with a paper napkin, and settled down to eat. "What a bloody mess. They used to have wogs to clean up this stuff, but I think they're all too big for their boots these days. They all want to be prime minister now."

Brandy looked around, blinking at the faces that swirled about her like shouts. A man sat hunched at the table next to them, his moustache drooping at the same angle as the newspaper in his hands. Some Indian women sipped tea farther on, darting their eyes to the small, brown children staggering at their feet. A baby behind them began to cry. Brandy bit into her salad roll, eyeing the cake longingly. "Liz?" she mumbled.

"Hmm?"

"Is it all right with Ron, me coming to stay an' all?"

24

"What? Don't talk with your mouth full."

Brandy suppressed a retort, reminding herself that she needed Liz. She slurped down some tea to clear her palate and, smiling obsequiously, repeated her question.

"Well, it will be a bit crowded, mind," Liz admitted, shrugging. "We made the sitting room into a bedroom for Bobby, you see, so we only have the two rooms and the kitchen. You'll have to keep out of Ron's way as much as you can. He needs a relax when he gets home." She rummaged in her bag, took out a pocket mirror and replenished her lipstick, putting it on thick and wet.

Brandy watched, carried back to their days on the estate when she used to spend hours sitting with Liz while her sister got ready for one boy or another. Liz still had that same pointed face, but otherwise she looked so sophisticated now. She'd become a real woman, and the change made Brandy feel empty and worn. "Can I have a turn with that, Liz?" she said. "Please?"

"Eat your cake first, then you can have it."

Brandy picked the cake up, still in her Borstal habit of obeying. It was yellow, with white icing and a layer of jam in the middle, and was crusted and stale on top. She wondered what the cake she was supposed to have stolen looked like, and the resentment burned in her again. Brandy gulped the cake down, aware of Liz watching her disapprovingly, and reached for the lipstick.

"Gawd, what happened to your manners in there?" Liz shook her head and handed it over. Brandy squinted into Liz's pocket mirror and put on the lipstick carefully, as if it were a magic wand that would turn her into someone else.

"It should be all right with Ron so long as you behave yourself," Liz continued. "Think you can manage it?"

"Course I can!" Brandy snapped. "I'm not a fucking kid!"

Liz clicked her bag shut. "Come on," she said, "Bobby's waiting for us. And for Christ's sake, girl, watch your language."

When they got to Liz's flat, the ground floor of a small house on Highcroft Villas road, they found Ron and Bobby in the front room watching Saturday football on television. The room was half bedroom, half sitting room, with a double bed under the windows and a television and armchair in the opposite corner. Ron had closed the curtains against the sun and the TV was sending a blue glare over his and Bobby's faces, making them look pale and unhealthy. As soon as Bobby saw Brandy, he hid in his father's ribs.

25

"Hello, Ron," Brandy said loudly as she stood in the doorway. She looked him over, trying, as she had with Liz, to connect him with her memories. His face hadn't changed much—it was still beefy, with heavy jowls, small black eyes, and freckles—but his body was quite different. His arms were thick and brown now from his work as a bricklayer, and a beer belly the size of a pillow bulged out over his tight trousers. His hair, too, had changed, its black curls thinning on top. He looked years and years older than the awkward boy Brandy remembered, and she felt, suddenly, how much of life had passed her by while she'd been shut away. Ron kept his eyes on the television set and grunted an unwelcoming hello. Brandy squinted at his back. "You've got fatter," she said.

Bobby poked his weasely face out at that and grinned. "Dad's fat, Dad's fat!" He laughed, and Brandy laughed with him.

"Just you watch it!" Ron said, although it was not clear whom he was addressing.

Ignoring him, Brandy bent towards Bobby. "Hello, you little blighter," she said, winking. "D'you know who I am?" The boy grew serious and hid against his father.

"Come on," Liz said, pulling Brandy out of the room. "You mind your cheek, young lady, or Ron'll have you right out on the street otherwise!" She led Brandy down the hall. "Look, here's where Bobby sleeps. You'll stay with him, all right? You can have that bed." She gestured at one of the narrow beds, covered in a pink and blue quilt. The room was light, with French windows that faced out into the garden, and was littered with cheap plastic toys. It smelled faintly of urine.

Brandy sat down on the bed and threw her bag to the floor. She looked around the bright room and a piercing happiness shot through her, so sharp it almost hurt. God, the room was pretty. Toys all over the place, bits of color flashing in the sunbeams. She looked up at Liz, her eyes glistening, and smiled, genuinely this time. "It's a fucking sight better than that cell, I can tell you. Thanks a lot, Liz, y'know, for fetching me and bringing me here and everything." She ran her hand over the soft quilt and bouncy pillow, then bent down to pick up an empty water pistol. She pointed it at Liz and pulled the trigger. "Bang," she said, and grinned.

Half an hour later, Liz insisted on taking Brandy and Bobby for a walk by the sea. "It's a beautiful Saturday and all you can do is sit around like a bloody caveman," she said to Ron, drawing back the curtains. "I'm taking them out." Cramming Bobby into the pushchair, she bustled him and Brandy through the front door.

"I want ice cream," Bobby said immediately.

"Shurrup or I'll smack you." Liz turned to Brandy. "Come on, we're going to walk. It'll do you good. You're as pale as death."

She led Brandy down a long, steep hill lined with junk shops and little houses painted in peeling, bleached pastels. The sun bounced off the walls, making Brandy wince, and the cars zoomed by so close she jumped. Out of the house, she once again felt lost and confused, as if her limbs were floating off her.

At the bottom of the hill they walked around a corner and along Western Road, a busy street crowded with Saturday shoppers. Clothes, jewelry, and records glittered invitingly from shop windows. Brandy looked down at the pavement for relief but even that was overly bright and crowded, legs pouring past her in all shapes and sizes, litter and dog droppings and cast-aside newspapers threatening to tangle in her shoes. "The salon's up there," Liz said, pointing to a narrow side street.

Brandy looked up, squinting, and saw a sign hanging out that said HAIRLINE in wispy purple letters. "Looks flash."

" 'Tis. We get a lot of students there. Crawling with money, they are. Brighton's full of them."

"Where's the sea, then?" Brandy said, looking around.

"This way." Liz led her across the road and down the hill until Brandy finally saw it: a line of deep blue flashing in the sun. She put her hands over her brow. The sun was low in the sky, shining off the water so brightly that it hurt, and the vastness of the horizon made her feel dizzy again. She wanted to buy some sunglasses from one of the stalls, but it had been so long since she'd bought anything that she was afraid. And she didn't like to ask Liz.

They crossed the wide, reddish street of the Esplanade and looked down over the beach. A green railing separated the road from the sea, giving Brandy the sense that the town had been cut in half and a beach stuck on, like the halves of two different pictures. They walked slowly, feeling the sun on their cheeks and chests. The air smelled of salt and suntan lotion, with an occasional whiff of rotting seaweed. Bobby began wailing for ice cream. "All right, all right, anything to shut you up," Liz sighed and stopped at an ice cream van on the corner to buy him a cone of softwhip. "None for you," she said, catching Brandy's eager look. "You're a tub and you know it."

They parked Bobby by a railing and leaned their elbows on it to look down. Below them hundreds of greased bodies lay out on the stones, glistening in the sun. Brandy caught sight of several bared breasts. She breathed in and shut her eyes for a moment, then opened them slowly. It was all still there. Suddenly her giddiness gave way to elation. She felt the walls of the Borstal fall away from her like husks, yielding her to pure, empty sky. "This place is fucking gorgeous," she whispered.

"Yeah," Liz said proudly.

"Can we go down there and sit? Maybe Bobby'd like to run about a bit."

Liz looked at her son. His face, shirt, and hands were covered in ice cream. "You little bugger." She sighed and began scrubbing him with a handkerchief.

"Stop, Mum! Lemme go!" Bobby cried, squirming.

"All right, but if I catch you throwing stones like last time, you're going straight home." She released Bobby from the pushchair and he catapulted down a ramp to the beach. Liz and Brandy followed at a trot. "Watch out for the tar," Liz said as they hunted for a clean place to sit. "I don't usually come down here without a mat." They found a passable patch and sat down between two clumps of people, a crowd of teenage boys in dark tans and a middle-aged couple so white their flab glowed. Brandy arranged her skirt and her thick, stockinged legs awkwardly. Her flesh looked pink and mottled with the heat, like bacon.

"Where's that brat gone?" Liz muttered, running her eyes over the crowd. She caught sight of him playing with some other boys near the sea, flinging stones at one another. She sighed but didn't move.

For a time the sisters sat in silence. From the back Liz looked slim and straight, her small waist tightly encased in a wide plastic belt and her hair spiked on top and straggling down in fashionable points of bleached blond, but Brandy looked like no possible relation. Her back was pudgy, her hair limp, and sweat was beginning to show under her armpits. Their faces, though, squinting against the sun, were similar: long-jawed and narrow-eyed, with heavy flat noses and pockmarked cheeks. "Have you heard from Mum?" Brandy asked at last.

Liz shifted her skinny bum on the sharp stones. "Not since I told her I'd fetch you. Don't want to, either."

"Did she say anything about me?"

"Nah."

Brandy stared down at her feet. They looked squashed, crammed into her best black shoes and swelling in the sun. "She never told you about me, then?"

Liz shook her head. "I never would've known you were in that place if me old mate what's-her-name hadn't told me. Betsy. Mum never said a word about you."

"Never?" Brandy looked at Liz, squinting.

"Nope. Even when I wrote to her about Bobby she didn't mention it. She just started trying to ponce money off us. 'Send us a tenner so's I can come see me grandson,' sort of thing. Best thing I ever did was leave that old bag."

"Wish you'd taken me with you," Brandy muttered, but she quickly laughed, trying to pass it off as a joke.

"Maybe I should've," Liz mused, "but how could I really? I mean, all that stuff about me and Ron getting married—well, we were underage, weren't we? It took me two years of tagging 'round after him to get him to marry me. I'd never have done it with you there."

"Yeah, I s'pose." Brandy suppressed the urge to ask Liz whether Ron was worth all that trouble, and picked up a stone instead. "But, Liz, why didn't you write to us for so long, then?"

Liz yawned and stretched. "Oh gawd, Brandy, don't bring all that stuff up now. I meant to, honest, but somehow I got so busy with Ron and moving and such. Anyway, I didn't know you were in all that trouble, did I? I would've done something if I had."

"Would you?" Brandy said, pleased.

"Course I would." Liz patted her on the shoulder.

Brandy picked up another stone and weighed its smooth warmth in her palm. "Liz?" she said again.

"Now what?" Liz had her eyes closed and her face up to the sun.

"Jeff should be getting out soon. You know, that bloke I wrote to you about."

Liz turned her head sharply. "Listen, girl, you're not seeing that lout again! I'm not having any of your Brummy mates 'round here. If you know what's good for you, you won't even tell him where you are."

"Why not? He's a good bloke."

"Good! Look, you bleeding fool, those bastards got you into this thieving business in the first place. If you want to straighten yourself out, Brandy, you've got to drop them. They like nothing better than to get some fool of a girl like you to do their dirty work for them. I know the type, I saw enough of them on the estate."

"But Jeff's not like that! It wasn't him got me into it, it was his friends. He's a good bloke, Liz—we're going to get married when he gets out. He promised!"

"Gawd, I thought Borstal was supposed to wise people up!"

"It's true! He wrote it all in a letter. I have it right here, look." Brandy put her hand down her shirt, which by now was sticky with sweat, and pulled out a damp, crumpled note from her bra. She held it out to Liz. "You read it."

"I'm not touching that filthy thing. How'd you get that from him, anyway?"

"I got it before I was nicked. Look, he says right here: 'You're the best thing I ever had. Let's get married when I get out.'"

"Hah! I'll see the sodding sun turn blue before that happens. Look, Amanda"—Liz had always used that name when she played mother—"don't be daft about this thing. That letter is two years old! If you're going to straighten up you've got to concentrate on one thing at a time. Get a job. Save some money. Stay away from blokes like Jeff and from Brum and from everything else you used to be mixed up with. And clean yourself up, for Christ's sake. Then maybe you'll meet a normal bloke like Ron, not some sodding juvenile delinquent."

Brandy muttered and looked down at the stones.

"What? Go on, speak up."

"You don't understand a fucking thing!" Brandy shouted suddenly. "Jeff's the only person's ever treated me decent. He loves me, he says so in this letter. See?" She unfolded the letter again and thrust it under Liz's nose. Liz saw the words "Luv you babie" before Brandy snatched it away again.

"He can't even bloody spell." Liz stood up to brush off her trousers. "I'm going to fetch our Bobby before he blinds someone. Bobbyyyy!" she screeched, and hobbled off down the beach on her high heels.

Brandy watched her sister for a while, fury tightening her throat. Liz didn't know anything! She didn't know what Brandy had seen, what Jeff had been like. She didn't know anything about how it had felt spending all those months inside making do with girls when all she'd wanted was him. Maybe Reardon had been right when she'd said people outside were different, that they wouldn't understand. "I'll show you," Brandy muttered. "I'll find Jeff and then you'll bloody well see." She stood up, dizzy for a moment from the sun, and looked down to inspect herself. "Fuck," she said aloud. Her stocking had run.

Liz came back up the beach a few minutes later, dragging a wailing Bobby by the hand. "He's got sand in his hair and sand in his eyes and sand everybloodywhere else he could think of," she said. Brandy looked down at him. Under his tangled blond hair she saw a purple shadow.

"What's that?" she said, pointing.

"What?"

"That lump on his head."

Liz crouched down to look. "What happened?" she screamed.

"A b-boy," Bobby sobbed. "St-stone."

"Did a boy throw a stone at you?"

Bobby nodded, sobbing louder.

"I told you not to throw stones, you stupid git!" Liz yelled, shaking him. "It's your own fault!" Bobby wailed louder. "Shurrup or I'll whack you so hard that stone'll feel like a kiss!"

"Ah, come on, Liz, leave him alone. He's only three, poor kid."

Liz turned on her. "Mind your own bloody business! What do you know about raising kids, eh? You stand there criticizing me and you can't even look after yourself without ending up in the nick!" Yanking Bobby by the hand, she dragged him off the beach. Brandy picked up the pushchair and stumbled after them.

On the day that Brandy turned thirteen, four months after Liz had left home, she decided to run away, too. She hoped to find Liz and move in with her, even though Liz had never written, for Brandy had found her sister all kinds of excuses. "She's probably sent a letter that got lost," she told herself. "Or she's waiting to get some money to help me with."

Brandy's mother was snoring in bed that morning, sleeping off her Friday night booze-up, so Brandy had an easy escape. She filled a small bag with her best clothes and her mother's makeup, took the money her mother had hidden in a tea tin, and caught a bus to the center of town. She'd worked out that she was most likely to find Liz along New Street, where her sister had always done her Saturday shopping.

For hours Brandy haunted the boutiques, jostling through the usual thick Saturday crowds with eager impatience. She stopped to stare at every blond, skinny young woman she saw and went into all the shops and cafés she remembered Liz taking her to. At first she kept herself going with pictures of how delighted Liz would be to see her, of Liz remembering that it was her birthday and taking her out for cake and a present, but as the hours stretched on, the pictures began to fade, gradually replaced by Brandy's habitual brooding resentment. Even if she found Liz, she began to think, her sister would only laugh at her and send her home.

When afternoon fell, darkening the streets, Brandy found herself back in her old haunt in the Bull Ring, the huge underground shopping mall where she had taken to hanging about with other children instead of going to school. She walked through the tunnels lit in gloomy fluorescent, past the shop windows turned dull and greasy by the artificial light, and fought back angry tears. The loneliness of the past four months ate into her and, at last, as her birthday hopes crumbled, she began to hate Liz for abandoning her.

By nine that night Brandy was hungry, tired, and broke. The shops had closed, the streets were emptying, and only the pubs were alive with voices. Yet she didn't want to go home. The thought of crawling back to her preoccupied, grumbling mother, who always seemed to be out at her job cleaning offices or in one of her self-obsessed drinking moods, filled her with despair. She walked down a dark, rubble-filled street and looked longingly at the bright window of a pub on the corner, smelling the smoke and beer and feeling a wave of warmth each time the door swung open to let someone in or out. She yearned to be able to enter, to be part of the laughing, hot crowd. She pushed the doors open and walked in.

Inside, a few people glanced at her curiously, but mostly she was ignored. The pub was packed and steamy. She stood for a moment, uncertain of what to do next, then elbowed her way to the bar. She'd been in pubs before, of course, even though she was legally too young, but always with Liz or older friends. When she reached the bar she tapped a man on the shoulder. He turned to look down at her.

"How about buying me a drink, mister?" she said, attempting a wink.

"Get outta here!" He laughed. "How old are you, nine?"

Brandy was insulted. She was used to being taken for fifteen, for she was well developed and in the habit of wearing makeup. "Up yours, mate," she growled.

The man turned serious. "Go on, out with you. We don't want any foul-mouthed little girls 'round here. Oy, Johnny!" The bartender looked up from the pint he was pulling. "Look what we have here." The man cocked his head at Brandy.

"You're underage, lass. You have to leave," the bartender said.

Brandy's eyes stung. "It's a free country, isn't it?" She'd heard Liz say that to their mother whenever she was being made to do something against her will.

"I'm warning you," the bartender said. "Don't stir it up. Just get out."

"You try an' make me, you wanker!"

The bartender ducked under the counter and sprang up next to her. Taking hold of her arm, he pushed her towards the door. "Go on, out—before I call the coppers!"

Brandy struggled but was unable to break free. The bartender shoved her to the door, opened it, and propelled her through. "Now bugger off," he said, and slammed the door behind her.

Brandy stood staring at the pub, clenching her fists. She longed to scratch and hit and kick at that sodding bartender and his mate. Looking around for relief, for anything to grab hold of and pound, she saw a broken board lying in the gutter. She picked it up, intending to bash it against the wall, but as soon as she felt the weight of it in her hands she had no doubt what to do—she'd watched such scenes on television enough times. With a great yell of glee she smashed it against the window with all her strength, shattering a large hole in the glass. Pieces of window rained into pints of beer and gins and tonics. One shard pricked a young woman on the nape of her neck, causing a single drop of blood to slide down her back. Brandy laughed aloud. "It's me fucking birthday!" she shouted, and waited for something to happen.

When Liz and Brandy got back from the beach, they found Ron still watching football in the exact position they'd left him, only with four more empty beer bottles beside his chair. The room stank of cigarette smoke. "Must be a good match," Liz said pointedly. Bobby, whose tears were long forgotten, jumped onto his father's lap.

"Did you have a good time, little fella?" Ron lifted Bobby up for a kiss. "What happened to your head?"

"A boy hit me!" Bobby squirmed with delight at the attention.

"Did you hit him back?"

He nodded proudly and Ron laughed. "Come on, you watch telly with me, love." Liz left the room to make tea and Bobby nestled into his father's big stomach, happy again. Brandy sat down to watch with them. Ten minutes passed before Ron finally turned to her and spoke.

"Well then," he said, "how's it feel to be outta the cage?"

She shrugged. "All right."

"Are you going down to the dole tomorrow?"

What's it to you? Brandy wanted to say, but she only shrugged again and looked at the floor.

"Well?"

"Yeah, I s'pose," she mumbled. "I don't see how else I'm going to get any cash."

"Didn't they give you any at the prison?"

"Only a bit. It was Borstal, if you don't mind, not a prison."

"All right, Borstal. It's all the same, innit?"

"It's not the same!" She looked up, her face flushing. "We wear our own clothes if we want and the trainees get a lot more freedom than ordinary cons. I know 'cause one of me mates was in Holloway once and she told me."

"Trainees!" Ron hooted. "Is that what they call you?"

"Yeah!" Brandy didn't know why she was defending Borstal all of a sudden.

"Well, it's all the same to me. A con's a con, a thief's a thief as far as I'm concerned. You just start drawing that dole and paying for your bed and board, that's all. I'll be blowed if I'm going to support any sodding delinquents in me own house."

Brandy was just about to protest when Liz came back into the room. "Ah, leave her alone, Ron. Tea's ready."

During Brandy's first two weeks out of Borstal, she spent most of her time in the house. After all the years she'd lived in institutions—the community home she was sent to as a result of the window-smashing incident, and the two Borstal sentences she'd served for attacking the home's matron and mugging an old woman respectively—she was so bewildered by possibilities, by not having her every moment dictated, that all she could bring herself to do was either stay at home watching television, or wait in the queue for her dole. Sometimes she forced herself down to the beach, but once there she found she could only huddle on a mat, unable even to stretch out her limbs and abandon herself to the sun. The open sky, the sight of the sea stretching to the horizon, the number of choices she had to make, made her sick with vertigo. In the shops it was even worse, for she felt as if the shopkeepers knew all about her from one glance, so once her money started coming in she hardly dared spend it and gave most of it to Liz for food and expenses. That first fortnight was a slow awakening. The only place Brandy felt safe was in Bobby's room, where she could either leaf through magazines alone or play with him for hours without feeling judged.

Liz, meanwhile, was getting used to having her sister in the house. At first she'd resented the amount of space Brandy took up and had been suspicious of her every move. Each morning she had surreptitiously hidden her jewelry and spare money before dropping Bobby off at nursery school and going to work, and in the evenings had rushed back to make sure that Brandy wasn't up to mischief. But now Liz was coming to like the way Brandy got on with Bobby and the way she helped around the house. "Y'know," she said to Ron as they were getting ready for bed one night, "it's rather a lark having Brandy here."

Ron looked over at her. He was sitting on the bed pulling off his shoes. "Are you serious?"

"Yeah." Liz brushed her hair slowly, frowning into the dressing table mirror. "It's nice for me having some company. Makes a change from talking to a three-year-old all day."

"Company? It's more like having a motorcycle moll in the house, if you ask me. She doesn't half look rough, Liz. Nothing like you." Standing in his bare feet, Ron padded up behind her. He put his hands on her shoulders and nuzzled the back of her neck.

Liz smiled, shrugging him off. "Well, give her a bit of time, love. She is only seventeen. Anyway, she's been a big help to me. It gets lonely for us women doing all the shopping and cooking alone, y'know. She makes it much easier on the days I have to work late."

Ron slipped a hand inside her robe and cupped her small,

hard breast. "You didn't look like that when you were seventeen."

"I should hope not!" Liz laughed. "But even I was a bit spotty then, Ron, you must admit."

"Weren't we all!" He grinned and bent to lick her ear, his curls tickling her cheek. "Come on, love, let's go to bed." He opened her robe and they both watched him caress her breasts in the mirror. Raising her arms, Liz put them around his neck and closed her eyes. He tumbled her off the stool and onto the floor, making love to her eagerly, his bulk heavy and hot as he pressed her into the carpet.

The next day, Liz asked Brandy to look after Bobby that evening while she and Ron went out. Brandy agreed readily. She relished the chance to have Bobby to herself, to be able to let go and be silly with him without the danger of adults interrupting them, and she was sick to death of Liz watching her all the time.

"He'll have baked beans for supper," Liz told her, "then give him a bath and get him into bed by eight. All right? You can park him in front of the telly if he's too much trouble."

Brandy nodded.

"Ta, love. We'll give you a quid for the favor."

"All right." Brandy paused. "Liz?"

"Yeah?"

"Have you talked to them about me working at the salon yet?"

Liz looked at her with amusement. "So, you're ready to do a bit of work after all, are you?"

"Well, yeah. Soon." Brandy shifted her eyes from Liz's face. "I told you before I was."

Liz put her hands on her hips and looked Brandy over. "I think we better wait another week or two first, ducks. You don't look half normal enough yet. You'd frighten away the customers!" Chuckling, she went into the bathroom and closed the door.

After Liz and Ron left, Brandy took out some baked beans for Bobby and got him laughing straightaway by pretending not to be able to open the tin. She struggled with it, twisting herself about, turning red and even falling to the ground, until he was pink with glee. Once she had him eating, she continued to clown by climbing up on a chair, tearing open one cupboard door after another, and rifling through old packets, pots and pans, rags and empty boxes, all the while muttering in a pirate accent about buried treasure. She was really hoping to find a bottle of booze somewhere, but Bobby thought it was a great lark.

"Look in that one, Aunty!" he cried, pointing his fork to a cupboard above the refrigerator. His peaky face looked particularly elflike at that moment, excited as he was with mischief, and Brandy watched him affectionately. After two years of staring at Borstal faces, of sly eyes and phony grins, the joy in Bobby's face seemed to shine out at her as if there were no evil in the world.

"All right," she said, shifting the chair and climbing back onto it. "What d'you think I'll find, matey, golden doubloons?"

"What's duboons?"

"Money."

"Nah," he said, a baked bean sliding down his chin. "Not money. Chocolates." Brandy opened the cupboard and found a big box of chocolates sitting inside. An expensive one, in black velvet with a gold ribbon, which Liz must have been saving for guests. "You clever little bugger!" She took it and climbed down.

"Open it, open it!"

"Finish your beans, then I'll let you see. Go on, eat up." Bobby shoveled a forkful into his mouth.

"I've finished, Aunty, look!" he mumbled, his mouth full.

"Swallow them first." Brandy opened the box and lifted off the tissue. Except for six missing pieces, the box was full. She took two chocolates, crammed one in each cheek, and made a face at Bobby.

He laughed, jabbing his fork near her eye. "Gimme one!"

"Here you are then." She picked up a fat, soft-centered one and popped it into his mouth. He chewed noisily, his blue eyes sparkling like Liz's when she was in a good mood. The two of them didn't stop eating until they'd finished a layer and a half and Bobby complained of a stomachache.

"All right, into the bath with you." Brandy buried the chocolate box in the dustbin.

After Bobby was settled into bed, and Brandy had smoothed his hair down and watched him drift off, she wandered into Liz and Ron's room to look around. She had planned to turn on the television as usual but instead found herself standing in the middle of the room, relishing her solitude. Being alone by choice was so different from the solitude of punishment. This was secretive, delicious, almost naughty. She walked over to the window to gaze out at the darkening street. She was more comfortable at night, she felt protected by it, less exposed, and, suddenly, for the first time since her release, the excitement of evening and all it promised splashed through her. The night was hers. She was free to take it for her own. The realization made her feel high and greedy. It made her feel brave.

She went to the dressing table, her heart racing, and rifled through its drawers, trying on Liz's makeup and jewelry with the same guilty thrill a child gets when sneaking through her mother's things. She pocketed the loose change she found mixed in with safety pins and cotton wool, streaked rouge over her cheeks, outlined her eyes in heavy black, and pushed deep purple lipstick over her mouth until she looked like a plump, exaggerated version of Liz. When she'd finished, she sucked in her cheeks like a model and stared at her reflection, then shook her head, chuckling at herself, and turned to the wardrobe.

Most of Liz's clothes were so small that Brandy didn't even bother to try them on, although she fingered them longingly, but she found a pair of purple platform shoes that fit and a matching silk scarf that she could toss around her neck. She pulled the money out of her skirt pocket and counted it: two pounds eleven. Glancing at the hallway clock, she walked down to Bobby's room and peeked in. He lay curled up under the blankets, one leg dangling off the edge of the bed, so she tiptoed up to him and gently lifted it back. He looked so peaceful. "Bobby?" she whispered, but he didn't stir. She hesitated, the sight of his frailty holding her back. But she needed laughter and booze now, she told herself, not another boring night at home with a snoozing kid. She started out of the room, stopped, and glanced at him again. "You'll be all right, won't you?" she whispered to him. "I'll just have one drink." And she strode down the hall, put on the front door latch, and slipped out.

Outside it still wasn't quite dark, being only half-past eight on a summer night, but the sky was a deep blue and pink streaks of cloud wormed out from the direction of the sea. Brandy wobbled down the road on her unaccustomed platform heels, looking for a pub. The street lamps glowed their fog orange, still dim but gathering strength, and everything was quiet. As she passed the little houses lined up along the pavement she caught sight of a television glow once in a while, or heard the drone of voices, but otherwise there wasn't a sign of life. She shivered even though the air was warm. She missed her Birmingham friends and Jeff, with their booze, dope, and loud music; she didn't like all this peace. She even missed Reardon and the danger of their secret courtship for a moment—anything but this deadening silence.

The first pub she looked into was full of toothless old men. They stopped talking when she poked her head in the door and turned to stare at her, their mouths crumpling into thin, suspicious lines. "Evenin', you old geezers," she called cheerily, and pulled her head out. "Bloody hell, it's like a fucking graveyard 'round here."

She walked down the hill and into an alleyway, enjoying the sound of her heels echoing against the walls, until at last she got to a main street. There she saw another pub, this one promisingly big and noisy. When she entered the public bar, she was immediately enveloped by heat and smoke, red light and the welcome smell of beer. A group of laborers, washed and dressed in their Saturday night gear, were playing darts at one end of the room, and the few seats were filled with their women, vivid in loud colors and laughter. A crowd of men stood between Brandy and the bar, knocking back their pints and shouting jokes. As she squeezed past, one of them said, "Hello, love," and winked. She winked back. This is more like it, she thought, and laughed aloud.

At the bar she ordered a pint of the cheapest cider and drank it down fast. "Just one more and I'll get back," she told herself, and ordered another. Her stomach swelled, unused to the volume and fizz, but she ignored it and kept drinking, waiting for the lightening in her brain, that delicious loosening that made her want to shout and dance and bed whomever she could find. She cadged a cigarette off one of the blokes and leaned back against the bar. Screw you, Liz and Ron, she thought, I'm fucking free! Over the top of her glass she eyed the men challengingly. They weren't Jeff, but they were men. Real ones. She felt her body signal like a red flag.

Bobby awoke feeling sick. His stomach was cramping and waves of nausea swept up his throat. He groaned and opened his eyes. The room was dark except for something shining and white that stared at him from Brandy's empty bed. "Mum?" he croaked, his eyes widening. "Mum!" His voice floated away and dropped into silence. He sat up quickly, alarm quivering through him, and his stomach lurched at the movement, cramping and heaving. The vomit spilled out all over him and the bed. "Mum!" he cried through his retching. "Mum! Mum! Mummy, Mum, Mum!" The silence sucked away his sound. He heaved and vomited again, then curled up in the wet bed, shaking. "I want you, Mum," he whimpered to the darkness. He wanted to get up and go find her

39

but he was too afraid. Why didn't she come? Where was his aunty? He stared at Brandy's bed; the white thing shimmered. "Mum?" he called again, his throat sore and burning, but his own voice frightened him even more. It sounded loud and menacing, sweeping around him in a black whirl. He felt his chest heave and his eyes fill with tears. He clutched his pillow and sobbed.

On her third cider Brandy began to feel right. It was doing what she wanted, blotting out all those months of gates and locks and spyholes, of squealing feminine voices and hot, damp hands. It was getting her ready for life again, for men who were lean and scratchy, for the challenge of scrabbling for a living and getting through the chaos. She felt big and brave now, hard and savvy. She looked down at her knuckles, still plastered with bandages where the doctor had cut out her tattoo, and, holding her glass in one hand, tore at the bandages with her teeth. She wanted to see if it still showed, if she could still read the word LOVE, a letter on each knuckle, now that it was only scars.

"Hello there, what did you do to yourself?" A thin young man with a greasy moustache, a cockney accent, and the tan of an outdoor laborer stepped towards her. "Cut yourself, did you?"

Brandy quickly lowered her fist out of sight. "Uh, yeah, on the kitchen knife. It'll be all right. It's just itching a bit."

"Mmm, I know what that's like. I got a nail through me foot last summer on the site. Need another drink, love?"

"Yeah, thanks, that'd be lovely. Whiskey and ginger ale, please."

The man eyed her cider glass but nodded and ordered. "I haven't seen you 'round here before, have I?" he asked, lighting cigarettes for both of them.

"Nah, I just arrived this week." She blew smoke up into the air.

"Oh, yeah? Where from?"

"Birmingham."

"Thought so. You on holiday, then?"

"That's right. I'm staying with me sister. What about you?"

"Oh, I'm working on the Marina. Most of these blokes are." He waved a hand over the pub. "My name's Frank. What's yours?"

Brandy eyed the room nervously, hoping Ron wouldn't show up looking for his friends. "Susan," she said.

"What d'you do when you're at home, Susan?"

She handed him her empty glass. "I'm a hairdresser. I work in a salon on Corporation Street. D'you know Birmingham?"

"No, I've never been there." He bought her another drink. "You like the work then, do you?"

"Oh, yeah, it's a great job. It's a real art, cutting hair right. It takes talent. Not everyone has the flair for it, y'know."

"You good at it then?"

"Oh, yeah." Brandy smiled nonchalantly, and polished off her drink.

Brandy and Frank chatted for over an hour. She told him that her boyfriend was a guitarist and that she was getting married next month, and didn't notice the skeptical looks that crossed Frank's face, or the time. She even forgot about Bobby until Frank began to fidget and glance at the door.

"You fancy a walk outside, Susan?" he said at last, leaning over her and breathing whiskey down her face.

Brandy blinked, suddenly back to earth. "Christ, what time is it?"

"Almost closing time. Come on, drink up." He picked up her fourth whiskey and held it out to her. Brandy swallowed it, trying to ignore the lurch in her stomach. The few pills she'd managed to get hold of in Borstal hadn't kept her in practice for a night like this, and the chocolates she'd eaten earlier weren't helping, either. When she stood to go, the room danced around crazily and the lights slipped from their sockets.

"Coming?" Frank said, linking his arm through hers. She staggered as he led her through the door.

Out in the alleyway, by the dustbins at the back of the pub, Frank quickly pushed Brandy against the wall and kissed her. She recoiled from his sharp teeth and wispy moustache, a shock after the soft lips of Reardon and the other girls, but she quite liked the feel of his hard body pressing against her. Suddenly she remembered Bobby again. "I've got to go," she said when Frank lifted his mouth off hers to take a breath. "I've got to get back."

Frank grunted, pressed his teeth on her again, and pulled up her skirt. Soon she felt the scratchy brick wall on her behind as he pushed off her tights. He unzipped himself, lifted her legs and entered her, pushing her against the wall with each thrust. Brandy gasped at his suddenness, and grabbed his shoulders to steady herself. Hurry up, she thought as he grunted in her ear. Hurry the fuck up. But he wouldn't. He kept going so long she

41

thought her legs would drop off. At least she and Reardon would get each other worked up a bit first, she thought—this bloke was like a machine! She was still trying to decide whether she hated what he was doing or just didn't mind when, with a final groan, Frank shoved into her and crumpled. Only Brandy's feet, planted on the ground again, kept the two of them up. She pushed him off her against the wall, pulled up her tights, and staggered away. By the time he opened his eyes, she was gone.

Liz and Ron stumbled up the hill to the house, weaving and giggling. Liz kept falling off her platform clogs and thought this was the funniest thing that had ever happened to her. "Oopsy-daisy," she said, tumbling off the curb and laughing hysterically. Ron grabbed her, laughing, too, and hiccupped, which sent both of them off into further paroxysms. When they got to the front door and Ron had finally managed to locate the keyhole, Liz kicked her shoes into the hall, stumbled inside, and leaned against the wall. Ron fell against her and gave her a wet kiss, trailing it all the way down her neck. She moaned, her head giddy, and ran her hands over his rump. He was just getting to her cleavage, sliding her dress off her shoulders and kicking the door closed with one foot, when they smelled the vomit. "Phoo, what a stink!" Liz said, pushing him away. She flicked on the light and followed the smell down the hall to Bobby's room, hitting her shoulder against the wall and tittering as she lost her balance. When she opened his door the smell was stronger than ever. She stumbled over to Bobby's bed and stared at it for a while, trying to figure out through her drunken haze and the darkness what was different. A small pile lay in the middle of the bed, but it was curiously flat and still. She reached out her hand and patted it. "Bobby?" She hiccupped. "You awake, love?"

Her hand sank into the folded sheets. She grabbed them and whisked them off. The bed was empty, its bottom sheet gone. "Fucking hell, what's going on here?" She staggered over to Brandy's bed, her eyes just getting used to the dark. "Brandy, wake up!"

Brandy moaned.

"Wake up! Where's Bobby?"

"What?"

"Wake up!" Liz's words were slurred. "Where's Bobby?"

"I'm sleeping," Brandy mumbled.

Liz hit her on the shoulder. "Where's Bobby?"

"Shhh." Brandy rolled over slowly and pulled back the covers. Bobby was curled up beside her in clean pajamas, his hair damp, his breathing deep and even.

Liz smiled woozily and bent down to kiss him, but when she got near she smelled the vomit in his hair. "What happened?" she said.

"Those baked beans made him sick," Brandy whispered. "I put the sheets in the bath to soak but he was scared, so I let him in with me."

Liz frowned. "That's funny, I never knew him to get sick on them before." She burped. "All right. But don't make a habit of letting him into your bed, love, or you'll never get him out again." She gazed down at him, still puzzled. "Well, night then." She started out of the room, hiccupping.

"Night."

"And thanks for minding him for us, love."

Brandy smiled. She felt so happy. Bobby cleaned up and safe in her arms, her freedom roaring around inside her like an animal on the loose. Her life looking up. She put her arm around Bobby's small, hot body and pulled him close. "That's all right, Liz," she said. "Anytime."

3

"You feel like starting work Wednesday?" Liz said one evening a week later. The sisters were lounging in the bedroom, reading magazines and smoking.

"You what?" Brandy looked up. "Did they say yes, then?"

"Yup, they did."

"That's great!" Brandy gazed at her sister admiringly. "It'll be a lark working with you, Liz."

Liz smiled. "It's only a tryout, mind you, so you'll have to be on your best behavior. If it works out though, Jenny said she'll need someone to help with the sweeping up and stuff. I just want you to promise me something first."

"What?" Brandy squinted at Liz through the cigarette smoke.

"Don't start gabbing about Bullwood Hall, all right? They wouldn't like it. Hairline gets some posh customers, y'know, and it wouldn't look good."

"What, don't you think they'd like a little excitement 'round

44

the place? A quick B an' E during the shampoo, maybe? Or some GBH with the blue rinse?"

"Come off it, Brandy, I'm serious. If Jenny and Peg guess what you are they'll sack us both."

"They sound charming," Brandy said, but she relented. "All right, all right. As long as the moolah keeps coming in, I'll be a good girl."

Liz looked her sister over. Brandy was slouched back on the chair with her legs wide apart and her socks falling down. Her clothes were crumpled, her fingernails bitten to the quick, and her hair a shapeless, dull blond. Every inch of her looked the con. "Can't you sit right at least?"

"What's wrong with the way I'm sitting?"

"Look at yourself, Brandy! You're sitting like a man, knees all akimbo. People can see right up your skirt."

"Lucky them."

"And can't you hold your fag properly?"

Brandy looked down at the butt she held clamped between her thumb and forefinger. "What d'you mean?"

"You're holding it like a sodding hod carrier! Gawd, what did they teach you in that place?"

"Ah, leave off, for Christ's sake."

"Well, just try, will you? I mean, anyone who's in the know will be able to tell straight off you've been inside. It's written all over you, girl."

Brandy shrugged. She knew it and she relished it. It was part of her pride.

Nevertheless, she did allow Liz to make an effort to disguise her. Liz cut Brandy's hair short in a Sassoon-like style she'd learned at the salon, bleached it a bright metallic blond, and even lent her a few pounds to buy clothes with. By the day Brandy was due to start at Hairline, she was completely made over. She wafted into the shop, squeezed into new jeans and a tight blue shirt like jelly in a bag, and turned around proudly for Liz to admire her. Liz nodded. "That's better," she said.

The morning began badly. When Brandy entered the shop it seemed so glamorous to her, with its fancy customers and delicate smell of perfume and soap, that she wanted to turn around and flee. She didn't belong in this place—Liz's sharp eyes boring into her back told her as much. She felt like a trapped bear, sure she would stumble and knock into things. So when Liz introduced her to the two smart women who ran the shop, Brandy stared at them with an uneasy grin and, falling back on the cocky tone she'd protected herself with in Borstal, blurted, "What a coupla lookers you are!"

Jenny and Peg were startled. "Nice to meet you," they replied and turned their meticulously made-up faces away.

"Brandy," Liz hissed, "come over here." She led her across the room. "You can start by sweeping up. The bin's in the corner. All right?" She frowned at Brandy, trying to signal to her to behave herself, but Brandy only smirked at her. "Now what're you gawping at?" Liz said irritably.

"We have got a lot of plums crammed into our gobs this morning, haven't we?" Brandy jeered.

"Get out of it!" Liz shoved a broom into her hand, glancing over at Jenny and Peg to see if they'd heard. It was true that she tried to suppress her Birmingham accent more than usual in the salon, but she didn't want people to realize it. "Will you shut up?" she hissed. "D'you want this job or not? Can't you behave like a normal person for a change?"

"I was just trying to be funny," Brandy said, the glint of revenge in her eye.

"Well, if that's funny, I'm a sodding hat rack. You're out in the civilized world now, Brandy."

"All right," Brandy muttered, "but I don't see what's wrong with a bit of a laugh."

Liz shook her head. "I dunno," she sighed, "I dunno about you."

But soon Brandy became excited about the work. She felt important, swathed in a pink overall, busily lining up bottles and brushes on the shelves. She listened eagerly to the chat of the women, picking up their hairdresser jargon and rehearsing it in her head, and followed Liz around like a flea, watching her do the shampoos and trims as if they were wondrous feats. Liz showed her where the towels were kept and how to prepare special rinses, even how to take down appointments politely on the phone. Brandy enjoyed wrapping herself in a busy, officious air, as if to say "Look at me, I'm a real woman with a real job!" She imagined her friends in Borstal watching her with envy, the girls who'd never had a job, either, or Reardon, who didn't believe Brandy could be anything, and she performed perfectly for them.

That afternoon, half an hour after lunch, a tall blond came in and took a seat by the mirror. Hairline had a lot of students as customers, and they were often quite glamorous, tending to come from the privileged and moneyed classes, but this one was the most stunning to ever enter the door. She had the build of a model: tall and thin with absurdly long legs, and hair that looked as if a cloud of blond bubbles had dropped over her head. She sat in front of the mirror and primped while everyone watched, turning her head to one side so that the sun hit her in the face. Her eyes were big blue pools of smugness and her small, sharp nose was as delicate as a petal. She stopped when she saw them all looking at her. "Can anyone help me?" she said in an American accent.

Liz rushed over. "Yes, madum, certainly. What can we do for you today?" The woman pulled at her hair and said she wanted it curly but more shaped, like Barbra Streisand's. Nodding, Liz called to Brandy to bring her an overall.

Brandy trailed across the shop with the overall, then stood a few inches from the American, staring at her perfect face. Not for years had she seen anyone this beautiful—creatures like this never came near Borstal. She wanted to reach out and touch her skin, to see if it would really feel like flesh.

Liz saw the woman glance at Brandy and draw back. "Come over here," she whispered, pulling Brandy to the back of the shop. "Stop acting like a half-wit, will you? You're going to scare the pants off her."

Brandy winked. "I'd love to scare the pants off that one."

"Don't be disgusting!" Liz glanced around anxiously. "Look, pop out and get us all a Coke, all right?" She gave Brandy some change. "And stop gawping at that Yank like a bloody Pekingese!" Snickering, Brandy took the money and flounced out of the shop.

Liz lowered the woman's head onto the sink and rubbed shampoo into her hair, still squirming at Brandy's joke. "Is this your natural color, miss?"

"Hmm," the woman replied, her eyes closed. Liz supposed that meant yes.

"And the curls, are they natural, too?"

"They're natural, too. I thought you hairdressers were supposed to be able to tell." Liz shut up at that and rinsed out suds. Even the woman's voice was thick and sort of curly, Liz thought, although she was a snotty bitch.

Brandy came back in clutching two Cokes and a 7-Up. When she saw what Liz was doing she walked straight over. The American's eyes were closed.

"Where are you from, miss?" Brandy said, right in her ear. She'd be damned if she was going to let Liz have all the fun.

The woman jumped and opened her eyes. "Uh, North Dakota."

"Oh, yeah? Is that in California?"

"No, it's a state. It's pretty far north, on the Canadian border. It's real cold there in the winter."

"What a coincidence! I'm from the north, too." Liz couldn't believe Brandy's cheek. "Birmingham. Have you ever been there, miss?"

The American laughed. "No, only here and to London. I love this city though, it's so cute."

"Well, we don't exactly call Brighton a city but it is nice." Brandy cocked her head to one side like a little girl. "Are you a model, then?"

Blushing, the woman laughed again. She was lapping it up, Liz noted with disgust. "No, but thanks for asking."

"You should be, y'know. You'd make a bloody fortune."

The American put a hand up to her face and touched her high cheekbones. "Thanks, but I wouldn't want to be a model. I've got better things to do with my brain." She smiled at herself in the mirror. Liz pushed her head forward rather violently and rubbed her hair with a towel.

"Get to work, Amanda," she said through her teeth, "you're bothering the customer."

"No, she isn't," said the woman, muffled in the towel. "Let her stay."

Brandy flashed a grin at Liz and winked.

After the American had gone, the women gathered around to discuss her. "Do you think she was born that way or did someone make her?" Jenny said.

"I reckon she came out of a mold. Y'know, like the things they make plastic dolls in," Brandy offered.

" 'I've got better things to do with my brain,' " Liz mimicked, and they all laughed. It did them good to take the piss out of her.

When the sisters got home that evening, however, Liz turned serious. "Look," she said to Brandy, "you might have got away with all that cheek this time, but I know your tricks. Staring at the Yank like that! That's no bloody way to keep a job, is it? Jenny and Peg weren't too pleased, I can tell you. They'll sack you if you keep it up."

Brandy laughed. "Ah, don't worry so much, Liz, I'll be a good girl. Anyroad, at least I talked to her. The resta you tiptoed 'round like she was a visiting angel or summat."

"You call that talk? Firing questions at her like some sort of twirp? She only put up with you out of pity."

"That's what you think! These Yanks want to talk to the natives, y'know. You just don't have the gift of the gab."

"Don't make me laugh." Liz made her voice syrupy and high: " 'You should be a model, miss.' You call that gift of the gab? I've never been so embarrassed."

Brandy looked at Liz with amusement. "She liked it and you know it. You're jealous."

"Jealous! What of, I'd like to know? You just fancy her, that's all. You're disgusting, you are." Liz knew as she was saying it that she shouldn't, that Brandy had only been out three weeks and was still feeling rocky. She knew she should be more gentle with her. But Brandy had a way of making her so furious that she couldn't stop herself.

Brandy stopped laughing. "What's that supposed to mean?" she said, her voice low and threatening. She was trying not to fight with Liz, she was trying to keep her own corner undisturbed. But the bitch was making it impossible.

"Well." Liz lifted her hands. "It was just the way you gawped at her, that's all. I didn't mean much."

"So what if I did? You all did, too."

"I know. Look, drop it, will you? Jesus, you're so bleeding sensitive." Liz stood up and grabbed her bag. "I've got to fetch Bobby. You coming?"

Brandy scowled and shook her head. "Just get off my back," she muttered, "just leave me alone and mind your own fucking business. I've got to fucking live, don't I?"

By the evening, however, Brandy had calmed down enough to agree to look after Bobby again while Liz and Ron went out. She wanted to be alone, to get her meddling sister out of the house so that she could breathe without being scolded and judged. She took Bobby into his room and shut the door. Just the sound of her sister's voice made her want to scream. She began to play with him while his parents were getting dressed, but although Bobby usually loved the attention he got from her, he ran to the door and tried to open it.

"Mum!" he cried, struggling with the doorknob. "Mum!"

"What's the matter, Bobby?" Brandy said, surprised. The boy was crying by now, wrestling with the doorknob as if he were afraid of her. She got off the floor and went over to him. "What's the matter, little lad? It's just me, your aunty."

Bobby looked up at her, his face blurred with tears. "Let me out, Aunty," he pleaded, sobbing. "I want me mum." Shrugging, Brandy opened the door and he ran out to grab Liz's legs. "Don't go, Mum, don't go!" he wailed, holding her so tightly that she could hardly walk around the room.

"What's wrong, love?" Liz said, kneeling beside him. "Aunty will be here to play with you. Dad and me'll only be gone a bit."

"No! Don't go!" Bobby grabbed onto her arm. "I'll be good, Mum, I will. Please don't go, please."

"I know you're good, lovey, don't cry." Liz hugged him and gave his little back a pat. "What's wrong? You didn't mind being left with Aunty last time." She took his grubby face in her hands and turned it upwards so that he had to look at her. "Come on, love, tell me what's the matter."

Bobby couldn't talk clearly because he was crying too hard, but he said something about a white monster eating him when Aunty was gone.

"There's no monster, little fella. Monsters don't exist in real life, only in stories. Maybe it was a dream."

Bobby shook his head. "There is, there is!"

"Liz, come on! We're going to be late," Ron called. He was already in the hall.

Liz patted Bobby on the head and stood up. "You just tell your aunty to chase that monster away, all right? Whenever you see it, just tell her to gobble it up. She's a good monster eater, she is, you'll see." She expected Bobby to smile at this, but he didn't. She had to pry his arms loose from her and he was still wailing when they went out the door.

As Ron and Liz walked down to The Queen, where they were meeting friends for a drink, Liz continued to think about her son. He was not the type of child to be afraid of imaginary things; he was usually more concerned about when he'd get his next sweet than whether there was something waiting to catch him in the dark. The change in him worried her.

"Oy, Liz, are you listening?" Ron said, and gave her a shove with his elbow that almost knocked her off the curb.

"Watch it!"

"I've been talking to you."

"What? Oh, sorry."

"What's wrong with you, anyroad? Are you going to be like this all night?"

"Simmer down, Ron. I'm worried about Bobby. He doesn't usually make a fuss like that when we go out. Maybe we shouldn't leave him so much."

"So much! This is only our second time out in fucking months! Anyroad, you said yourself Bobby loves his aunty." Ron put his arm around Liz and gave her a squeeze. "Don't worry, love, it's probably just too much ice cream. He's a happy little kid, our Bobby. He'll be fine, you'll see."

The people they were meeting at The Queen were old friends, Dave and his girlfriend Valerie. Dave and Ron had known each other in Birmingham, and now worked together on the Marina. Valerie had met Dave on his first night out in a Brighton pub and they'd been together ever since. Liz liked Valerie. She was a tough little woman, short and buxom, with black hair and a wide, laughing mouth. She kept Dave from going overboard with his teasing and Liz had even seen her get the best of Ron once or twice. Liz knew that Ron fancied Valerie—she could tell from the way his eyes drifted to her breasts like dust to a shelf—but she trusted Val not to let him come near her. Val was her best friend, and they both knew that friends have to stick together.

When Liz and Ron reached the pub they found Dave and Val playing darts. Liz ordered a port and lemon like Val's and the men were both on Guinness, so it wasn't long before they were all a bit tipsy, laughing as usual at Val's dart playing. Val was so short that she had to shoot the darts way above her head, and whenever it was her turn Ron would shout, "It's the Blitz!" and Dave would make air-raid noises because her darts flew all over the place like paper airplanes. They played for a few hours until they were ready to go dancing at The Palace, a disco below the tiny, winding streets known as the Lanes. Val and Liz linked arms and stumbled down the road, giggling, the men following them. It was a nice night, brisk, with a bit of a sea breeze, and Liz felt relieved. The day at the salon with Brandy had been a strain.

At The Palace Val and Liz went to the ladies' room while the lads found them a table. Liz loved the ladies' there. It was a bordello-like place with a scarlet carpet, gold velvet walls, and dressing tables draped in red cloth. The mirrors were impressive, too, large fancy ovals painted in gold, their frames held up by cupids with tiny penises. There were times when Val and Liz spent most of the night in there, chatting with other women and having a drink. They relished the chance to get away from the lads' boring talk about the site and the horses, and it was a treat for Liz to be alone with a friend without Bobby.

While they freshened their makeup, Liz admired Val's dark skin in the mirror. She had always envied Val's ability to turn a deep brown in the sun—whenever Liz tried to tan she just burned and faded, so was always either bright pink or dead white. Liz had indoor skin, the kind that's bred under electric lights; council estate skin. If she didn't have a good figure, she often thought, she'd be as ugly as Brandy.

"How are things at home, Liz?" Val asked. Liz had told Val about Brandy, although she hadn't mentioned the Borstal; there were some things she just didn't want known.

"Brandy started with me at the salon this morning. Did I tell you she was going to? Jenny's letting her sweep up and such. She's going to give me half her pay for rent and board, though actually I'm planning to save some of it for her. She'd probably spend it all on sweets and fags otherwise."

"You're an angel, Liz, you really are. I hope she appreciates it."

Liz gazed into the mirror, considering. She wished she could tell Val the truth about Brandy, for she did want someone to pat her on the back and tell her how generous she was being. But she couldn't. Brandy was like a dirty secret, she thought, walking 'round for all to see. "I dunno," she said finally. "I think she might appreciate it a bit more if she had a chance to meet some people her own age—she's been stuck at home an awful lot. I'm going to ask Ron to look after Bobby for an evening soon, so I can take her out. She needs to meet someone, Val, a bloke who'll treat her decent. D'you know anyone?" Liz didn't say how hard it was to picture matching Brandy up with a man. What bloke would be interested in a pimply seventeen-year-old who'd spent two and a half years in the nick?

"Not offhand but I'll think about it. Still, if I were you Liz, I wouldn't ask Ron, I'd tell him. She's your sister, after all. He can't keep her a prisoner in the house all the time, you know."

"She isn't a prisoner, Val! She could go out if she wants. She's just never asked."

"Yeah, well, don't forget, she's a teenager. I mean, it wasn't that long ago for us, was it? How old are you, twenty-two? Would you have stayed in every night when you were her age? Just tell

Ron the two of you want a night out together. He needs a shove to look past his own nose once in a while."

Liz flushed, annoyed that Val spoke like that about Ron, but she knew Val was right. She always was.

The women finished fixing themselves up and walked back out to the dance floor. Liz liked slinking out of the ladies' on high heels, lips freshly greased, hips swinging. It made her feel sexy.

The Palace was a huge place, its entire ground floor given over to dancing except for a bar and a strip of stage at one end where the go-go girls wiggled about. Above the floor was a balcony where people sat and drank, looking over the railing to the dancers below. A giant ball covered with glass chips revolved slowly in the middle of the ceiling, sending rainbows over people's faces. Sometimes the management turned off the lights and put on an ultraviolet one, making everyone's dandruff glow in the dark.

Val and Liz went upstairs to join the lads, who had chosen a table in the middle with a good view and had the women's drinks waiting. Both men were staring at the go-go dancer, a black woman in hot pants with legs like billiard cues. She had a way of moving her hips as if they weren't attached to the rest of her. "Oy, wake up," Liz said, nudging Ron. "How about a dance, then?"

Ron blinked and kept staring. He was getting that nasty look around his mouth that came when he drank too much, so Liz decided to let him be. She sat down to watch.

Often, discos made Liz happy. The music and the drink would mix together in a blur, spinning her around in a kind of giggling tizzy like the bubbles in a Babycham. She would become involved in the story of each song when she was in that mood: the boy losing the girl or the girl losing the boy or the boy wanting the girl, and she'd really believe it for a while. Sometimes her eyes would fill with tears because the song was so sweet or sad. It was like watching a string of films all in a row, story after story catching her up and making her believe. That night, though, The Palace depressed her. She looked down at the youngsters dancing, most of them only fifteen or so, and thought about how she had cut her own youth short. There had been plenty of lads after her at home, but none of them had ever had the money to take her to discos, or anywhere much but to the local cinema, then she'd run off with Ron when she was only sixteen, barely old enough to know anything. She glanced at Ron resentfully. He'd been her ticket out, all right, but what a price she'd had to pay! Putting up with his moods, burdened with a kid already. It's all right for men, she thought. Why, he even had the odd one-night fling when he needed a break; she could tell by the way he'd creep into the house late at night muttering about poker games and insist on taking a bath before he'd let her touch him. But she . . . she couldn't even get away for a bit of clothes shopping on a Saturday morning. And now, on top of everything, she had Brandy to worry about.

A new song came on, "Rock You Baby," which Liz loved, so hoping to drive away her souring mood, she leaned over to touch Ron on the arm. "Ron? Aren't you going to dance at all, then?"

He turned to her, his eyes blank.

"Well, are you?"

"Am I what?"

"Going to dance?"

"Not now. Later." He turned back to the go-go dancer.

"I want to dance now!"

"Leave me alone, woman. Stop nagging."

"What's the bloody point in bringing me here, then?" Liz said loudly. "I'm not sitting here like a lump of dough all night while you lust after that wog!" Val glanced at her uneasily.

"Don't start," Ron said.

"Look, if you're going to act like that I'll just bloody go home."

"Shurrup, will you? I'm trying to relax."

"Relax from what, I'd like to know?"

Ron looked at her, his eyebrows raised. "What are you talking about, you stupid cow?"

"Don't you dare speak to me like that!" Liz shouted, and she stood up. "I'm going home."

Ron glanced at Dave with embarrassment. "No, you're bloody well not. Sit down. What's the matter with you, anyroad?"

"I will not stay here while you use that tone with me," Liz said in her salon accent. "I'm going home and that's that."

"You're not going anywhere till I say so. Sit the fuck down and stay there. What are you, pissed or summat?" He grabbed her arm.

"Let go of me!" Liz shouted. She saw people turning to stare. "I'm going!"

"I'll go with you," Val said, getting to her feet. She glared at Ron's hand until he let go of Liz's arm. Liz wished she had a stare as powerful as that. "It's not exactly a load of fun in here anyway if neither of you blokes'll dance. Come on, love." Val put her arm around Liz, not touching her but just cushioning the air, and walked her towards the stairs.

"Wait up," Dave called. He trotted after them, leaving Ron alone at the table. Grumbling, Ron drained the last of his pint and got up, too.

The four of them walked in silence up the hill to Ron and Liz's house. None of them knew what to say. The night had grown colder and Liz shivered. It was only eleven, closing time, much too early to go home from a disco. Liz sped up to get it over with. She had ruined the evening in a fit of pique and she knew it. She felt like a fool.

When they got to the house, Liz knew immediately that something was wrong. At first she couldn't tell what, she just knew it looked different, but when they reached the door she saw it was ajar. Someone had put the latch on and the hall light was shining through the crack—anyone could have walked in! She flung open the door and ran down the hallway, looking for Brandy, but as soon as she was inside she knew that her sister wasn't there. She could tell from the silence—there's a special sound when a house is empty, a kind of hollow swallowing. She didn't even call out but ran right into Bobby's room.

The room was so dark that it took some time for Liz's eyes to get used to it. At first all she could see were the beds, glimmering a dim white against the walls, but soon she saw all she needed. Both beds were empty.

"Where's Bobby?" she screamed, and reeled around to crash into Val, who was right behind her, looking frightened. She pushed her aside and ran into the kitchen. Empty. The bedroom. Emptier. "Bobby!" she shouted. "Bobby!"

"Maybe Brandy took him out for a minute," Val said. "I'll look." She ran out the front door, past Ron, who was standing stock still in the hallway, blocking the light.

"Do something!" Liz yelled at him. "They've gone!" She turned around and dashed back into Bobby's room to open the French windows to the garden, hoping Brandy had just taken it into her head to show Bobby the stars or something. But the garden, too, was empty, nothing but a black patch in the moonlight. She stumbled onto the grass and stood staring at the bushes, trying to see beyond them, her mind whirling with frightful pictures. Bobby under the wheels of a car, Bobby floating facedown in the sea, Bobby missing for weeks while television appeals flashed on the screen and police filled the house. What had Brandy done with him? And as she was wondering, she realized what a stranger Brandy really was. Liz hadn't seen the girl for five years; what did she know of her really? What did she know of the effect Borstal might have had on her? Brandy could have been turned into a monster.

"Ron's calling the coppers, Liz." She felt Dave's hands on her shoulders. "It'll be all right, you'll see. I'm sure they haven't gone far. Maybe she just took him out for a walk." He turned her around and steered her back into the house. Liz took a deep breath and felt her arms trembling.

Inside, Ron had finished calling the police and Val had come in from running up and down the road. They all gravitated to the hallway and stood there in silence. packed between the walls like coats in a cupboard—four huge and helpless adults.

"Well, fuck me, look at this! Is this a party or summat?"

They looked up. Brandy was weaving through the front door, smiling a lopsided grin. She crashed against the wall and propped herself up on one shoulder. Her lipstick was smudged and her face was a rubbery blob. "Uh-oh," she said, trying to cover up her nervousness with a laugh, "now I'm in for it."

"Brandy!" Liz lunged at her. She wanted to tear her eyes out. Ron leapt in front and grabbed Brandy by the shoulders.

"What the fuck have you done with Bobby?" He shook her and her head wobbled like a doll's. "Answer me!"

Brandy blinked but the grin stayed. She wasn't going to let that overweight old wanker scare her. "He's in bed," she said. "I was only out a minute. What's all the fuss?"

"Oh, he is, is he? Have a look then." Ron swung her around and half shoved, half carried her down the hall to Bobby's room. He pushed her against the wall a couple of times, hard, and Liz heard her grunt. "See? Now tell me where he is, you fucking whore." He whirled her around, took hold of both her shoulders, and shook her again. "Where is he?" he roared.

"Leave off! I don't know!" Brandy cried, and tried to push him away, but Ron's big hands were controlling her as easily as if she were a puppet. He shook her and slapped her hard on both cheeks, over and over. Her head swung around like a spring, right, left, back, sideways, right, left. She tried to kick out at him and to struggle, her face red and twisted, but he just hit harder.

"You stupid fucking cunt!" he shouted with each slap. "How long've you been out?"

"Only a coupla hours." Brandy gasped, the pain blurring with

56

her drunkenness. "Stop!" She swore at him but he slammed her up against the wall and hit her again. Something cracked and her nose began to bleed, the blood fusing with her snot and running down her face. Liz watched, confused.

"I'm going to keep looking for him," Val said in her ear. "I can't stand this." She went out the door.

Dave looked from Val's disappearing back to Ron, not sure whether to stop him or go after her. "I'll go and help," he said quickly, and followed Val out. Liz heard their footsteps running in different directions down the street, heard them shouting "Bobby!" and suddenly she didn't want them to be the ones to find him. She wanted to be there herself.

"I'm going to look," she told Ron.

He glanced at her, his hands still pinning Brandy to the wall. "All right. I'll wait here for the coppers."

Val had gone across the road and Dave up the street so Liz ran down the hill in the direction of the sea front. That was the way she and Bobby usually walked when they went out, on their way to the shops or his nursery school. Liz ran along calling him, then stopped to listen. The streets were quiet and she could hear her voice disappearing down the hill, echoed occasionally by Val or Dave shouting Bobby's name. At each corner she looked down the side streets, straining against the dark to see a small shadow or a hunched little figure. All the time she was sobbing "Please, please, please," trying to push away images of him lying in a gutter somewhere, crushed, or struggling in a kidnapper's arms.

When she had reached the fifth street down, panting and straining, her body a rod of fear, she heard the police sirens. They were racing up Dyke Road, and the new fear filled her that in their hurry they'd run over Bobby. She wanted to shout at everyone to stop, to be quiet, to tiptoe slowly and carefully. "He's precious, my little one," she wanted to tell them, "he's delicate. Don't go tearing about or you'll smother him." Then, as she listened to the sirens, her heartbeat and panic increasing with their volume, she heard another sound blending in with them. A high, interrupted crying, like the wail of a toy fire engine. When the police sirens died down for a second and the wail went on, she knew it was him.

"Bobby!" she cried, her breath catching in her throat. "Bobby, it's Mum! Where are you?"

"Muuuum!" she heard, weak and high, scared and tired. "Muuuum!" She followed the sound around a corner and there, huddled on the steps of a house, sat Bobby in his pajamas, shivering and sobbing with the kind of dry, despairing heaves that children have when they've cried all the tears they can make.

"Bobby!" Liz threw herself around him and picked him up and sat on the steps with him, trying to cover every inch of him with her arms and skirt. "Bobby, what're you doing here?"

Bobby sobbed and shook in her lap. "I"—he hiccupped—"I couldn't find you."

Liz held him tight and rocked him back and forth on the steps. "Ah, me poor little love. It's all right now, poor sweetie, your mum's here now." He sobbed anew, his teeth chattering, and buried his face in her breasts. His skin was cold and hard, like the side of a sink. Liz rubbed and cradled him while he clutched her with his stringy arms.

When she got home, having carried Bobby all the way, the place was full of lights and people. The neighbors were hanging out of their windows and police cars were parked all over the road. Liz walked into the kitchen, where Ron, Dave, and Val were helping the police to fill out forms, and just said, "Look." They all stopped and glanced up at her from the kitchen table. She smiled, fresh tears starting down her face. Unable to speak, she hid her face in his hair.

Ron jumped up and ran over, putting his bloodied hands around them and hugging. "Bobby, Bobby," he said over and over, "thank God, Jesus Christ, thank fucking God."

Bobby snuffled, "Dad," and put his arm around Ron's neck. "Aunty left me again. The white monster came. I had to find you . . ." His voice squeaked and trembled.

"It's all right, love, we're not angry," Ron said, kissing him all over his cheek.

"It was going to eat me, Dad. Is it gone, is it?"

"Yeah, love, it's gone. Come an' see." Ron shoved past the police, who were standing about with soppy smiles, and led Liz and Bobby to Bobby's room. He turned on the light. There was no sign of Brandy. Ron took the quilt off her bed and wrapped it around Bobby, who was still shivering in Liz's arms. "Don't worry, little fella, you're safe now," he said. "The monster's gone. It's gone forever."

4

Brandy awoke as the first gray fingers of dawn touched her eyelids. It took her a moment to orient herself, for she was confused by the black slats of wood above her, the smell of seaweed, and the feel of the hard, wet stones grinding beneath her shoulders. She yawned and pain shot over her face but she didn't dare touch herself, afraid of what she'd find. Her nose was so swollen that she couldn't breathe through it, one eye was puffed almost closed, and her jaw and cheeks ached as if someone had been sitting on them. Her head throbbed from last night's drink and this morning's hunger.

She stood up slowly, shivering from the cold ground, and looked about her. When the police had pulled up in front of the house and Ron had finally left off beating her to bring them in, Brandy had run. She'd sneaked into Bobby's room, stuffed a few belongings into her duffel bag, and escaped out the French windows, staggering down back alleys to the beach. She'd found a hidden spot under the West Pier, already occupied by an unconscious tramp, and had huddled into the shadows, too drunk and sore to go any farther. There she had sat, shaking, until she'd fallen asleep.

With the morning Brandy realized that no one would come to look for her. Liz and Ron had called the police to find Bobby, not her. "After all," she told herself, "I didn't commit no sodding crime." But when she glanced at the tramp, still asleep in his bundle of newspapers, she felt afraid. She'd never actually had to spend the night out like this before—there had always been Jeff to go to, or her mother's flat, or a cell. She had never been quite this alone. She picked up her bag and walked towards the sea.

Nothing was stirring yet, not even the early fishermen. A heavy mist hung over the beach, tinted pink from the dawn, the seagulls' cries echoed in the empty air, and the stones crunched loudly under Brandy's feet. She cursed the high heels and tight skirt she was still wearing from her night at the pub. Her heels caught on the stones, turning her ankles, and the crisp sea breeze penetrated the thin cloth of her jacket. She stumbled towards the waves, wanting to hide in the pink clouds.

When she got to the edge of the sea, gray-green and murky under the mist, she stood on a wet patch of sand, her heels sinking, and stared into the waves. The sea was calm in that early-morning way, before boats and wind and busy daytime have stirred it up, and the waves caressed the beach gently, sucking at the stones. She watched the usual Brighton flotsam float by: a piece of wood, a Styrofoam cup, misshapen lumps that the locals said were sewage. A seagull swooped down, startling her, and pecked at something in the seaweed. A rotting stench wafted under her nostrils and passed, leaving fresh, searing air in its wake. Brandy thought of her cozy room in Liz's house, of cuddling in bed with Bobby, so warm and soft, of the kitchen smells of toast and coffee, and her head ached all the more. She wondered what had happened to Bobby and her throat constricted at the thought that perhaps he really had come to harm because of her. "I thought he'd be all right," she whimpered. "I never thought he'd leave." And as she stood facing the sea, her feet getting wet, her cold legs bulging out of the runs in her stockings, she became filled with rage at herself. Liz had been her lifeline—she'd had a real job because of Liz, a home, maybe even the chance to become the sort of person who could find Jeff and hold on to him . . . how could she have been such a fool as to fuck it up? Brandy looked at the waves creeping towards her feet, at the seagulls with their silly bobbing heads, at the tangle of rusted tins and seaweed around her, and all these things seemed to have a place but her. Maybe Murdock had been right when she'd cracked that joke about Brandy coming back. Maybe freedom wasn't for girls like her.

Hearing voices, she looked around, up the beach to where the mist had cleared and the sun was burning through. Some fishermen were pulling their boats down to the sea, arranging their nets and shouting to each other. She watched one of them, a red-faced man in his fifties with coarse gray hair and hands like bared muscle. As he shoved his boat past her, he nodded and mouthed, " 'Mornin'," casting a sidelong look at her battered face. He splashed into the water, protected by thigh-high rubber boots, and leapt into his boat. Brandy swung her bag over her shoulder and teetered back up the hill to find something to eat.

Most of the stalls along the beach, small grubby places built like rabbit warrens under the road, were still closed, but a couple of the cafés had opened to cater to the fishermen and other early risers. Brandy dug into her pockets to find 20p, all she had left of her dole money, and regretted the cash she'd handed over to Liz. She stopped at the window of one of the cafés and squinted through the glass to read the prices up on a noticeboard. Her 20p would buy only tea and a bun, but it was something. As she drew back she saw her face dimly reflected in the salt-glazed glass. This wasn't the first time she'd been beaten up, but it was the worst. Dried blood was smeared under her nose and around her mouth, the white of one eye was a bright red, and the left side of her face was purple and distorted with swelling. She started to smile—her resemblance to a horror film poster amused her—but smiling hurt her swollen lip. Hoping her appearance would win her some food, she walked in.

When the group of men in the café saw this bloodied, scruffy girl wobble in on high heels, they stopped chewing to stare. Brandy noticed them but kept her eyes averted. She even tried to swing her hips sexily as she walked across the room, unaware of how this added to her grotesqueness. "Cup of tea, please, and a bun," she said to the blue-haired old woman gaping at her from behind the counter. Her words came out stiff and slurred because she couldn't move her swollen mouth properly and her throat was sore from her night out in the fog.

The woman blinked, nodded, and went to pour the tea. As she handed it over she said, "You all right, ducks?"

61

Brandy shrugged and looked down. The kind words made her feel squelchy inside but she fought the feeling off with practiced speed. She picked up the tea and shakily carried it to an empty table. Grateful for the steamy warmth of the café, she sat down and put her cold hands around the cup, hunching over the tea to sip it and trying not to spill a precious drop. Each sip stung the cuts inside her mouth.

The men in the café remained silent. Brandy felt them staring at her but wasn't bothered. She was used to being stared at—the times she was arrested, the time she attacked the matron at the community home, various times in Borstal when she'd caused trouble—being stared at meant nothing to her. She sipped her tea and began on the bun, moving it gingerly around her sore tongue and lips. When she finished, she felt hungrier than ever. She gazed into her empty cup, feeling the warmth come back into her limbs, and thought about what had happened.

When Brandy had left Bobby for the second time, she'd never foreseen any trouble. Why should she? They hadn't eaten any more chocolates, she'd put him to bed—he seemed perfectly safe. And she really had only nipped out for a couple of hours. Even when she'd got back and found those people clogging up the hallway, looking like death had come for supper, she hadn't expected them to turn on her like that. Christ, Brandy thought, that Ron is off his rocker. She shook her head and moved her teacup around in its saucer. Well, maybe she had taken a risk, she admitted, but that was no call to treat her like a murderer. For a moment the worry that Bobby was hurt flitted across Brandy's mind again, but she quickly dismissed it. Liz should have taught him not to go out on his own, that's all. Any mother should know that—Brandy herself would do it if she had a child. "Anyroad," she muttered, "what did they want me to do, spend me life squeezed up in that poky flat like the two cheeks of a bum?" Brandy clicked her tongue and hunched her shoulders against a new chill, wondering what Reardon would have made of all this. Inside, Reardon had liked to talk about how people decide what's right and what's wrong. The woman thought she had it all sorted out, with her ideas about how God teaches people to be good. Brandy snickered, thinking of Reardon's image of God sitting up there in the clouds, so smug and sure of Himself, dispensing goodness to all below. If God's spreading love and goodness, I could show him a few places He's missed! she thought. Maybe she was nothing but a Borstal bird, but she did know a few things.

Outside it's wrong to nick a packet of sweets off a fat man's shelf, inside you're a fool if you don't. Outside no one minds if you help yourself to a bit of cake in the fridge, inside they lock you up for six months. Maybe it was stupid of her to leave Bobby, but if there was one thing she'd learned in this stinker of a life, it's that what's right and what's wrong all depends on who's making the rules. And whatever Reardon said, Brandy was sure that the rule maker was not God.

The men in the café had forgotten Brandy by now and were talking again in low grunts. Some of them got up to ask for more tea and some of them left, banging in a cold draft each time they opened the door. Brandy sat and sat. The warmth was seeping out of her again now that the heat of the tea was wearing off and her nose was beginning to throb with a new intensity. She touched it again, gently. It felt puffy and smooth—she was sure Ron had broken it. Glancing at a table next to her, where the men had left toast crusts and pats of butter, she wished she'd chosen a busier café so that she could have taken the leftovers without being noticed. Suddenly a fresh cup of tea was slapped down in front of her. "Here you are, girl," said the old woman. "You look as if you need it."

Brandy glanced up, blinking. "Thanks, yeah, thanks," she mumbled. "Uh, you couldn't spare anything to eat, could you?"

The woman narrowed her eyes. "I don't usually let you girls come in here, y'know, but you look like you've had a rough time of it. Can you pay?"

Brandy shook her head and found her eyes filling with tears. Gawd, she thought, a couple weeks outta the nick and I get all soppy.

The woman averted her face. "All right, all right. You better clean up, too. There's a washroom in there." She pointed to a door in the corner and went back behind the counter. Brandy muttered her thanks, swallowed the tea and got up.

The washroom was a tiny toilet and sink, far from clean, but at least it had hot water and a pile of paper towels in it. Brandy wiped her face off as best she could, wincing into the mirror, and combed her hair. It helped to wash away the blood and smeared makeup, but she still looked a fright and her face ached mercilessly. She went through her duffel bag to pull out her jeans but then changed her mind: If she was going to hitchhike to Birmingham, and she didn't see what else she could do, her tight skirt might help, so she just took off her torn stockings and threw them away, putting on socks instead. Her makeup and other shoes were still at Liz's, but she reckoned the socks and high heels might appeal to drivers. The worst thing was having no money.

Back in the café, the woman had given her a plate of sausages and toast. Brandy sat down and ate them greedily, her spirits rising with each bite. When she got to Brum, she decided, she'd go back to the squat in Balsall Heath where she used to live with Jeff. She had written to Jeff's Borstal giving him Liz's address and had planned to wait until she heard from him before returning to Brum, but she could just as well meet him there. Once he was released he'd probably go to the squat anyway, or his friends would. The hopelessness she felt earlier lifted a little. Reardon had always told her not to dwell on the bad things in life: "Look ahead, not behind, and God will help you," and Brandy could see the sense in that now. What's more, she'd screwed up so badly with Liz that there was nothing for it but to try something new anyway.

When she'd finished eating Brandy asked the woman which road she should take to Birmingham.

"Birmingham!" The woman laughed. "What do you want to go up there for?"

"That's where me mum lives," Brandy said, putting on a little girl act. "I want to go home."

The woman sniffed and looked her up and down. "I'm not surprised you do, although I don't know what kind of mother you must have to let you get into this state. You should go to hospital first, if you ask me."

Brandy knew the woman thought she was a prostitute and felt indignant, but not wanting to antagonize her or her generosity, she merely shrugged. The woman told her how to get to the London Road, then hesitated and said with an embarrassed air, "Do you have any money?" Brandy shook her head. "All right. I don't know why I'm doing this but you remind me of the daughter I never had or something. Here." She handed Brandy 50p. "Go on, then, get out of here." Brandy picked up her bag and scuttled out.

It took Brandy all day to get to Birmingham, it being unconnected to Brighton by any direct route. She had to spend many hours walking from one motorway junction to the next or waiting by the road with her thumb stuck out. Only lorry drivers would stop for her—even single men in private cars were put off by her swollen, rapidly discoloring face. The drivers all asked her how she'd been hurt, but she put them off with discouraging grunts until they turned surly, so most of the journey went by in silence. Brandy almost enjoyed herself after a while, sitting high up in the cabs, serenaded by the steady rumble of the lorry engines, looking over the flat, unchanging fields that flanked the motorways. Sometimes she caught a driver eyeing her cold bare knees, mottled pink and pudgy all the way up under her skirt, but that's as far as any of them went. She sat with her hands under her legs, looking out of the windows, and let the long rides ease her away from her worries, into dreams about Jeff.

Only the last driver got any conversation out of her. He was a wiry man with dirty hands and a blond moustache. They had just caught sight of a glow of lights he said was Birmingham when he asked her if she had been away long.

Brandy muttered and stared out of the window, wanting to preserve the numb daze she had wrapped around herself during the long journey.

"What was that? I can't hear you over the engine."

"I said yes."

The man glanced at her. Brandy was glad it was night so that her bruises weren't so visible—she was tired of making up stories to explain them.

"Where'd you grow up? Round Solihull, was it?"

"No, London."

"London?" The man laughed. "Where'd you get that Brummy voice, then?"

"What Brummy voice?"

"All right, all right, I get the message. Christ, I was only trying to make conversation. You're bloody lucky I don't do anything more. You should know better than to hitch by yourself at night. I'd never let me daughters do it."

"Why'd you pick me up, then?"

"Better me than some pervert, eh?" He winked.

"I can look after meself," Brandy said fiercely. "I got a black belt in judo, y'know, and an orange in self-defense."

"Orange? No such thing."

"Oh, yeah? You want me to prove it?"

"Never mind!" The man looked at her again. "You're a real charmer, aren't you?" He swerved to the side of the road, pulled to a stop, and jerked his head towards the door. "Go on, get out," he said. "I'm going the other way."

"Fuck you!" Brandy climbed out and slammed the door behind her.

The man had dropped her off at a motorway junction, and she watched the back of his lorry disappear into the night with a sudden sense of desolation. The motorway stretched in front of her, surrounded by nothing but empty black fields and rubble. She shivered, cold again after the warmth of the cab, shouldered her duffel bag, and walked along the edge of the road towards the glow of lights in the distance. Ahead of her, at the end of a small street, she saw a single street lamp casting a pool of white light on the ground, the color of ice.

At first Brandy hoped to find some recognizable street signs. Although she knew central Birmingham well, she was not familiar with its outskirts and had no idea where she was. She walked for almost an hour, sticking her thumb out at the occasional passing car, but the suburban scenery didn't change much and the signs meant nothing to her. She felt light-headed with hunger, her face ached, and her feet were throbbing from her high heels, but the street was too dark and filthy for her to take off her shoes. On she walked, noticing only that the city lights were getting denser so that she must, she reckoned, be heading towards the center of town. She was surprised that she hadn't come across a pub or any people: Except for the odd circle of light from a street lamp and the click of her heels, there was no sign of life.

As the walk stretched on, Brandy tried to sing. Snatches of music from the Borstal radio ran through her head and she crooned them softly to herself, stepping in time to the beat. But gradually the sound of her voice echoing in the silence began to spook her, much as a child is frightened by its own crying after a nightmare, so she fell silent. Bending her head, she watched each foot lift and step and wobble, one in front of the other. Now that she was so tired, she found it harder to fend off the memory of Ron's fist slamming into her eyes, or the thought that Bobby might have been run over or lost.

As Brandy's mood darkened, her sense of adventure sank gradually into fear. Her mind began to flicker, passing from images of Jeff turning his back on her to pictures of him sneering at her from the arms of another woman. She tried to comfort herself with thoughts of the good times with him, although what was real memory and what the fantasy she had polished during the endless, empty months in Borstal was no longer clear to her. She did remember how he looked, pale with sunken cheeks and a pigeon chest, his arms stringy but strong. She also remembered how he had felt, a skeleton covered with soft, downy skin;

sharp bones that dug into her, ribs like a fence that always made her feel fat in comparison. She could even remember his voice, a deep Brummy drone with an accent that went right up his nose, and the way he always called her love or ducks, a bit like an old woman. But what had he actually said? Brandy remembered silences, when there hadn't been much worth saying. And Jeff's stories about how he'd stolen money or a leather jacket, about how he'd kicked his older brother down the stairs, or the trips he'd gone on with his pills. And mutterings of revenge against another gang member, or a copper or any of the other numerous people who were his enemies. But she couldn't remember the important talks. She shook her head and looked up again, still walking although now her legs ached with a sharp pain that spread all the way up her back. Even if she couldn't remember the exact words, she decided, she could remember the feelings she'd had with Jeff: that sense of being accepted and understood, even protected. The sense of being curled up together in a warm nest, fending off the world.

Brandy had a theory about herself and Jeff. She'd developed it inside, after one of her talks with Reardon. She believed that true love got started before people were born. If, as Reardon had told her, people move about as formless souls, like shadows, before they come into the world, then Brandy reckoned they must find mates in their soul life just as people do in human life. And once the souls have found those mates, she believed, they fuse together—perhaps they are born holding hands, or connected by their feet—after which they belong to each other forever. Brandy had decided that she and Jeff were like that. Anyone could tell by looking at them because they were such opposites. Where she was short, he was tall. Where she was plump, he was skinny; they had all the parts of each other the other one was missing. So when they were separated, locked away in different cages, it was as if they were being starved of sections of their own selves. That was why, Brandy thought, a part of her had died inside Borstal; why she sometimes felt as flat and gray as a shadow.

At last Brandy got to a bus stop. When she saw the numbers on the sign she at least had a vague idea of where she was. No bus had passed her since she'd been walking and she had no money, having spent the blue-haired woman's 50p on a packet of cigarettes earlier in the day, which she'd long since finished, but she stopped anyway and slumped against the post. She felt giddy and nauseated. Her legs buckled under her and she slid down the post and landed in a crouch, dropping her head onto her knees. In Bullwood Hall she would have been in bed by now, at least with the nightly cocoa and bread that passed for supper in her stomach. A quick nostalgia for the coarse blanket, the familiar square walls and window of her cell shot through her, but she shook it off. "I'm not that fucking desperate," she told herself, and struggled to shift her mind to other things. She felt her knees press into her brow as her head grew heavier, and her backbone curve and settle as if she would never be able to straighten up again. Her toes shoved down to the ends of her shoes, crushed into unnatural points as they took the weight of her body, and her head spun, lifting her towards the dark summer clouds floating mildly above.

Brandy was awoken by the roaring of an engine. She looked up just in time to see the bus approaching, a blue and cream ship blazing light and warmth, and she grabbed her bag and leapt at it, waving one arm wildly. The bus streaked past but stopped, its brakes squealing. She stumbled on and up the stairs to the top deck, where she could at least breathe smoke if not actually cadge a cigarette off someone. She flopped into a seat at the front, took off her shoes and socks and put her feet up on the window, cooling them on the sooty glass. Her toes were red and rubbed raw, stinging like fresh wounds. She turned around to see who else was there: a middle-aged woman, worn down in the way of a factory worker, smoking a cigarette and staring out the window, and two men reading newspapers. Leaving her bag on the seat, Brandy got up and hobbled in bare feet to the nearest one. "Got a fag you can spare, mister?" she croaked.

He jumped and looked up at her over his tabloid. His eyes widened at her battered face but he reached in his pocket and pulled out a packet, holding it out to her. "Help yourself," he muttered.

Brandy took one, fumbling, her hands stiff with hunger and fatigue, and put it in her mouth. The man lit it for her with a lighter. She nodded and returned to her seat, praying the conductor wouldn't come up to collect the fares too soon. Inhaling the smoke, she felt it cut down her hunger a little and gazed through her wobbly reflection out of the black window. She liked buses at night. They were cozy and bright and they blocked out the world—she could hardly see anything except shop lights and refracted glare. Sitting up on the top deck was like riding a blimp, sailing along warm and safe above the city. No sounds but the ticking engine and coughs of the people inside, no disturbances except the sway of the bus as it turned a corner, the slight interruption of the stopping and starting, the ringing of the bell. Brandy leaned her head against the window and dozed.

She rode three long stops before she was thrown off. The conductor wasn't angry, just weary. "Come along then," he said, once she'd confessed to having no money. "Off you get." He held the bus at the stop, watched her squeeze her swollen feet back into her shoes, and ushered her firmly down the steps and off the platform before ringing the bell and swaying away into the distance. Brandy took a last drag of her cigarette and threw it into the gutter. She had at least got into the town proper now—she could see the train station. She knew where to go from there.

For another hour Brandy walked. She was heading towards Jakeman Road in Balsall Heath, a part of Birmingham where many houses had been abandoned, left either to be claimed by the latest wave of immigrants or knocked down by the city. It was there that she'd lived for the year between her two stints in Borstal, squatting with Jeff and three of his mates in one of the tiny, brick houses that ran along the road like a string of crumbling orange beads. They had broken into a house at the end of the row by tearing open the plywood boards that covered a window in the back and crawling through the smashed glass.

The gang had decided not to occupy the front of the house because they were too visible through the windows and they liked to think of the place as their criminal hideout, so they crammed their beds between the narrow walls of the two small back rooms. They furnished their new home with scraps found on rubbish dumps or stolen during their periodic burglaries: drawers without chests for their clothes, pillows they scattered about for chairs, blankets they hung over strings for privacy, and patches of carpet they used to block out the drafts. They lived without electricity or water, so had nothing but candles or matches to see by and nothing but each others' bodies for warmth, but they managed. Brandy had always liked the coziness of the squat. She'd liked living secretively among the ruins, scurrying through the dirt and loose bricks like a mouse.

As she drew nearer to Jakeman Road, however, she began to feel afraid. She remembered Reardon saying to her "It's one thing to make dreams, Brandy, but don't expect to live them," and she understood the wisdom of this as she approached the squat. She stopped for a moment and reached into her bag for her cough drop tin, pulling it out and holding onto it for luck. Inside was Jeff's letter, talking of love and marriage. Brandy knew most of the girls inside lost their blokes while they were rotting away behind bars, unable to fight rivals or remind anyone of their existence, but she'd always expected to be different because of the soul shadows. Not until now had she acknowledged how thin this expectation was. She brought the tin to her lips and whispered, "Be there, please," as if she were trying to evoke a spell, then clutching it tightly turned a corner to enter Jakeman Road. As exhausted as she was, her body was alive with sensations—the pain in her legs, feet, and face, the hunger cramping inside her, the headache and dizziness, the cuts still raw and stinging in her mouth. She held the tin to her chest and stumbled on, breathing quickly.

Brandy walked to the end of the dark road and around the corner before she realized that something was wrong. She stopped, confused, and looked around. I must have the wrong bleedin' place, she thought, surprised at herself. Apart from the occasional drunk sprawled against a wall, and one or two prostitutes smoking on the corner, the street was deserted and silent. Brandy turned and walked back, looking for a landmark. There was the old grocer's, locked and dark now. There was the newsagent's on the corner, where the gang had bought their cigarettes when they couldn't steal them. There were the same old rows of dingy little houses, filled with Indians. Brandy stood still and looked again. The buildings, a murky black in the darkness, breathed silently around her as if waiting for her to discover their secret. She took a step forward and stared. Her building was gone. The street simply ended a house earlier. There was nothing but a patch of rubble and a few tufts of grass. It wasn't even like the old war-bombed buildings Brandy remembered from her childhood, where she could see the layers of wallpaper from each sheared-off room and find the broken toys of a dead baby in the bricks. The building had simply been whisked away.

5

Liz and her family clambered onto a green double-decker bus and up the stairs to the top. They chose seats in the front to please Bobby, and Liz watched affectionately as he pressed his face against the window and reported everything he saw: the cars weaving beneath him, the people out at their morning shopping, the trees heavy with summer leaves. The higher the bus climbed, past houses and lawns, flower beds and bushes, cricket fields and woods towards Devil's Dyke, a peak among the chalk downs of Sussex, the more excited Bobby grew. He seemed to have forgotten all about the traumas of the night before.

The morning started off damp, chilled by the sea breeze that always swept through Brighton before eleven, and at first Liz worried that she and Ron had taken the day off for nothing. But by the time the bus was halfway up Dyke Road the sun had come out and the morning was promising to turn into one of those bright, summer days the British long for all year. Liz smiled out of the window, still basking in the relief of averted tragedy.

The bus let them off in front of an ugly sprawl of modern buildings that contained a pub and some tourist information. It was too early for opening hours so Liz suggested that they take a walk and work up a thirst. "You could do with a bit of exercise," she said, nudging Ron's large belly. "Come on, let's go over that hill."

"What d'you think I get all fucking week?" But he agreed and they headed across the fields. The view around them was green and comforting—undulating hills, clumps of soft trees, velvety crevices. Liz studied it carefully, as if its vivid, summer innocence were too lovely to be anything but an illusion. To one side lay the Sussex farmland, patches of fields outlined by hedges and dotted with the tawny colors of harvest; to the other was the sea, spread out like an aquamarine sheet, bright, shimmering, and vast. Bobby ran ahead of them, leaping and running and tumbling, his arms held out like the wings of a scrawny bird.

Liz and Ron walked in silence. They felt awkward, not having spent leisure time alone and sober like this for years, and Liz hardly knew what to say. Her thoughts were full of the previous night—how they had almost lost Bobby, why Brandy had left, what Ron had actually done to her—but she was afraid to bring these things up. She looked down at the grass, searching for safer subjects. The only ones that occurred to her were foolish, trivial stories about life at the salon.

"I'm glad we're doing this," Ron said, making her jump. "I think it'll be good for our Bobby to have a day with us."

"Yeah, poor love."

They watched Bobby leaping about in front of them, and Ron chuckled. "Well, he seems happy enough now, doesn't he?"

"Yeah." Liz sighed.

Ron looked over at her. "What's wrong, love?"

She hesitated, glancing at him to see if he seemed willing to hear her thoughts.

"What? Go on, you can tell me." He reached out and patted her shoulder.

Liz shrugged. "I dunno, Ron." She paused, still uncertain. "It's just that I can't help blaming meself a bit, that's all. Both of us, really. We should've known better than to leave Brandy in charge like that."

72

"You what? You're not trying to say it's our fault now, are you?"

"Well, no, but I mean the girl hardly knows how to buy a Tampax, let alone mind a child. She's been doing time since she was fourteen, remember."

"She knows too much, if you ask me."

"No, listen. I mean she's stunted, in a way. She hasn't had time to learn much about the real world. In Borstal they don't teach you how to fend for yourself, y'know. They just treat you like a child. They don't let you make decisions about anything. Brandy was telling me you can't even choose when to have a bath."

Ron grunted and hitched up his trousers. Bobby was a few feet in front of them, intently digging into the ground with a stick. "I don't think that's an excuse," he said at last. "It isn't as if we never gave her a chance, is it? I mean, we had her home for a whole fortnight before we went out—any decent person would've known not to leave a little kid by himself. She's just bloody selfish, Liz, you've got to face it. Our mistake was taking her in in the first place. We're not a bleedin' home for delinquents, are we?"

"Yeah, well, she is me sister."

"There are some relatives you'd best do without. You've got a bad lot in your family. I'd drop 'em if I were you."

Liz tightened her lips. Drop them! she thought. That's what I've been trying to do for years.

"Mum, look what I found." Bobby ran up holding something in his hands. It was a translucent white stone, flecked with gray. He held it out to her proudly, his pudgy fingers already stained with earth. "Keep it in your pocket for me, Mum, will you?"

Liz took the stone and inspected it. "It's lovely," she said. "All right, but don't load me up with the whole bloody hill. I won't be able to walk otherwise!"

Bobby laughed and ran off to gather more treasures. "You're a good mum, y'know that?" Ron said quietly. He put his arm around her shoulders and gave her a hug. Liz blushed, thinking of all those days she screamed at Bobby and slapped him when Ron wasn't home.

"You know summat, Liz?" Ron said, still walking with his arm around her. "I've been thinking about last night. That was so fucking awful, the idea of losing Bobby an' all, that I thought it's time we had another. You know, as a sort of safety valve." He pinched her bum and grinned.

Liz wiggled away from his fingers.

"I know we keep talking about it," Ron continued, more serious now, "but don't you think it's time? I mean, not only for safety's sake, but 'cause Bobby's getting of an age to need a brother or sister. What d'you think?" Liz looked up into his reddened face, slack now in the jowls but still handsome in a heavy sort of way. She frowned.

"Well?" he persisted.

"Yeah, I suppose so." She sighed, looking away. "You know, soon." She'd said this many times before and knew that Ron's patience was wearing thin, but the idea of another reason to never be able to go out, another load of chores and nuisances and weights on her freedom had always filled her with dismay. Now, however, fresh from the fear of losing Bobby, she thought maybe Ron was right.

By this time they had reached the cliffs, and Liz ran over anxiously to take Bobby by the hand. They were so high up that when they lay on their stomachs to peer over the edge, they could see seagulls wheeling about beneath them. Liz stared down over the rough grass and patches of chalk to the rocks below, listening to the bird cries mingling with the crash of waves. Normally she wasn't afraid of heights, but here the rocks jutted up as if waiting to impale a body, and the waves smashed hungrily. She put an arm around Bobby and held him so tightly that he squealed and wriggled. The sea air burned her lungs, and the wind seemed about to sweep them off the cliff.

Ron touched her foot, startling her. "It's opening time!" he called. "Come on, Bobs-me-Bob, I'll race you back to the pub!" When he took hold of Bobby's hand and led him away, Liz felt reprieved.

At the pub they sat outside in the sun and drank beer. Bobby perched on a chair next to them and munched on a sausage, singing while he ate. "Shut your mouth when you chew," Liz said, but she couldn't help smiling at him. He looked so happy, his blond hair blowing about in the breeze, his little chin smeared with sausage grease. He hummed to himself and kicked his legs. Once he stopped and said loudly, "This is fun!"

Liz let herself drift into a pleasant daze. Leaning back, she turned her face to the sun and shut her eyes. She felt lazy and sensual, a soft blur cushioning her from worries, as if they were one of those upper-class county couples she sometimes saw in pubs, people who never seemed to have a care in the world.

74

"Oy, Mum!" Bobby climbed onto her lap, jabbing her stomach with his sharp knees. "I'm finished. Come play with me."

"You go and play by yourself, Bobs," Ron said. He pointed to the end of the pub garden where a rusted pedal car was nestled in the grass. "Look, there's a car just your size. Go on, take it for a drive. Your mum and me want to talk."

Bobby ran to the car while Liz took a few more swallows of beer and looked down. A slight haze hovered over the grass and she was beginning to feel hot. The silence between her and Ron throbbed.

"Want another?" he said, getting up. She nodded and while he was gone ate her flabby cheese sandwich slowly, wallowing in the sudden quiet of the garden around her. She looked at the green bushes, dense with color, at the grass bright and fresh, and wished she could be alone sunbathing in a garden somewhere, listening to the radio. Or just lying in a field where no one could see her.

"Cheers." Ron handed her a half of shandy and sat down again. "This is the life, eh?" he said, sounding unsure, and drank through his second pint. Liz nodded, smiling.

When Bobby finally got too bored to stay at the pub any longer, they walked back into the fields. They had the hills to themselves, it being a weekday, and Ron said he'd like to find a sunny, secluded spot to lie down in. Bobby ran ahead of them, still as full of energy as when he first woke up, leading them away from the cliffs and down into a valley. "Look, Mum," he shouted, and Liz trotted beside him. He had found a small, brown river meandering along the valley bottom. "Can I have a swim, Mum, can I?"

"Let your dad try it first, love. You can't go in if it's too deep. Ron, d'you fancy a swim?"

Ron chugged up, his face red and sweaty. He looked around, grinning. "Why not? Might do me some good." He stripped down to his red briefs. Bobby had already taken off his clothes and was running around naked, his little hips as slight as a wraith's.

"You wait here with me for a minute," Liz said to him. She sat down on the bank and pulled Bobby onto her lap, caressing the smooth insides of his legs and rubbing her hands over his tight, round belly. With grunts and curses, Ron lowered himself into the water. His face, neck, and arms were all a roughened, reddish tan from his work outside but his torso and legs were a pasty white. He slipped on some mud and fell in, gasping from the cold, and Bobby squealed with laughter, rocking back and forth on Liz's lap. She laughed, too, at the pure joy in Bobby's face. Ron clowned for their benefit, dipping up and down, spouting water and pretending to drown.

"I wanna go in!" Bobby said.

"Is it shallow enough?" Liz called when Ron emerged.

"I'll hold him, it's all right." Ron waded up to the edge and Liz handed Bobby over, thinking that he looked more like a woodland sprite than ever next to Ron's bulk. Ron dipped him in and out of the water, making him shriek, and Bobby retaliated by pulling his father's nose. Liz sat back down on the bank and gazed fondly at Bobby's tiny, sharp shoulder blades and the ribs rippling under his tight skin.

"Aren't you coming in?" Ron called.

Liz shook her head. She couldn't swim well and she was afraid of the river, its murky water and the invisible plants and creatures underneath. "It's all right," she called back. "I'll be all right here."

Watching Ron and Bobby from the bank, Liz experienced that rare chance to see her family from afar. Normally she was never farther than five feet away from them and she'd grown used to seeing their faces and bodies close up: Ron with his stubble and drying skin, Bobby with his downy cheeks. Now she realized that Bobby wasn't a baby anymore; he had become a wiry boy, filled with his own dreams and ideas and desires, packed with a will that was fiercely independent. Ron, on the other hand, was not as far from a pudgy lad as she'd thought. In spite of his big arms and gruff voice and the way he so easily tossed Bobby up and down, there was something comic about him, something almost babyish about the way he looked in the river, white and tubby like a hairless teddy bear.

Liz sighed and let her mind drift back to the previous night. She was still shaken by how close they had come to losing Bobby. She couldn't imagine how she would have gone on if she had lost him, how she would have continued to breathe or talk or walk— she was sure that her chest would cave in, or her body collapse into dust. She couldn't see herself carrying on with all that pain inside her, even though she knew people did it every day. Brandy must be really warped, Liz thought. Anyone who could leave a child like that must be evil or numb right through to the bone. She tried to imagine her sister's thinking, how she must have planned her jaunts as Liz was blithely telling her what to cook for tea, how she must have convinced herself that Bobby would be safe. Or perhaps, Liz thought, she just didn't think about him at all. Anger at her sister boiled up in her again and she clenched her fists, pressing them into the earth and reveling in the way Ron had hit Brandy and hit her and hit her and hit her. Then, abruptly, she shuddered. The memory of Brandy's head whipping back and forth, of her face covered in blood, suddenly horrified her. After all, it didn't seem so long ago that Brandy was Bobby's age—acute memories of her at three had been coming back to Liz lately whenever she smelled Bobby's sugary breath as he slept, or felt his pudgy limbs. Liz drew her knees up, pressed her face into them, and finally, for the first time since Brandy had disappeared, let herself wonder where her sister had gone.

"Liz, take him, will you? I'm knackered," Ron said. Liz looked up to see him holding Bobby out to her. She took him, patting his cold body dry with Ron's shirt. Bobby's teeth were chattering and his lips were quite blue.

"You're such a skinny little thing, you are," Liz said. "No wonder you get so cold." She dressed him quickly and held him on her lap, rubbing his arms and back vigorously until he giggled. His back was still so small that she could span its width with her hand. "Come, give me a cuddle." She held him tight, needing some shelter from her thoughts. He nestled against her and put his thumb into his mouth, sleepy at last.

Ron got out with much grunting and splashing and lay down in the sun, his belly spilling over and wobbling as he moved. "Whew," he said, and closed his eyes. "I'm going to catch a few winks." The sun gleamed white on his skin and droplets glinted in the hair on his chest. Liz moved over and laid her head on his cool shoulder. Bobby wriggled between them, sucking his thumb with his eyes closed. The three of them lay on the grass, hovering on the edge of sleep while birds and flies moved quietly around them.

On the way home that evening, the family was subdued. They were still dazed by the sun and Liz had a headache from the beer and heat. They sat on the bus in silence, watching the shadows lengthen and turn the grass a dark, vivid green. Ron lit a cigarette and gazed out of the window, allowing the sway of the bus to hypnotize him. Bobby sat on Liz's lap and basked in the comfort of her warmth and musty smell. "I'm sad," he said.

"Are you, love?" Liz stroked his hair. "D'you know why?" He shook his head. "You're sad 'cause the holiday's over. Right?" He nodded and rested his cheek against her chest. Ron looked at them and smiled. Liz rubbed her nose in Bobby's hair and looked back at Ron wistfully, hoping he would understand her mood.

When they got off the bus Ron suggested buying fish and chips for tea to prolong the special day. "I don't want you to have to cook," he said to Liz. She nodded gratefully and took Bobby home while Ron went down to the shop. But when she stepped inside the house, her heart sank. Everything was back to normal now. The same old house, the same old telly, the same routine. At least Brandy had livened things up.

Bobby went into his room to find a toy he'd been wanting all day, and Liz took out some dishes and cutlery for tea. Being back in the house made her worry about Brandy again. Liz realized that her sister couldn't have had much money, especially since she'd come back so drunk from the pub. She put down the knives and went into Bobby's room. Brandy's bed was stripped—Liz had done that first thing in the morning—but lying in the corner were her flat shoes and the cardigan Liz had given her the week before. And on the counter, in a pathetic array of chipped and smeared containers, were the few bits of makeup Brandy owned: a worn-down lipstick, a stick of pancake to cover spots with, a small compact of rouge, and a pot of the garish green eyeshadow she always insisted on wearing. Liz walked over and picked up the lipstick, turning it around in her fingers. She lifted it to her nose and sniffed, recognizing its cheap perfume from Brandy's breath. Brandy was out there with no place to sleep, no money, and hardly any clothes. Shit, Liz thought. I've gone and done it to her again.

6

Mary Botley lay in the bath, pinching her stomach. She'd been lying there for an hour, adding hot water whenever she needed to, sighing and singing. She couldn't get over how enormous she'd grown, how round and loose like a great rubber pillow. She'd been slim once, like Liz, even after she'd had the children, but over the past few years she'd let herself go. She sank farther into the hot water, closing her eyes and humming, her tired face relaxing for once, smoothing out of its swollen grooves. Mary believed that baths were good for the body and spirit, steaming one clean like a purge. They were also the only way she could get rid of the smell of ammonia and furniture polish that clung to her skin like a curse.

She would have lain musing for hours had she not been interrupted by a banging on the front door. She sat up, swearing "Jesus, won't that bloke ever leave me alone?" and clambered out of the bath, her vast breasts swinging. The banging grew louder, "Hold on a mo, for Christ's sake!" She quickly patted herself dry, put on a worn, pink dressing gown and stumbled out of the bathroom. "Hold your bloody horses, George!" George was a married man who lived three floors up and had been carrying on in secret with Mary for years. She glanced at the clock—half-past one in the morning. "Don't you know what time it is?" She unlocked the door, pulled it open and shrieked.

Brandy stood there, leaning on the wall, as pale as paper. The bruise around her eye had deepened through the day to a vivid purple, her jaw was distended with swelling, and her nose was an uneven, puffy blue. "Hullo, Mum," she said, her tone sarcastic, and pushed past Mary to stagger into the room and collapse on a worn armchair. Kicking off her shoes, she closed her eyes and waited for the spinning in her head to subside.

Mary shut the door and fell back against it. "What the hell are you doing here?"

"I've come home, haven't I?" Brandy's voice was low and weary.

Mary raised her arms, as if trying to hug the air. "I thought you were with Liz. Bloody hell, what a shock!"

"Mum, I've got to have summat to eat."

"Get it yourself. Jesus, you could have warned me."

"Mu-um." Brandy opened her eyes and looked at Mary. Gawd, she thought, what a wreck. Standing there all bulgy in her pink dressing gown, her hair straggling damp and orange. She ran her eyes over her mother's familiar face, puffier than ever around the cheeks and nose. Poor old sod, Brandy thought, she looks like a lump of dough pushed any which way. She sighed and shut her eyes again. Her mother had always looked like that to her, malleable, with a face that changed every minute. Even her features weren't reliable. "Come on, Mum," Brandy said again.

The whine triggered vague maternal memories in Mary, so she pulled herself away from the door. "Oh, all right," she said, plodding towards the kitchen. "I don't have much. Baked beans do you?"

"Anythin'." Brandy kept her eyes closed. Even the slightest movement started a rushing in her head and the nausea of fatigue and hunger kept breaking over her in waves.

"This should help." Mary came back in with some bread and butter on a plate and handed it to Brandy. She sat down opposite her to stare.

Brandy stuffed the bread into her mouth. "Got summat to drink?"

Sighing, Mary stood up. She went to the kitchen, fetched a bottle out of the cabinet, and took a swig. There wasn't much left but she brought it to Brandy anyhow. "Just a little swallow, mind. Leave me the last."

Brandy took it and tossed down the lot. It burned her gullet, making her eyes water, but she felt the heat hit her stomach and spread. "Ta." She handed the empty bottle back and crammed more bread into her mouth.

Scowling, Mary sat down again. "What the hell happened to you?" she said.

"Nothing."

"Don't nothing me, my girl!" Mary's voice wobbled. "You can't come waltzing in here in the middle of the night, looking like you've been run over by a steamroller, and expect me to sit here without an explanation. You better bloody well tell me what you've been up to or you're right out again!" She slumped back, feeling unpleasantly sober.

"Just let me finish eating." Brandy chewed the last of the bread and sniffed. "The beans are burning."

"Damn them to hell." Mary got up wearily. It was so hard for her to move these days, with her exhausted limbs weighing on her like sandbags. She shuffled into the kitchen, pulled the beans off the stove, and slopped them into a bowl, burned ones and all. She took a spoon from the dishrack and brought the food to Brandy.

Brandy slurped down the beans eagerly, scalding her tongue. Her stomach still felt empty but at least now the nausea was gone. The orange tomato sauce dribbled down her chin, enhancing her ghoulish appearance. "Bloody hell, Amanda," Mary objected, turning her eyes away. "Come on then, out with it."

"It don't matter what happened, Mum." Brandy spoke in a low monotone; it was an effort even to talk. "I'm home, all right? Things didn't work out with Liz."

"I'm not surprised. She wouldn't put up with the likes of you for long, I shouldn't wonder. She's got a decent life, she does. What does she need some juvenile delinquent hanging about for, eh?"

"Well, she isn't as perfect as you think," Brandy snapped. "She's married to a fucking maniac, I'll tell you. He makes Dad look like a sheep."

Mary put on a well-worn pained expression. "Don't remind me of that bastard," she moaned, and looked at Brandy again, her eyes watering. "How is Liz?" Her voice was plaintive. "She all right, is she?"

Brandy put down her empty bowl and staggered to her feet, swaying from fatigue. She wandered towards the toilet. "Liz is always all right," she said. "I need a piss."

While she was gone, Mary stared at the floor, muttering. She'd never expected to have Brandy home again so soon, especially after Liz's letter promising to take the girl in, and she felt invaded. Mary liked having the place to herself, where she could enjoy her small comforts undisturbed. She didn't want this hulking great teenager mooning about and bothering her. Still, someone had to take responsibility for the girl. She was clearly a mess.

"I'm going to bed," Brandy announced, coming back into the room. "See you in the morning." She picked up her duffel bag and headed for the old bedroom she used to share with Liz.

"Wait!" Mary commanded. "What're you going to do, Amanda? I mean tomorrow and after that?"

"I dunno," Brandy said, shrugging. "You got any spare cash? I'm skint."

Mary shook her head. "You better go down to the dole Monday, first thing. And then you better look for a job, young lady. I'm not having you hanging about here all day getting into mischief."

"Jesus, give me a chance, will you!" Brandy turned back to the bedroom. "I'm looking for someone, that's what I'm doing. This is my home, too, y'know. Fuckin' hell!" And with that she left the room, slamming the door behind her.

Brandy awoke late the next day and lay in her old bed for a while, listening to the squeals of the neighbors' children through the walls and the creaks and thumps of the decaying building around her. She judged it must be afternoon, for the light had a faded cast to it, but in spite of her long sleep her limbs still ached from all the walking she'd done the night before. She gazed at the wallpaper, still peeling, and at the burnt orange curtains, still creased with grime, and tried to feel some sort of affection for the place. When Liz had lived there, she had at least made an effort to cheer it up by keeping it tidy and pinning pictures on the walls, but now it looked deserted and shabbier than ever. Brandy glanced over at the other twin bed, not much more than an iron cot, rocky on its legs and sagging in the middle. She and Liz had spent hours playing on those beds as children, making tents with the sheets and hiding from ghouls and goblins. It was there that Liz had told Brandy stories about witches who changed people's hearts into stone, or wind that blew down children's mouths and turned them inside out. It was there that Brandy had adored Liz with the same kind of purity she saw in Bobby, that natural love that was the color of milk, not polluted with the stinking oil of hurt and betrayal she'd found in everyone else. Brandy sighed, for even though Liz was different to her now with her quick temper and sharp tongue, she didn't want to lose her again. Not when Liz meant so much.

When Liz had started writing to Brandy in Bullwood Hall, Brandy had been astonished to find she had a normal sister. The relatives of all the other girls inside were as messed up as they were—sisters on the streets, brothers into dope or thieving, mums and dads in the nick, or disappeared, or never known in the first place—but Liz was an exception. She had work and a child, a husband—she didn't even have a record! Up until Liz's letters, Brandy had passed the time inside like all the other girls, spinning dreams of impossible fame and extraordinary luck, but Liz's normality had brought her a real hope. It had enabled Brandy to believe, for the first time in years, that a simple, ordinary life was within her reach, and that was better than any dream. Brandy closed her eyes and rubbed them gingerly, her jaw still pulsing from Ron's beating. The amazing thing was, the thing that still surprised her whenever she thought about it, was that her dreams about Liz had almost come true. Reardon had warned her to keep a watch on those inside dreams, to gird herself for disappointment and not to expect too much of Liz, but this time Reardon had been wrong. Liz had not turned out to be a saint, of course, but she hadn't been a lie, either. Brandy smiled, thinking of her astonishment that first day in Liz's flat. That little shining boy, that room full of sun and toys, the cupboard stuffed with clothes. She had never been in a house so nice. She'd never sat on a warm bed, surrounded by color, and just felt the sun seep into her skin, or heard that soft quiet houses have when the people are in a different room. She had never felt so at peace with the world.

Brandy stretched and got out of bed, wincing as her muscles clenched. There was nothing she could do about Liz now, she told herself. What's gone is gone, as Reardon used to say. Sighing, she went into the kitchen. On the counter she found a note from

Mary scrawled on a paper napkin. "I'm out shopping. Don't you dare pinch any of my stuff. There's food in the fridge. Be back from work after midnight." Pinned to the napkin was a one-pound note. Brandy pocketed it and rifled the kitchen for food. She found a loaf of bread, a pot of jam and some butter, and sat down to eat. Her plan was to take a bath, rest until evening, then get back to town to search for some of her old mates. As soon as she found out where Jeff was, she promised herself, she'd get out of this place for good.

Across town, Mary slumped into an office chair to take a breather before she began working. The giant vacuum cleaner lay coiled at her feet like a tamed serpent and the fluorescent tubes on the ceiling cast a harsh light over her heavily made-up face. She reached up to adjust the yellow scarf she had tied over her head to keep out the dust, and yawned. It was only six o'clock and already she was exhausted.

The office building where Mary worked was in the main part of town, on Corporation Street. The building was large and shabby, prone to attract dust from the slowly crumbling plaster of the ceilings and soot from the traffic outside, and Mary loathed her job of keeping it clean. She was supposed to mop the floors with ammonia, dust down bookshelves and windowsills, polish the brass, wipe the toilet seats, vacuum the carpets, rub the bent and peeling mirrors, and empty the wastepaper baskets. Instead, she flicked her duster about, explored desk drawers for anything she could pinch, and took plenty of breaks.

At half-past six, just as Mary was about to nip out for a quick cup of tea, Brandy sauntered in. She hadn't visited her mother at work since she was at school but she remembered the building. She clattered up the stairs in her now loose and ruined shoes, her plump legs in a pair of Mary's stockings, and almost bumped into her mother at the top. "Evenin', Mum," she said, looking Mary up and down. Her mother's face was shiny under the eyeshadow and rouge, the veins broken across her swollen nose, and her hair was straggling out of her scarf in its usual orange strands. "You look a right treat in that smock, like a nurse."

Mary scowled. "I'm going for my tea break. What do you want?"

"Tea? I didn't think you touched the stuff. Got any spare cash?"

"I gave you a quid."

Brandy sat down on the steps, leaned back, and splayed her legs out on the floor. "Well, thanks, Mum, but what can anyone do with that? It cost almost a quid to take the frigging bus here."

"Get up!" Mary shouted. "I'm not having you coming here and bothering me at work! What do you think I am—a money machine? I don't spend all night scrubbing to give you what I earn. You come with me." Mary moved like a parrot when she was angry, in quick, exaggerated bursts, and her movements contrasted peculiarly with her heavy face and unused body, as if someone had attached a lively mechanical head to a dummy. Sighing, Brandy got up and obeyed. Mary led her to an off-license, where she bought half a bottle of whiskey, and then down the road to a grimy café on the corner. She ordered two cups of tea and, once she had hers, poured a large dollop of whiskey into it. Brandy sat opposite her on a rickety chair, watching. They both sipped their tea in silence.

"Look, Mum," Brandy said finally, "I'm not going to bother you for long. I just want to stay awhile to sort things out for meself. I have to find me boyfriend, you know that bloke Jeff I told you about. Once we're together I'll be off your hands forever. And that's a promise." Brandy blinked and put on a phony smile that looked particularly out of place on her bruised face. Mary turned her eyes away and finished her tea. "All right, Mum? I'll go down to the dole on Monday and I'll pay you back. But I can't do a sodding thing without some cash, can I? I walked so many bloody miles yesterday me legs feel like they're going to drop off, and me feet are covered with fucking blisters. They look like bits of raw meat. Look." Brandy slipped a foot out of her shoe and held it up above the table, oblivious of the view she gave the café up her skirt. Mary grunted in disgust. "It kills me just to walk, it does. I need a few bob for the buses."

Mary sighed and reached in her pocket. She felt better now that the hot toddy was spreading through her. She couldn't be bothered to argue anymore, and reasoned that if she didn't give Brandy some money, the girl would only steal it anyway. "All right, all right. You're a right little begger, you are. You should have more respect." Mary pulled out three pounds and some change. "Here." She gave Brandy all but one pound. "When I was your age I already had a husband, a baby, and a home. I knew what I was doing!"

"Ta, Mum. I'll pay you back, honest." Brandy grabbed her jacket and stood up.

"Hold on a mo, not so fast." Mary reached out a fat arm and pulled her down again. "You still haven't explained what happened with Liz and who did that to you." She nodded at Brandy's face. "Someone gave you a right going over, I can see, though I daresay you deserved it."

Brandy looked her mother in the eye. "It was some bloke picked me up hitching," she said. "He tried to rape me but I fought him off. It was a hard bleeding fight, though."

Mary tut-tutted and shook her head. "I wish you wouldn't hitchhike, Amanda. It's a dangerous world out there." She sighed, suddenly aware of how little she'd done to protect her daughters.

"Tell me about it," Brandy muttered, then stood up again. "Tra, Mum, see you later."

It was too early to find her friends in the pub, so Brandy strolled through the streets, stopping frequently to compare the clothes in the boutiques to what had been around before she was locked away. Each step was like pressing on a bruise and she had to take several rests, but she wanted to save her money for the pub, not spend it on a bus. She was excited about going back to her old haunt, certain that she'd find at least one or two of the gang there. She longed to boast of her life in Borstal, to talk about her escapades and bravado, subjects she hadn't been able to raise with Liz at all—her sister would never have believed that Brandy had been one of the top girls inside, that some inmates had even fought over her. Brandy couldn't wait to compare notes with Jeff, to talk about the screws and the scandals and the way his Borstal differed from hers. She couldn't wait to be with her own kind.

After fifteen minutes of walking, she stopped for a rest beside a boutique called Bus Stop and looked in the window. The mannikins were dressed in tight satin clothes and bubbly hairstyles like that American's in the salon and the sight of them made Brandy feel sad again, reminding her of how much fun her one day in the salon had been. She suddenly missed her sister and Bobby, and the unexpected softness beneath Liz's scolding tongue. Turning her back to the window, she leaned against it and watched the people scurrying by and the buses and cars edging along the busy road. If only she could twist back time, the way she'd seen done in films. The hands whirring backwards, undoing everything that had happened over the past few days. If only Liz would give her a second chance.

At half-past seven, Brandy caught her bus, climbed to the top deck, and sat down in her favorite seat at the front. She opened the handbag she'd borrowed from Mary and took out a mirror. She'd done her best to camouflage her bruises with Mary's powder that morning, but they still showed through like birthmarks, her nose was puffy, and the white of one eye remained a glaring red. She combed her hair and put on the lipstick she'd also taken from Mary. At least she had a bit of a tan, she thought, and most of her pimples were gone. Perhaps the bruises would impress the blokes. She wanted them to know she was tough now, that she was ready to find Jeff and keep him. She put away the lipstick and took out her cough drop tin, opening it to look at Jeff's letter yet again. The letter was crumpled, limp, and ripping along the folds. She knew the words so well they sometimes echoed in her dreams but she reread it anyway, for reassurance.

The pub Brandy was headed for was a small, decaying place called the The Sun and Moon, traditionally occupied by Irish laborers and underworld types. She and Jeff had been introduced to it by Larry, the bloke who had found the squat, and the pub had become an integral part of the gang's new life. Whenever they'd made a successful burglary or collected some money in one of their other dubious ways, they'd gone there to celebrate. Brandy smiled at the memory. That year between her two Borstal sentences had been the best of her life. She'd had Jeff, her own home, excitement, occasional money, the pub. Even during the frightening times, when Larry had got angry, some other bloke tried to screw her, or the coppers had come snooping around, she'd had Jeff to hide behind. It had been a good time while it lasted.

Jeff was arrested the week before Brandy's sixteenth birthday, when he and Larry were out stealing diet pills from a chemist's shop. He had scouted out an open window, which he thought he could, being so skinny, just fit through, and Larry was to be the lookout. Larry said afterwards that things had been going fine, Jeff slipping in the window like grease through a crack, when a beat copper strolled around the corner. Larry whistled a warning, or so he claimed, then took off before the copper could get him, but Jeff didn't hear. He was caught, as the gang used to say, barefaced and shitless.

Without Jeff, the squat had quickly turned from a safe, private place to a terrifying hole. Larry kept pushing Brandy to do more and more dangerous things, not just shoplift the way she'd done for Jeff, and he even tried to pimp her. If she didn't cooperate, he'd told her, he'd throw her out. Brandy started going home for shelter, as much as she hated it there—the choice was either a night in Mary's flat, watching her mother drink herself unconscious, or a night of being bullied by Larry and his friends. And on one visit home she found Jeff's letter. She didn't tell the others about the letter—she was afraid to let them know that she went home occasionally in case they thought she'd been grassing on them—but after that she began to think about how long it would be until Jeff was released and about her first time in Borstal, where at least it had been light and safe with people to talk to. Then one day when she was out shoplifting, she caught sight of a policeman coming up the road and saw a way out of it all. She pushed over an old woman right in front of him and grabbed her handbag. It was as easy as that.

Brandy got off the bus and walked around the corner to the pub. The doors were open, it being summer, and only a few people were inside. She went in, accustoming her eyes to the darkness, and took a quick look around. The Sun and Moon was a cozy place, with a low ceiling, deep red walls, and a nice glow of old wood and glass about it. It had known better days—the carpet was matted with dirt to the point of having no color and the wooden bar was nicked and scraped—but it smelled comfortingly of beer and cigarette smoke. Brandy recognized the bartender, an old paddy who'd been there most of his life, but no one else. "Hullo, Mick," she said, going up to him. "How are you keeping these days?"

"Why, it's you, lass! I haven't seen you for a donkey's age." Mick pulled her a half of cider without asking and put it down in front of her. "On the house for a welcome back. Where have you been hiding, then?"

Brandy thanked him and took a swallow. "I went away for a while," she said, winking.

"Oh, I see. You're all right, though, aren't you?"

"Well . . ." Brandy pointed to her face. "I've had me ups and downs."

Mick laughed. "That I can see. I haven't seen your lad around, either."

"Not at all?"

Mick shook his head. "Larry still comes in once in a while, but the old gang seems to have scattered." Someone shouted an order and, still talking, he turned his back and filled a glass from a gin bottle hanging upside down behind the bar. "Are you looking for them, lass?"

"Yeah." Brandy took another drink. "D'you think Larry might come in tonight?"

Mick shrugged, slapping the gin down and ringing up the till. "Why don't you stick around and see? I'll stand you another if you want."

"Thanks. I can pay a bit." Brandy gave him a couple of shillings, then lit a cigarette. "Who's Larry with now?"

"A bird called Maureen, I think. Long hair, brown. Know her?"

Brandy shook her head.

"I don't know, though," Mick said, leaning near her and dropping his voice. "That lad's in for trouble. He's getting a big mouth. Comes in here, gets pissed as a parrot, and starts gabbing away like an old woman."

Brandy sucked her cigarette intently, listening. She loved this kind of talk, this confiding, secretive business. It made her feel so important. "Yeah," she said, "he always did have a big gob. Too much pride."

"Too true." Mick smiled at her, his cigarette stuck in one side of his mouth and his grizzled face screwed up against the smoke. "You'll be all right, though. Sensible girl, you are. Bet you miss your laddie, eh?"

Brandy nodded. "I got a letter here." She patted her bag. "Soon as I find him, we're getting out of this together."

Mick cocked an eyebrow but didn't say anything.

For the next hour Brandy sat in a chair by the jukebox, waiting. Sometimes she wandered up to chat to Mick, but the rest of the time she just listened to the conversations around her, hoping someone she knew would show up.

At about half-past eight, a familiar-looking girl came in by herself. She had long black hair with a fringe that hung over her eyes, tight jeans, and extraordinarily high platform shoes. Brandy caught her eye and grinned at her, a little tipsy now from the cider. For a moment she couldn't quite remember who the girl was, but an instant later she placed her—the girl was from Martyn House, the wing for first-timers, nutcases, and middle-class misfits at Bullwood Hall.

At first the girl ignored her, but in a minute she did a double take. She picked up her drink from the bar, stuck a cigarette in her mouth, and sauntered over. Brandy looked at her coolly, giving her the Borstal once-over. "Do I know you?" the girl said, putting her head to one side and eyeing Brandy. She kept her face deadpan. It was a pretty face, dark and smooth.

"I dunno," Brandy said. "Do you?"

The girl took a drag of her cigarette and stood looking down at her.

"You better park your carcass before you fall," Brandy said, glancing at the girl's feet. "I don't know how you can walk in those things." The girl sat down and put her beer on the table. The two of them smoked silently, avoiding each other's eyes. When the girl reached out for her drink Brandy saw scars all over her knuckles. "When did you get out, then?" she asked finally, as if asking the weather. The girl looked up, startled, and Brandy winked.

"I remember you now," the girl said. "You're Brandy, right? You were in House One. Your hair's changed."

"Yup, that's me. You look different, too. Did you just get out or what?"

"Yeah, two days ago." The girl looked around nervously. "It's a shock, innit?"

"Telling me. I only got out about three weeks ago and it feels like fucking years. A lot more happens on the outside."

The girl eyed Brandy's battered face and grinned. "It looks like it. Who did that to you, then?"

"Ah, no one. So how's Lucy and Mags? Doing all right?"

"I s'pose. I haven't seen much of them lately. They canceled house association last week 'cause of fights."

"Oh, yeah? Who?"

"Ah, the usual sodding stuff. Summat to do with someone's fags, I think."

"What about Reardon? Got any new favorites?" Brandy gazed nonchalantly over the girl's shoulder.

"Who? Oh, that big screw you mean? I dunno. Barmy as ever, I s'pose." The girl paused and looked around the pub again. "Did you used to come here a lot, then?"

Brandy hesitated before answering, still wanting to hear about the Borstal. She couldn't think of a way to ask anything more without seeming too interested, however, so she let the subject drop. "Yeah, but I don't remember you being here before."

"I used to come here with me boyfriend, Pete Scargill. Know him?"

Brandy shook her head and both girls looked disappointed. Brandy remembered now that the girl's name was Molly and that she'd had a reputation inside for being an easy screw. "Where'd you get all that gear?" Brandy said, nodding at her outfit.

"Nice, innit?" Molly looked down at herself, then tossed back her hair. "Me mum bought it for me. A welcome-home present—to keep me good."

Brandy leaned towards her. "An' are you going to be good?" She winked and ran her eyes over Molly's body. She couldn't help it. The girl looked delicious.

Molly drew back, blushing. "I'm waiting for Pete," she said.

Brandy blushed, too, ashamed of herself, and took a long drink to cover up. "He coming in here, then?" Molly nodded. "Does he come here a lot?"

"Yeah. He lives near here. And arranges some of his, you know . . ."

"Yeah, I know." Brandy's hopes lifted. Maybe this Pete bloke would know something about Jeff.

Molly and Brandy boasted about their exploits in Bullwood Hall through another couple of drinks. Brandy enjoyed being able to talk about what she really knew at last and warmed to her inside role of the witty tough. It was such a relief not to be bossed by outside people for a change and not to feel the uncertainty that had been plaguing her ever since her release. But at the same time she had the unpleasant sensation of being pulled backwards, as if the Borstal were reaching out tentacles and trying to reclaim her.

"Pete!" Molly squealed suddenly, and waved to someone across the room. Brandy watched in disgust—she never had gone in for that feminine squeaky act. "Come over here!" A tall rangy bloke walked over and he, too, looked familiar. Brandy thought for a moment he might be the same Pete who used to feel her up in the school gardening shed. "Pete, this is Brandy. One of me mates from inside."

Pete nodded at Brandy, barely taking her in. "Listen, Moll," he said, turning to her. "I can't stay long. Summat's come up. All right? I'll just have a quick pint. Want anything?"

Molly looked disappointed but she asked for another half. "Men," she said to Brandy, and shrugged. Brandy smirked. Jeff had never done things like that. When he'd had a job, he'd told her about it.

Pete came back, handed Molly a drink, and sat on the bench

next to them. The pub was filling up at last and the noise had risen to a busy hubbub. He stared at Brandy's face but didn't make a comment.

"D'you know Larry Dobson?" Brandy asked him.

Pete shook his head and took a swallow of beer.

"What about Jeff Whitely?"

He shrugged.

"Come on, it's all right. Jeff's me boyfriend."

"Oh yeah?"

"Yeah! We was together before we got nicked. I'm looking for him. Is he out yet?"

Smiling, Pete leaned back and ran his eyes over Brandy.

"Come on!" she said. "If he's out he'll want to know where I am."

"Who says he's out?" He lowered his smile to his glass.

"Don't give me that crap. I know he's out. It's written all over your weasely face."

Pete raised his eyebrows. "You've got a pretty tongue on you! No wonder someone did you over."

"Leave off, Pete," Molly said, much to Brandy's surprise. "She only wants to know where her boyfriend is. How would you have liked it if no one told you I was out, eh?"

"I can't tell her where he is," he said sullenly. "She can ask Larry if she wants."

"So you do know Larry then. Where is he?"

Pete wouldn't answer.

"Look, you wanker, we all lived together in the same place before I got nicked. In that squat on Jakeman Road. What d'you think I am, a grass or summat? Fucking hell!"

At that news Pete sat up and looked at Brandy with more respect. "All right, all right. I'll tell Larry you're here and see what he says. That's all I can do."

"What's the bleeding mystery, anyroad?"

"I'll tell him, all right? You got an address?"

"I'm not waiting 'round all year for you to carry some fucking message. Just tell me where to find him."

"Have it your own way." Pete got up and put on his jacket.

"Wait!" Brandy snapped. "Here." She fished in her bag for a pencil and scribbled her mother's address down on a beer mat. "It's important." She handed the mat to Pete. "Jeff's going to want to know where I am."

*   *   *

For three days Brandy waited at home for something to happen. Sometimes she went back to the pub to try to find Larry herself, but he never showed up. She was getting bored and irritable, and increasingly anxious about why Pete had been so secretive. Her only comfort was wheedling more money out of her mother and buying herself some new shoes. Her bruises faded gradually from purple to yellow.

On the third day at seven o'clock in the evening, there was a knock at Mary's door. Mary was out at work and Brandy was scraping the dirt out of her nails, wishing her mother had a television. She jumped up and opened the door eagerly.

"Hullo," Molly said.

"Oh, it's you." Brandy ran her eyes over Molly again. She was wearing the same sexy clothes she'd had on in the pub. Brandy reckoned that was all she had. "All right, come in." Molly nodded and followed her. "You want anything—tea?" Brandy heard the gruff voice she used in Borstal coming out again. Molly had that effect on her.

"Nah. It's all right. Pete sent me with a message."

"Oh, yeah? About time."

"I know. Sorry. He almost wouldn't do it but I changed his mind. Still, he wouldn't have done it if I hadn't . . ."

"Yeah, yeah. Thanks. What is it?"

Molly looked around, chose a sagging armchair, and sat down in it. Her long legs bent up in a graceful arc. "I got Larry's address for you. He says you can go see him tomorrow at eight."

Brandy sat down, too. "What's all the fucking mystery? Does he think he's Robin Hood or summat?"

"I dunno. I think the coppers are after them. You know how it is." Molly moved her great, dark eyes around the room. "This your mum's place, then?"

"Yeah. Disgusting, innit?"

Molly laughed. "I've seen better." She looked at Brandy for a moment. "What're you doing with yourself these days?"

"Nothing much." Brandy gazed over Molly's shoulder at the blank window. "I'm waiting to find Jeff. See what happens then."

"Well, maybe when you do find him the four of us could go out one night. Go dancing maybe."

"Yeah, maybe." Brandy paused and looked directly at Molly. "I'm lined up for a job as a hairdresser, actually," she said. "I'm supposed to start next week."

"Oh yeah? That sounds great."

"You've got lovely hair. I'll do it for you if you need it any-time."

"Are you really good then?"

"Oh yeah. Me sister works in a very posh place in Brighton called Hairline. That's where I got me training."

"Well, it is a bit long in the front. D'you think you could trim it for me?"

"What, now?"

"Yeah."

"Course I can. Come on, there's a mirror in here." Brandy led the way to Mary's bathroom, perpetually damp from all her baths, and shut the door so that Molly could see herself in the mirror hanging on the back.

"See this bit here?" Molly said, pointing to her fringe. "It curls under, see? Right into me eyes. It keeps making me blink. Think you could cut it straight across? Y'know, just a tiny bit so it still looks long but so's I can see?"

"Easy. I'll get the scissors and a towel. Why don't you sit on the bed in there, so I can reach you?"

"Sure you can do it straight?"

"Course I can. They trained at that Sassoon place in London, the people in Hairline, y'know."

Molly wandered into Mary's bedroom and sat on the edge of the old, double bed. At least that room was presentable, with a faded pink quilt, a fluffy rug over the worn carpet, and female things like pink furry slippers and perfume bottles littered about. "Your mother likes pink," Molly called.

Brandy came in with scissors and a towel. "Yeah, I know." She put the towel on Molly's lap, tilted her face up by the chin, and scrutinized her. "Right then, close your eyes."

Molly shut her eyes and Brandy raised the scissors to her face. Molly looked so trusting, her face blank and smooth, her chin tilted up like a child's. Brandy ran her eyes down Molly's neck, exposed and white, and over her small, pointed breasts, outlined under her tight T-shirt. She longed to kiss her, to push her back on the bed. "Anyone ever tell you you're beautiful?" she said.

Molly smiled, keeping her eyes closed. Brandy reached up and caressed her cheek, seeing that she wasn't resisting. "Keep your eyes shut," she said, her voice low. Molly obeyed. This is just what Brandy had done to Reardon. It had been nice, having such a bulk of a woman yield to her so easily, soft and obedient in her hands. It had made Brandy feel so powerful. She ran her hand over Molly's face to her hair, then took the thick, shining fringe between her fingers and snipped it along the edge. The scissors caught, being blunt, but she sawed away anyhow. Putting her knee between Molly's legs, she bent closer and cut from one side of the fringe to the other in uneven, jagged snips. When she finished, without even looking at what she'd done, she put the scissors down, slipped her hand around Molly's jaw and lifted her face some more. She bent to kiss her and Molly still didn't open her eyes or resist—she just started to breathe heavily. Brandy laid her body against Molly's, pushing her down on the bed and kissing her harder. She ran her hand over Molly's hips, undid her zip, and slid her hand into Molly's jeans. Molly did the same to her and soon the two of them were rolling and panting, gentle and hard, soft and sharp, until they had lifted beyond their worries, their bravado, and their phoniness to the only part of themselves they had ever trusted or loved.

Afterwards, as the two of them lay on the bed, their clothes half off and their arms around each other, Molly began to cry. At first Brandy didn't notice because Molly did it silently, the tears rolling sideways down her cheeks to the pillow. Brandy was wallowing in the luxury of being able to make love without being interrupted by a screw or a bell or another girl, but then she heard Molly sniff. "Hey, what's the matter?" she said, raising her head.

Molly turned away. "I didn't want to do this," she said, her voice squeaking.

"What d'you mean?" Brandy was hurt. "Course you did."

"Nah, I don't mean that." Molly turned her head back and gave Brandy a squeeze. "It was lovely. I always heard you were good. Nah, I mean I thought that was only for inside, y'know? What would Pete think?" She squeaked again and more tears came.

Brandy flopped onto her back. "Don't tell him," she said gruffly. "Look, babe, it doesn't matter. It's summat that happens once in a while, that's all. We learned it inside, right? What do they expect when they lock healthy girls away with no blokes, eh? It's normal, really."

"You think so?" Molly sniffed.

"Yeah!" But Brandy was not so sure. She thought of a conversation she'd had with Reardon once, when Reardon had asked her if she'd have ever liked girls if men had liked her. Brandy had been so insulted she'd almost shoved Reardon off the bed with her foot. "What's that supposed to bloody mean?" she'd said. "Plenty of blokes like me—what about Jeff?" Then she'd looked at Reardon, who had gone all quiet and was fiddling with her fat fingers in a certain way she had, and realized that the woman wasn't talking about her at all but only about herself. "Look, Moll," Brandy said more kindly, "there's no point in worrying about something you can't help, is there? You start questioning your sex life, babe, and all hell breaks loose. It just makes those marbles rattle around inside your head till they crack. I mean, what your body wants, it wants, see? There's no use screwing it up with your mind."

"You really think so?" Molly said again, her voice wavering.

"Yeah! And anyroad, once you've had more time with your bloke again, you'll probably lose interest in birds. You did just get out, remember."

"Yeah, probably." But Molly didn't sound so sure. Pete never made her feel the way Brandy had, soft and passionate like that. "I dunno though. I feel like a freak."

Brandy sighed. She'd felt like a freak of one kind or another all her life. She propped herself up on an elbow and looked down at Molly, noticing for the first time what a botch she'd made of her fringe. "Look, love, maybe we are freaks, but so frigging what? It isn't our fault, the way we're born, is it? Don't worry yourself about it."

"But what about your Jeff though? What would he say?"

Brandy frowned, trying to imagine what he would say. "I won't tell him," she replied. "Why should he know? It's none of his sodding business, is it? Anyroad, the blokes do it, too, y'know. They screw each other all the time inside, worse than us. And that really is disgusting."

Molly giggled. "Yeah." Then she sighed again. "It's all such a fucking mess."

"Too true." Brandy sat up. "So's your fringe, for that matter." And she picked up the scissors to continue where she'd left off.

7

Larry Dobson, the former gang leader, lived in the top two floors of a tall, narrow house in the suburbs of Birmingham. The house was old and in bad repair—the red brick crumbling and the roof shedding slate—and it stood on a corner, sticking up awkwardly out of its shabby garden like an outcast in a schoolyard.

To get to Larry's flat Brandy had to climb a splintering wooden staircase that zigzagged up the back of the building and wobbled dangerously under her feet. Clutching the unreliable banisters, she made it to the top and looked around. The suburban streets before her seemed smug and lazy compared to the parts of town she was used to, with their semidetached houses and carefully tended gardens. She turned to the door at the top of the stairs and banged on its mottled glass panel, her stomach feeling watery and loose. She heard a thump of feet, the clatter of a dish, and a curse. "Yeah?" someone shouted.

"It's me," she called.

"Me the fuck who?" She recognized Larry's voice: thin and high-pitched, almost a whine.

"You know who." The door opened a crack and Larry looked out. His eyes were set closely together, with a line of black eyebrow marching over them, and his nose was curiously flat, as if someone had sat on his face.

"Oh, it's you." He opened the door wider, glancing over her head. "Come in then, quick!" Grabbing her arm he pulled her in and shut the door behind them. "This way." He led her down the hall and into a shabby sitting room.

"This is worse than me mum's place," Brandy said, looking around. The room, large and perfectly square, was scattered with cast-off furniture: a beaten-up sofa in dirty yellow, two scratchy green armchairs with the stuffing sprouting out of them, and a painted orange crate with a brown mug on it, ringed with old tea. The wooden floor was bare and unpolished and the walls were a murky pea green.

"Keep your charming remarks to yourself." Larry waved at a chair. "Park yourself there."

Brandy chose the sofa instead and sat down to face him. He hadn't changed, she thought. Dressed in tight black jeans and a T-shirt with a cartoon of a naked, buxom woman on it, he looked the same dark, muscular bloke she'd been frightened of in the squat. Even his hair, cut in a shag—long on the sides, short and spiked on top—seemed evil. "So, what's all the bloody secrecy about?" Brandy said, eager to show him that she was tougher now, not the meek little girl he used to push around. "You're all acting like a pack of schoolboys playing spy."

Ignoring her question, Larry perched on the edge of an armchair and looked her over. "Well, well, here she is again. The little bird who keeps ending up in a cage. Who messed you up, then?"

"None of your business."

"Some nutter in Borstal, was it? I wonder what you were doing to deserve that."

"Fuck off, Larry. I told you, it's none of your business."

He grinned. "So how was it this time?"

Brandy shrugged. "Same."

"You're getting to be quite a regular, aren't you?"

Brandy shifted on the sofa. Larry had always talked to her this way, but she was determined to prove that she could handle it now. She kept her voice low and her face bored, the way she'd learned inside. "Don't count your chickens, Larry. A lot of people are saying you'll end up inside yourself before you know it."

"That's a loada crap. It's only the daft ones get caught."

"Jeff got caught, didn't he? And it wasn't him who was daft that night."

Larry scowled. "Who's been gabbing to you about me, then?"

"Everyone. I can't get away from it. 'Such a big mouth,' they say. 'He's going to end up with the whole of Brum in on his jobs if he doesn't watch it.' I'm only telling you what they say, Larry."

"Like fuck you are."

They both fell silent and stared down at the scuffed floor. Brandy was determined not to be the one to bring up the reason for her visit, although the longing to see Jeff was coursing through her like blood.

"Where are you living now?" Larry asked, his voice a bit kinder.

"At me mum's. I stayed in Brighton with me sister for a bit, but it didn't work out."

"I thought you hated your mum."

"She could be worse." Brandy glanced at him. "What about you, then? What're you doing these days?"

"Things are going all right for me. Very all right."

"That's nice." Brandy recrossed her legs and waited. She'd learned how to wait.

"So then," Larry said at last, "what did you want to see me for?"

Brandy faked a yawn. "You know."

"You think so, do you?"

"You haven't changed a bit, have you Larry?" Brandy leaned back and crossed her legs again, keeping her face a deadpan cool. "Two bloody years and you're still full of yourself. Like a little boy, you are. Well, I got better things to worry about than your stupid games."

"Oh, yeah? Like looking for some dyke to screw, no doubt."

Brandy allowed a small, contemptuous smile to creep over her lips. "That's all you know about it. Anyroad"—she faked another yawn—"I can't hang around here all day. You got Pete's message, didn't you?"

Larry raised a hand and picked at his teeth. "Oh, yeah, now that you mention it. So you're after your sweetheart, eh? How touching."

99

At that Brandy's control cracked. It was torture to sit there letting Larry play with her when she'd been waiting for this moment for twenty-one months, counting the days and the hours until she'd see Jeff again. Larry was acting like a screw, like Reardon and all those others did when they accused her of nicking the cake—taking the one thing they knew was important to her, her freedom, and messing her around with it. "If Jeff knew you was fucking me about like this he'd tear your bloody balls off!" she snapped. "You'd better tell him I'm back. You owe him a favor after all, don't you?"

Larry colored but quickly controlled himself. "Me an' Jeff sorted all that out long ago. What d'you want with him, anyroad?"

"Don't be daft!" Brandy slipped her hand into her bag and clutched the cough drop tin for luck, looking Larry straight in the face. "I bet you have him right in this sodding house."

"Like where? Tucked in the bread bin? You can go upstairs an' look if you don't believe me."

Brandy stood up. "You just tell Jeff I'm at me mum's, I got some money, and I got plans. I'm not wasting any more time with you. I know what you did to Jeff—you're about as trustworthy as a snake, you are. Better at running away than farting!" She began to walk out of the room but then she turned to look at Larry again. He was standing by now, his face clenched in anger. "You know what you really are, don't you? You're a fucking grass."

"You cunt!" Larry yelled, and lunged at her. She darted behind the sofa, feeling reckless now, ready to do anything to end this cruel game of his. "You're a fucking coward, Larry, that's what you are. A phony fucking coward!" Hearing her words, seeing their effect, Brandy didn't feel fear. She was sailing way beyond that, beyond any sense of self-protection. She'd always hated cowards—that's why she'd been so angry at Reardon, why she'd wanted to punch her and hit her when she saw her standing there, limp as a popped balloon, not raising a finger to help. "You're a fucking coward, and a bastard grass and a pimp!" she shouted, her face red and straining. She didn't even notice that Larry had stopped still and was only staring at her. "You know what they do to fuckers like you inside, people who turn in their mates and pimp their girlfriends? They fuck them up the arse!" Brandy's voice became a scream. She pressed her hands to her temples and screwed up her eyes tight, almost enjoying the way her voice roared and smashed inside her. "You'd probably even like it, you sodding poufter!"

"Brandy!"

She felt someone grab her and ducked, instinctively raising her hand to protect her face, but she kept on shouting. Arms shook her and a voice called her name, but she only shrank back, pulling into herself, and continued to pour out her fury. "Fucker, fucker!" she screamed. It wasn't until someone slapped her that she stopped yelling and reeled backwards into the wall.

"Brandy, calm down, will you?" She opened her eyes and tried to focus on the face in front of her. An emaciated, pale face, sunken in at the cheekbones and eye sockets.

"Jeff?" she said.

"The girl's a bleeding nutter," Larry said. He looked shaken.

"Get out of here!" Jeff hissed. Larry nodded and stumbled off. Jeff turned to Brandy. "You all right now?"

Brandy blinked. "Jeff?"

"Yeah, I just came in. Christ, what a scene!"

"I know," Brandy said shakily. "That bastard." She sat down on the sofa to catch her breath, wishing Jeff would sit next to her, hold her. She was trembling all over.

"Didn't he tell you I was coming home in a minute?"

"No. He wouldn't tell me where you were or anything."

"He was supposed to tell you to wait for me."

Brandy shook her head, sniffing. "He never said you lived here." Her voice trembled again. "He's a fucking wanker."

"Well, sorry about that. But there is some important shit going on right now, Brandy. We've got to be careful, y'see."

"Yeah, but not of me!" She looked up indignantly. "I didn't spend all that time inside to be treated like a bleeding copper. What's the matter with everyone?"

"Yeah, sorry. I told him to ask you to wait."

"But why wouldn't anyone tell me where you were, Jeff? What's going on?"

Jeff sat next to her on the sofa. "I can't answer that now, love. Look"—he smiled and patted her knee—"you want a cup of tea or anything?"

"Yeah, in a minute." Brandy took a deep breath and wiped her face on her sleeve. She felt hot and drained. "You got a tissue anywhere?"

"Hold on a sec." Jeff walked out of the room and came back quickly with a wad of toilet paper. "Here."

"Ta." Brandy blew her nose, then looked at Jeff again. He seemed older now, gaunter and wearier than she remembered him. He looked grown up. She felt suddenly shy. "Funny this, innit?" she said with another sniff.

"What?"

"You know. Seeing you again. Here. After everything. Like a dream, really."

Jeff turned away. He seemed uneasy and Brandy felt a tightening in her guts. He wasn't behaving the way she'd expected, the way she'd planned in her dreams. He hadn't even kissed her yet.

"What is it, Jeff? Is summat wrong?"

Jeff began pacing the room. He looked like a long, thin whip—his skinny legs striding up and down, his belly so flat it curved inwards. Brandy watched him, her heart squeezing with a new fear. "Well?" she said.

"Look, babe, I told you. There's summat going on now. Summat big." Brandy looked down. He'd never called her babe before. She didn't like it—that was something she did to the girls she screwed inside, the ones she didn't respect.

"So what?" she said. "You know you can trust me. I won't mess you up."

Jeff stopped to look at her. "I know, you're a good kid. I always could rely on you . . ." He took a step closer. "What the fuck happened to your face?"

Brandy picked at her fingers. "It was me brother-in-law, the one Liz married, remember? I went down to Brighton with them after I got out and . . . well, he did it." She didn't feel like telling Jeff the details. She wanted him to trust her.

"Poor kid." Jeff sat down and put his arm around her at last. His arms were as narrow as straps. "Sounds like you've been having a rough time of it. Even coming here to find me." He bent down to look into her face, his slitty eyes and string-thin mouth smiling the way she remembered. "That was quite a speech you gave our Larry," he said, chuckling. "Tough little bird, aren't you?" Brandy smiled, but Jeff turned serious again. "Still, you should watch it with him. That bloke's got a dangerous temper. He might've slaughtered you if I hadn't come in."

"Yeah, well, I wanted to find you, didn't I?"

At that Jeff took his arm off her again. "Listen, love, I'm touched you came out here to look for me an' all—you're a sweet bird—but . . ." He looked down at his hands, stringy and white, dangling between his knees like rags.

"But what, Jeff?" Brandy began to talk fast, certain that if

102

she just explained things, helped him, he would see how they belonged together. "Look, we just got out. I know things have changed. It's different now, it's been two years—I know all that. But give it a chance, Jeff. We were great before." She had that Borstal whine in her voice again, the one she hated in herself.

Jeff kept staring at his dangling hands. "Yeah, I know. But you're just a kid, Brandy. I'm into big stuff now. I met some blokes inside and they put me onto this deal . . . well, anyroad, it's serious stuff. Dangerous. Big money. A lot of people involved—I can't mix you up in it."

"You mean you don't want me, don't you?" Brandy watched him, trying to pin her eyes to his to stop herself from sinking through the floor.

Jeff looked at her and squirmed. He dropped his gaze from her face, taking refuge in her body. She was a short little bird, he thought, cuddly. But that bruised face, that mouth clenched up like a child's—a mixture of revulsion and pity washed through him. "Look, love," he said, laying a hand on her leg. "We are still mates. The truth is I have to lie low for a bit 'cause the fuzz are onto us, but when that clears I'll have some cash and we can do some things. You're better out of this, Brandy, honest you are. It's risky stuff."

"Mates! What about that letter, Jeff?" Brandy felt her world tipping, sliding around under her like loose tiles. She didn't care about her whine, she didn't care if she begged.

"What letter?"

"That letter you sent to me mum's house just after you got nicked. You said you wanted to get married."

"A lot of water's gone under the bridge since then, Brandy. You know what it's like inside. You know what it does."

"But I been counting on you, Jeff. I been waiting . . ." Tears choked her, and she got up to pace the room. "Please," she said, turning to him, mascara staining her cheeks, "please give us a chance, Jeff. You said I was the best. We was so close, like brother and sister. You remember, don't you?"

Jeff looked uncomfortable. "Brandy, you've got to grow up, kid. It's not a sister I want. I got another woman, haven't you worked that out by now?"

"Another . . ." Brandy inhaled. "Already? But you haven't had time!"

"I been out four months. There's been time."

"Four months!" During all those hours she'd spent dreaming

103

about Jeff, about the way they'd find their shadow selves and help each other get used to the world again, she'd always assumed they'd be released at about the same time. "Did you get early parole or summat?"

"Yeah. Y'know how they are with first offenders. And I was a real angel inside, you shoulda seen me. Why, did they keep you longer?"

Brandy slumped into one of the armchairs. "Yeah. An extra six."

Jeff whistled. "What the hell did you do?"

Brandy glanced at him and away. Six months earlier and she would have been out before him. In time to wait for him, to catch him before anyone else did. Whoever took that cake really owed her now. "Who is she?" Brandy mumbled.

"Who?"

"Your . . .'woman.' " She tried to sound mocking.

"No one you know."

The two of them sat in silence, staring at their laps. Jeff had nothing more to say. He felt sorry for Brandy but she was a ghost to him now, a part of his childhood. A sweet memory. Yes she'd been good for dreaming about while he was inside, but that was just something to do with his head, not real. And he'd been out for a while now, long enough to start living again. He'd grown out of Brandy months ago.

Brandy was breathing. That's all she could do at first, hang on to breathing. Her stomach pitched as if she were tumbling into nothingness. She gripped the cushion under her with both hands.

"Y'know, Jeff," she said eventually, "I used to have this one dream all the time inside. Almost every night, it seemed."

"Oh, yeah? Was it about me?"

"No, but every time I would wake up screaming. I'd be in a little dark room—like a box, it was, with tall walls and a floor so dark I couldn't see it. The ceiling was like a barred window . . ."

"Sounds familiar."

"And as long as I didn't look up, I'd be all right, I'd stay alive. But even though I knew that, I could never stop meself. It would be like some sorta spell was forcing me to turn me face up towards the only bit of light in the place. And as soon as I looked up and saw the grate, it would begin to come down on me. Slowly, y'know, like when you push a slicer down on a bit of cheese. It would come down and down till I could feel the bars pressing on me skull. Sometimes I'd scream and wake meself up before I got sliced, but sometimes I couldn't."

Brandy fell silent and Jeff looked at the floor, embarrassed. Finally he stood up. "Look, babes, I think you better go now, eh? Before Larry comes back. I can't have you tearing each other's eyes out again." He took hold of Brandy's arm and tried to pull her to her feet. "All right?"

"Jeff," Brandy said, ignoring him. "What's going to happen to me?"

"I dunno, don't ask me." He felt irritated, his guilt and her pathos suddenly getting to him. But then he looked down at her, a shivering bundle on a chair, and remembered their times together in the squat, huddled between the pipes like a couple of baby birds. "Look, love," he said more kindly, "you'll find another bloke to look after you, you'll see. And you're luckier than most. You've got a mum and a sister. Go on home now and watch the telly or summat. You'll feel better soon." He put a hand on top of her head. "And, Brandy, you've got to wake up, love. You're on the outside now, in the real world. You've got to make a new life. You're not in that dream anymore." He took his hand away. "All right?"

She nodded and felt for her bag through her tears. Jeff took her by the elbow and propelled her down the hall to the front door. Outside it was raining and dark, the heaviness of the night dropping to the gound in sheets. "Watch the steps," he called, and she stumbled down them, barely able to see where to put her feet. She turned around at the bottom and looked up. He stood silhouetted against the doorway, as black and thin as a shadow. "Bye, love. See you!" he called, and shut the door. Brandy gazed up at the house, the rain drenching her hair.

8

Liz awoke with a start in the middle of the night. She'd been dreaming about going back to Birmingham again and, as always, the dream left her sweating and anxious. She looked around the dark room trying to shake the dream's hold and pulled the blanket up to her chin. Ron's bulk felt hot next to her and he was wheezing in his sleep, but for once she was grateful. In these dreams she never had Ron, but was always returning to Birmingham alone and lonely, without a job, Bobby, or even a man.

She'd been walking the streets in this dream, looking for old friends but recognizing no one. The streets were a mixture of Birmingham and Brighton, busy and gray like Brum's but with the dancing light of the seaside playing over the cars. She'd stepped into a phone booth to ring her mother but the receiver had squirmed in her hand, echoing with the hoarse cries of seagulls. Stumbling out, she had found herself standing in a parking lot, trembling, and Brandy was there, her hands on her hips, laughing at her. In the back of her mind she'd had a vague sense that somewhere, sometime she'd had something better, but she couldn't remember who or what. She kept stopping to look about her, frightened, not understanding how she'd come this far in life without a husband or a home.

Liz pulled herself up on the pillows, adrenaline still trilling through her as if she'd heard a scream. All was silent though, but for the clock ticking and Ron's breathing. A street lamp sent a moonlike glow through the curtains, turning everything a bluish gray. She ran her eyes over the room: the clothes piled on a chair in a dark, tangled heap; the luminescent screen of the TV; the glass on her dressing table shining under its clutter of bottles and trinkets. The dream slipped away as she surveyed her belongings, solid proof of all she had—clothes, makeup, ornaments, a husband, a son. She put her hands under her head and gazed at the ceiling, darkened with a soft blur of shadows from the light outside. She liked these moments of peace when she awoke in the night; they were her only times alone, away from the whirlwind of customers or Bobby or street crowds or shopping queues—the only times she heard quiet. But no matter how hard she tried to settle into contentment, to congratulate herself on the nest she'd built, she couldn't stop her thoughts from returning to Brandy.

Two weeks had passed since Brandy had fled and Liz still hadn't heard a word. She'd written to her mother asking if Brandy was with her but she'd had no answer, and even though she knew Mary easily might not bother to reply, it worried her. When Brandy had first left, Liz had expected to hear from the police at any moment, thinking they would probably pick up her sister for shoplifting or for just looking the way she did, but as the time passed with no news she'd become increasingly frightened. She couldn't help picturing Brandy's head whipping back and forth under Ron's fist and imagining her alone in the streets, her face dripping blood and her pockets empty. Liz had even taken to combing the papers each morning, looking for tales of dismembered bodies and murdered girls. She tried to comfort herself with the thought that Brandy knew how to survive, that the girl was tough and streetwise, but she couldn't really believe it. Liz knew that for all Brandy's bravado and rough talk, she was only lost and confused. So as Liz lay in bed, her worries intensified by the late hour, she began to run through all the possibilities she'd imagined yet again. Perhaps Brandy was in custody but too proud to let anyone know. Perhaps she'd been kidnapped or murdered and the police hadn't been able to identify her body. Perhaps she was drowned somewhere along Brighton beach.

To distract herself, Liz got out of bed and put on her dressing gown—a delicate, long robe in wafting white. She went into the kitchen to make some hot milk and turned on a dim lamp in the corner. While the milk was warming she climbed onto a chair and reached for the chocolates she had hidden in a cupboard, a fancy box from Ron that she kept for comfort at times such as this. The box was gone. She was still standing on the chair when Ron came in. He looked up at her, yelped, and clutched his chest.

"Gawd, you gave me a turn! You look like a fucking ghost standing up there all in white. What're you doing, anyroad?"

"Did you eat me chocolates up, you devil?"

"What chocolates?" Ron's sleepy face was as rumpled as his pajamas.

"You know, the box you gave me for me birthday."

"Nah, I didn't take 'em. I don't even like the stuff."

Liz clambered down and took the milk off the stove. It had already boiled, which meant a skin she didn't like, but she poured it into a mug anyway. "What're you doing up?"

Ron sat down at the kitchen table and rubbed his face. "I woke up all randy, but when I rolled over to knob you one you were gone. What's the matter, can't you sleep?"

Liz shook her head and sat opposite him with her milk. "I'm still too worried about Brandy."

"She musta done it."

"Done what?"

"Took your chocolates." Ron looked triumphant.

"Oh." Liz stared at the kitchen wall, suddenly tired, and took a sip.

"Come on, love, sit on me lap." Ron pulled her over. She nestled on top of him, feeling his erection pressing into her thighs. He nuzzled her neck. "You smell like a baby drinking that milk."

Liz dropped her head back, letting him kiss her under the chin. He pulled her against him and she began to feel lazily sensual through her fatigue. He took the mug from her, put it on the table and slipped his hand under her robe, running his fingers over her stomach. His hand was warm and heavy, the palm rough, and Liz liked the way her skin felt under it, silky and delicate. She turned around, straddling his lap, and he quickly reached under her to open his pajamas. As they made love on the kitchen chair, with all the gentleness and ease of habit, worry about Brandy rocked along with them at the back of Liz's mind.

In the morning both Liz and Ron were deeply asleep when Bobby came staggering in, whining and tugging at his pajamas. "Take me peejamas off, Mum," he said, pulling back the bedcovers. "I wet meself."

Liz groaned and rolled away from Ron, whom she'd been clutching in her dreams. He grunted, slapped a pillow over his head, and went back to snoring. "Here," she said, pulling Bobby closer. With her eyes half shut, she took off his wet pajamas and mopped him dry. Bobby clambered over her, sticking a knee into her stomach, and wriggled between her and Ron.

"I'm cold," he whimpered, so Liz helped him under the blanket. He snuggled down and put his arm around her neck. She smiled, feeling its small weight resting against her jaw.

"Lie still, love, and get a little more rest," she whispered. "Me and Dad are tired." She tried to get back to sleep but Bobby kept shifting around, scraping her stomach with his toenails or thumping her groin with his heel. "Ow, lie still," she said again. With a mischievous grin he took her cheeks in both hands and began to push her face into different grotesque expressions. "Leave off, Bobby," she said, pulling away, but his fingers caught her lip and yanked. "Ow!"

"Will you two be quiet!" Ron pressed the pillow tighter over his head.

"Shut up, Dad," Bobby said, kicking him in the back. "Go away."

"Bloody hell." Ron rolled over, making the bed bounce under his weight, and glared at Bobby. "It's too early. Go back to sleep."

Bobby wrinkled his nose. "You smell like poo."

"Don't speak to your dad like that," Liz said, trying not to laugh. "What d'you think you smell like, pissing all over yourself like a baby, eh?"

"I am a baby," Bobby said, pouting.

Liz sighed and pulled him closer to cuddle him but he pushed her away, too awake now for that. "You be an Indian girl, Mum. I'll be the shoulder coming to capture you." Liz groaned. "Come on, Mum. I'll let you go, promise."

"I'm too tired, Bobby. I'll be an Indian girl later."

"Nah, now! Play now!" Bobby sat up, pulling the covers off his parents. "Yippy-eye-oh-kai-yay!"

"Bloody hell!" Ron said again, and sat up, yawning. He swung his legs off the bed and rubbed his hair. "It's like being woken up by a band of bleeding savages!"

"You're an Indian chief, Dad. I'm gonna shoot you!"

"I'll Indian you, me boy!" Ron tumbled Bobby on the bed, tickling him, while Liz got up sleepily and went into the kitchen to make breakfast.

Once Liz had navigated through the chaos of the morning, getting Ron fed and packed off to work and Bobby to nursery school, she had time to worry about Brandy again. She walked down the morning streets to the salon, her body tipped forward from the double incline of the hill and her high-heeled shoes, trying to decide what to do. "It's no use just bloody worrying about it," she told herself. "I'll get old before me time doing that. I've just got to do something." If only Mary had a phone, then she could at least get an answer from the woman. She could try writing to her again, she supposed, but that would take so long and not even guarantee a reply. She could call the police and report Brandy missing, but that might only get the girl into trouble with the law again. Or she could simply go up to Brum and try to find Brandy herself.

All morning at the salon Liz tried to decide whether to go to Birmingham. She hadn't been back there since she'd fled it with Ron, and the idea of returning was as repugnant as her dream, but as she mulled it over, it was the only thing that made sense. Where else, after all, had Brandy left to go?

That night, once Liz had the family fed, Bobby tucked in, and the supper cleared, she brought up the subject with Ron. They were sitting in the bedroom watching a soccer game on television.

"Ron," she said nervously, "I've been thinking."

"Did it hurt?"

"No, listen, this is important. Turn off the frigging telly, will you? I don't see how you can listen with that thing blabbing away."

Ron sighed, heaved himself off the armchair, and turned the volume down. He sat back, his eyes still fixed on the players. "I'm listening," he said.

"Well, I've been thinking about Brandy, Ron, and I decided I should go up to Brum and look for her."

"What?" He turned to her, already angry.

"Now don't get all worked up about it. Jenny said I could

have Monday off, so I thought I'd take the train up Saturday morning and come back Monday night. Don't worry, I'll pay for it meself."

"What with?"

"I'm getting me pay tomorrow."

"And where's the money for the groceries going to come from, I'd like to know? D'you expect me to work double time or summat?" Ron's sunburned face darkened with indignation. "You can't do it, Liz. Don't be daft."

"We'll manage. I can do it, you'll see."

Ron stood up. "What about Bobby?" he shouted.

"You can look after Bobby for just one weekend, can't you? I do it all the time."

"You're supposed to, you're his mum. I can't, anyroad, 'cause I've signed up for overtime Saturday. And what about me rest on the weekend, eh? I can't go running around like some bleeding nursemaid all the time. I'm too knackered, you know that. You must be daft, Liz. What d'you want to go up there chasing her for, anyroad?"

"What d'you think?" Liz wandered to the dressing table, picked up a pot of face cream and fiddled with it. "Look, Ron, we don't have the foggiest idea what happened to her after that night, do we? She could've been murdered or run over or anything, and it's getting so as I can't sleep for worry about it. We shouldn't've done it, Ron."

"Done what? She's the one who done it, in case you forgot. Have you forgotten what she did to Bobby, leaving him alone night after night, frightening the wits outta him? Supposing there'd been a fire? Supposing he'd got run over? What if he'd got sick?"

"I know, Ron, but it wasn't night after night, it was only twice or something. And nothing like that did happen, did it? I know he was scared, but it was our fault, too, Ron. I told you we were stupid to trust her so early."

"You were stupid, you mean. She's your sister. I thought you were supposed to know how to handle the girl."

"So it's my fault now, is it? Well, I don't care what you say, Ron, I'm going."

"I think you care more about that fucking con artist than you do your own son."

"That's a load of crap and you know it."

111

Ron stepped nearer to her, angry but cool. "You're not going, Liz, an' that's that. You're not even thinking straight. What if you do find her, what's the use?"

"I just want to see if she's alive, Ron, if she's all right. You really did her over, if you care to remember. She's probably with Mum but I want to make sure, that's all. Maybe help her out a bit."

"That nutter doesn't deserve any help. We gave her plenty of it and look what she did. Abandoned Bobby, pinched your chocolates—and that isn't the only thing I've found missing 'round here, I'll tell you. She's no good, Liz, and the sooner you face up to it the better."

"She's my sister, Ron. You don't have any right to tell me what to do about her." Liz was speaking icily by now, trying to match Ron's coldness, but her cheeks were flaming.

"Oh, yes I fucking do. You're the mother of my son, me girl, and I'm not having you walking out on him, or bringing home any more of your nutcase relatives to screw him up, you understand? You're staying right here this weekend, where you belong, and I don't want to hear any more about it." And with that Ron turned the television back up and stared at it for the rest of the evening.

On Saturday morning, after Ron had gone to work, Liz quickly packed an overnight bag. She put in two changes of clothes for herself, three for Bobby, their toothbrushes, toothpaste, and some snacks and toys. The bag was bulging and heavy by the time she'd finished but she knew that she'd need plenty of distractions to keep Bobby entertained on the long train journey. She dressed him neatly in navy blue shorts and a white shirt and combed his clean blond hair until it shone. If she was going to have to face her mother again, she thought, she might as well at least show off her gorgeous son. Then she wrote a short note to Ron: "We've gone to stay with Mum. We'll be back Monday. There's stew in the fridge. Don't worry." She liked that note. It seemed cool and mature, with no mention of their fight, no apologies. It made her feel brave.

Bobby was excited. He loved going on trains but hardly ever had the chance since the family rarely left Brighton. Liz had promised him sweets, too, deciding that indulgence would be the best preventive of tantrums. He hopped about her eagerly, bringing more and more toys for her to stuff into their bag. Even though her plans had not originally included Bobby, Liz was glad now that he was coming. His presence might make everyone behave better, perhaps even get her mother to sober up enough to see beyond her nose for once. And he would be proof of where she'd got in life in case she ran into anyone she knew.

"Where're we going on the train, Mum?" Bobby asked as they got on the bus to the station.

"On an adventure, love. We're going to look for your Aunty Brandy."

"Why, has Aunty run away?"

"Sort of. We're going to be detectives and find her."

"Ooh! Maybe some Indians got her, Mum! Or some Daleks! Maybe they tied her up in a cave."

"Yeah, maybe, Bobby."

They reached the station too early so Liz decided to walk Bobby down Queen's Road for a while, hoping he'd burn up some energy and so be more manageable on the train. They strolled along the narrow pavement, Bobby stopping frequently to gloat over toy shops or to pick up a cigarette or bottle cap off the ground. "Ooh, look, Mum!" he said as they came to the window of a glassmaker's shop. "Look at all those animules."

Liz looked in with him. The shop window was lined with dozens of glass figurines: glistening swans, miniature umbrellas, tiny animals as delicate as bubbles. She could see the glassmaker inside, a burly man in goggles bending over a white flame. "Let's go in, Mum." Bobby tugged at her hand.

"No, love, we don't have time." Liz looked at her watch. "We'll miss the train."

"I want to!" His voice was shrill. "Come on, Mum, please!"

"No. I told you."

"Ple-ease. Pretty please."

Liz laughed, wondering where he'd picked up that phrase. "Oh, all right, but only for a minute, mind."

Inside, the shop was dark and hot. The man had a long crystal tube in one hand and was dipping it in and out of the fire, his fingers dancing as gracefully as a magician's. As they watched he formed a tiny horse, complete with pointed ears, a tail, and four minute, transparent hooves. "Can I have it, Mum?" Bobby said.

"We don't have time, Bobby. We're going to miss the train. Come on, let's go."

"Ah, go on," the man said to Liz. "A sweet little boy like that should have a magic horse, shouldn't he?"

113

"We don't have time," Liz said, cursing the man under her breath.

"But it's magic, Mum. The man said it's magic."

Liz knew she'd be hearing about it all day now. "Well, how much is it then?"

"Just two pounds, madam."

"Two pounds! You must be joking. Come on, Bobby, we've got to go." She tried to pull him out of the shop.

"No! I want it, I want it! No, no, no, no!" Bobby began to cry, rubbing his dirty fists in his tears. Liz grabbed Bobby's hand and yanked him out of the shop. He screamed and dragged his feet all the way up the hill, pulling on Liz's arm until she was sweating and furious. By the time they reached the station, the London train had already arrived.

Liz hauled Bobby over to the ticket booth and, without letting go of him, bought a return to Birmingham, which left her with only six pounds for the whole weekend. She wanted to swat Bobby for making everything so difficult, for getting her all hot and flustered when she'd been so determined to keep calm. He was still sobbing with rage.

"Shurrup!" she hissed, looking around in embarrassment. "People are staring at you." She let go of him for an instant to pick up the bag and Bobby shot off towards the station entrance, shouting about getting his magic horse.

"Bobby! Come right back here this minute!" Liz shrieked, but he didn't pay any attention. Dropping her bag to the floor, she dashed after him, caught his arm just as he was about to run into the road, and whacked him hard across the back. He gasped, then resumed crying even louder. "Shurrup, you little bastard," Liz shouted, and shook him. "Shut up or I'll bash your face in!" She picked him up and ran inside, but when she tried to lift her bag, too, she couldn't manage both and had to put Bobby back down. His legs crumpled to the floor and he refused to move.

"Get up!" she screamed, but he sat in a heap, stubbornly limp. Liz yanked him to his feet by one arm. Her back strained and she felt a pain shoot up her spine.

"Can I help?" She looked up to see a young man in jeans and a leather jacket. He had a posh accent and a fashionably scruffy look—probably a student.

"Yeah, please," she said, panting, "it's the London train." She picked up Bobby and staggered after the student while the guard watched them impatiently, chewing the whistle in his lips. As the young man opened a door and helped her in, passing her the heavy bag, the whistle blew.

Liz pushed Bobby ahead of her down the aisle until they found an empty seat by a window. "Sit down," she said to Bobby, collapsing into her seat and closing her eyes. "You little bastard. What a fucking circus." Bobby put his face in her lap and cried dirty tears all over her newly cleaned skirt. Liz patted his head, giving up.

After apologies and hugs, the two of them settled down to enjoy the journey. Liz cleaned Bobby and herself up as best she could with a package of towelettes, and Bobby knelt next to her by the window, pressing his nose to the glass, munching on potato crisps and humming to himself. Liz took out the magazine she'd brought to read but left it unopened on her lap, letting her head fall back and closing her eyes. She felt the sun passing over her eyelids, flashing red and yellow, sometimes green, and waited for a sense of freedom to come to her, for some pride at her daring escape, but she only felt afraid. She had never defied Ron like this before.

Bobby pushed his forehead against the cool, vibrating glass, feeling it buzz over his face, and watched the world flash by. The landscape was lit up with morning sunlight, bright and clear, and it flickered past like a film. Before long the dazzle and rhythm of the train lulled him into a daze and he sank down to rest his head against his mother. He nestled into her, feeling the side of her breast cushion his face, and put his grimy thumb into his mouth. The sunlight spread across her lap and oddly shaped patches of shadow moved over her legs, like insects. She was hot from the sun and smelled of perfume and sleep, the kind of enveloping, protective smell a bed has in the morning. Bobby's eyelids drooped and the curtain of his lashes closed slowly over his vision.

Liz laid Bobby's head down in her lap and gazed at him. He still looked like a baby when he was asleep, his flawless skin round and firm, his nose tiny, his eyelashes fanning delicately over his cheeks. She pushed back his hair from his forehead, where there was a line of white skin untouched by the sun, and wondered at her temper a half hour before. She always swung to such extremes with Bobby, either weak with adoration or rigid with fury. Always kissing or hitting. That's the way it was with kids, she supposed. She lay back again, resting her hand on his small chest as it rose and sank beneath her.

By the time they reached Birmingham, it was two o'clock.

Bobby should have had his lunch by then but wasn't complaining, being stuffed with chocolates and crisps, and Liz was too jittery to need more than the cup of tea she'd had on the London train. The journey had gone well after their nap but she was tired. She tidied them both up in the station ladies' room, and walked him over to the bus stop.

"I'm cold, Mum," he said, shivering, and indeed it was much cooler there than in Brighton. Liz put him in a jacket that made him look like a miniature man and slipped on a cardigan. She looked around as they waited for the bus, recognizing the modern buildings and denseness of the city with a kind of excited dread, but she didn't feel defeated by the place as she'd expected—in fact, she felt triumphant.

On the bus, however, as they passed through the center of town towards the Highgate estate, Liz became increasingly nervous. She hadn't set eyes on her mother since she was sixteen, and had barely communicated with her since then, either, except for two letters or so. Had Mary grown worse? she wondered. Liz tried to remember the details of what her mother looked like, but oddly enough could only picture herself with Bobby—a slim mother in good clothes. She mostly recalled Mary's bulk and her smell, that constant stink of furniture polish and alcohol. Liz pulled Bobby to her protectively. Maybe she did lose her temper with him too easily, but that was nothing compared to what Mary had been like. Liz remembered those Friday nights when she would come home from her first job at a salon to find her mother in one of her bitter moods. Mary would spout insults, attacking Liz and Brandy for their looks, their postures, their ingratitude; then the self-pity would take over and she'd start blubbering and nagging until she'd made Liz hand over her pay packet. Liz clenched her lips at the memory.

The bus pulled up to the council estate at a quarter to three, just as the sun was making a last effort to pierce through the sticky clouds that had moved over the city. Bobby was groggy by now with fatigue and on the edge of giving her trouble again. "Come along, Bobby love," she said, helping him off the bus. "We're almost there."

"Carry me," he whined. "Me legs hurt."

"I know, sweetie, but I can't carry you, you're too heavy with this bag. And me back's killing me. Look!" She pointed at a tower of flats jutting out of the ground like a gray tombstone. "That's where I lived when I was a little girl."

Bobby looked around, squinting into the sky. "It's big here," he said, and clung to his mother's legs.

"Yeah, I know." Liz crouched down to hug him. "It won't be so bad once we're inside."

The two of them made their way slowly to Mary's tower at the front of the estate. Built on the crest of a hill and surrounded by wire fences, the Highgate estate had always looked naked to Liz, its tall gray towers interspersed with barracks-like buildings and patches of asphalt, its empty spaces filled with sky. The wind, as usual, whirled about her, scattering a 7-Up tin and a pile of sweet wrappers past her feet, but there was no other sign of life—not even a moving car or a line of flapping laundry. The place looked utterly abandoned, as if everyone had moved out or no one had ever lived there at all.

Bobby staggered beside Liz looking particularly small in the wide, barren landscape and Liz felt a surge of pity, as much for herself and Brandy at that age as for him. "That's where Aunty and I used to play when we were little," she told him, pointing to the industrial building at the back of the estate, now nothing more than a few crumbling walls and a pile of bricks. "It's got worse since then."

"Are there Daleks here, Mum?"

"No, love. You're safe with me."

"Did you like Aunty?"

"When I was a little girl, you mean?"

Bobby nodded.

"Course I did, love. She was me baby sister, wasn't she?" Liz felt a twinge of guilt. "Everyone likes their sisters."

"Will she be there, Mum?"

"I hope so. We're detectives, remember? We'll have to wait and see. But your gran'll be there."

"Does Gran have a telly?"

"I don't know, Bobby. We'll just have to wait and see."

At last they got to Mary's tower and approached the front door cautiously. The door was made of heavy glass covered with cross-hatched wire. Someone had twisted a tangle of coat hangers around the broken lock but that did not prevent Liz from pushing open the door easily. Inside, the lobby was dim and bare, its brown walls scrawled with graffiti, its light nothing but one naked bulb. The place was much worse than Liz had remembered. Bobby looked about him and hugged her legs.

"Come on. We'll go up in the lift." Liz pressed the button

and smiled nervously at Bobby, praying the lift worked for once. She heard it creak and rattle above her. Suddenly three teenage boys burst through the front door, wearing skinhead haircuts so short they looked almost bald, heavy black boots, and tattoos on their bare arms. They looked Liz over silently, the sound of their gum-chewing snapping against the walls. She pulled Bobby closer and fixed her eyes on the lift.

"Why're those men bald, Mum?" Bobby said, his voice piping out clearly.

Liz darted a look at them. They were all staring into space, their faces expressionless. "I dunno, ask them." Bobby grinned shyly and hid in her skirt. The lift door finally rattled open and Liz ushered him in. To her relief the skinheads stayed downstairs.

In front of Mary's door, Liz put down her bag and took a deep breath. Bobby was still in his fit of shyness, hiding behind her and holding onto her knees, and Liz's heart was beating hard. She knocked, waited, and knocked again. Bobby whimpered. "Shh," Liz said, and put her ear to the door. She heard nothing.

"Right then, no one's home," she said with some disappointment, and opened her handbag, rummaging through tissues, makeup, and sweet wrappers until she found the old key she'd brought with her. She fit it into the lock—it still worked. "Come on, love, let's go in." She swung open the door, flipped on the familiar light switch, and pulled Bobby in with her.

The biggest astonishment was that the flat hadn't changed. Not one iota. The chairs were in the same place, the carpet was as dingy as ever, and the wooden tables under the windows were as dusty and scraped up as when she'd left home. Liz shivered, chilled by the material evidence of how little her mother's life had progressed. Leaving her bags on the floor, she walked over to the side table by the sofa and turned on the lamp—an unwieldy orange pot topped with a plastic-covered shade that crackled when she touched it. She gazed around her. The sun had moved behind the building, sending a cold shadow over the room, and the place looked curiously flat, as if it had been sketched in with a pencil. There was no sign of life other than the well-used furniture—no magazines, no cups, no newspapers. People in this room obviously just sat and stared at the walls.

"Where's the telly?" Bobby whimpered, edging closer to her.

"It looks like there isn't a telly, love. I'm sorry. I s'pose Gran can't afford it."

"But I want to watch telly."

"I know, I know. Look, d'you want something to eat? Are you hungry?"

Bobby shook his head but Liz went into the kitchen anyway, a back room the width of a hallway. She searched through the cupboards and found nothing but tins of baked beans and a jar of Marmite. "Fancy some baked beans?"

"No." Bobby was near to tears, exhausted and bewildered by this cold, silent place. "Where's Gran?"

"I dunno, love. She'll probably be back later." She opened the bread bin. "How about some toast, then? With butter and Marmite?"

"Yeah."

"What do you say?"

"Please."

"All right, you sit down and I'll make you some." She helped Bobby onto a wobbly metal chair and poured him a glass of milk, putting on the kettle for herself. Soon she had him munching on the toast, his face brightening. Liz never could get over how Bobby's mood changed after only one bite.

"Mum," he said, his mouth full, "when'll the adventure start?" He pronounced it "adwenchu."

"You mean finding Aunt Brandy?"

"Yeah! We're going to rescue her, right?"

"Well, first we have to find out if she's living here, in Gran's home. Then if she isn't, we might get the police to help us."

Bobby's eyes grew wide. "She done something bad, Mum?"

"No, no. The police help find lost people, y'know, they don't just chase robbers." Liz smiled and reached out to smooth Bobby's hair. "Eat up, love. It's your nap time."

"Nah, it isn't." He picked up his glass and drank down the milk noisily. His cheeks puffed in and out and his smooth forehead frowned in concentration. "I want to find Aunty," he said, putting the glass down.

"We'll find Aunty later. Come on, I'll show you where we'll sleep."

"You going to stay with me, Mum?"

"Course I am, ducky. I wouldn't leave you alone in a strange place."

Bobby pushed himself off the chair and came 'round the table to Liz. He put his thin arms around her and hugged. "I love you, Mum."

Soon Liz had everything organized. The beds in the room

she used to share with Brandy were made with fresh sheets, Bobby was washed and tucked in, their bag was neatly unpacked, and Liz was lying in the dark with Bobby, stroking his hair while he sucked his thumb in her arms. She felt calm and in control. Liz liked to sweep into a confused place and sort it out, to exert her will over things and people. She'd been doing it since she was nine and she was good at it. She ran her eyes around the room. Earlier, Liz had found Brandy's clothes scattered all over the floor, and the now-battered shoes the girl had worn in Brighton lying toppled over in a corner. She had folded the clothes with relief, putting them on the sitting room sofa along with sheets for Brandy to sleep on, and now she took advantage of the quiet, dark room to make her plans. Not only was she going to clean up her mother's disgusting flat, with its greasy dust and bathtub ring that hadn't been touched for years, but she was going to sort out Brandy, too.

Just as Bobby drifted off to sleep Liz heard the front door being unlocked. She stiffened, willing Mary or Brandy, whoever it was, to keep quiet so they wouldn't startle him awake. She heard the door close, a release of breath, and footsteps thudding over to the toilet. She slipped her arm out from under Bobby's head and tiptoed into the sitting room. Brandy emerged, zipping herself up. "Liz!" she cried. "What're you doin' here?" And before Liz could blink, Brandy leapt over to hug her.

Liz returned Brandy's hug stiffly, then stepped away. "Shh, not so loud, Bobby's in there sleeping." She nodded towards the bedroom door. "Surprised to see me, eh?"

"Is he all right then?" Brandy asked anxiously.

"Yeah, he's all right . . . now."

There was an awkward pause and Brandy looked at the floor.

"Is Mum coming home soon?" Liz said.

"I dunno. She usually stays out boozing on Saturday nights. Why did you come, Liz?" Brandy felt wary now. What was Liz after, she wondered, some sort of revenge?

"Come on, let's sit down, we've got some talking to do." Liz led Brandy to the sofa. "I came to find you, Brandy. I just wanted to know if you were all right. I wrote Mum asking but she never answered. Did you see the card I sent?"

"Nah. The old crow probably dropped it down the bog."

Liz nodded and looked her sister over. Brandy didn't look well. She was thinner, which wasn't so bad, but her face was pale and her expression droopy. She seemed half-asleep, as if the life had been drawn out of her. "You all right, love?" Liz said gently.

Brandy shrugged and turned away. Her bruises had faded to a pale yellow and were only visible as dim blotches in the afternoon gloom. Brandy felt her lips tremble at Liz's sympathy but clenched them tight. After her initial joy at seeing her sister again, her resentment over their last encounter was returning with the sharpness of a fresh slap.

"What have you been doing with yourself?" Liz persisted. "What did you do that . . . that night you left?"

"What's it matter to you?"

"Well, Bobby and me came all this way to find you, didn't we?"

"Did you?"

"Why else d'you think we came? To see the sights?"

Brandy's mouth twitched at that. "D'you think it'll wake him up if I go take a peek at him?" she said.

"Not if you're quiet. Be careful though, he's knackered after that long train journey, poor kid."

"Don't worry." Brandy tiptoed across the room to peer in. She could just make out Bobby's white face in the dark. She listened to his delicate breathing and snuffling sounds and crept up to his bed, bending down to smell his hair. He smelled of milk and shampoo. She felt so relieved to see him all right and whole, not lost, not run over, that she wanted to gather him to her and squeeze him tight. Instead, she rested her lips on his head, ever so lightly. "Hello, little love," she whispered. She wished she could get into bed and cuddle him the way she used to in Liz's house, just hold him and hug him until the world went away. When she finally crept out of the room, she left behind the first sense of peace she'd felt since seeing Molly.

"He's a darling, your son," she said to Liz, sitting back on the sofa. "Wish he was mine. I'd love a kid of me own, one day."

Liz smiled cautiously. She didn't like the way her sister moved, as if she wasn't all there. Even right out of Borstal she'd had more life to her than this, a grin and a cocky joke. "Come on, Brandy, tell us what you've been up to. I been worried, you know."

"Does Ron know you're here?" Brandy said.

Liz flushed. "Yeah, he knows."

Brandy hunched her shoulders. "I haven't been up to much. I hitched here the day after your charming husband smashed me up, and I've been here ever since. Seen a few mates. Not much to tell, really." She spoke distantly, as if referring to someone else.

"What're you doing for cash?"

Brandy shrugged. She felt herself slipping away again, back to the glum daze she'd been in since Jeff. "Mum gives me some and I've signed up for the dole."

"Brandy, you can't rot here forever doing nothing, y'know." Liz looked at her sister's heavy-lidded eyes. "You on something?"

"What?"

"Are you on some drug? You look doped up to the eyeballs."

"Wish I was. Where am I supposed to get anything like that with no cash, eh? I can hardly afford a sodding pint of cider."

"All right, all right." The sisters were silent for a moment. "What're you going to do with yourself, then?"

"I dunno." Brandy's voice was dull. "Don't care, either."

"What mates have you seen?"

"No one important. Just this girl from inside. And . . . no one important."

"Is your bloke out yet? What's-his-name?"

Brandy looked down at her lap. "Jeff. Yeah, well . . ." She tore at her cuticles. "I saw him but I didn't fancy him no more. You know how it is, two years an' all."

"I thought you were all set to marry him!"

"Well, I'm not, see?" Brandy's voice turned fierce and she glared at Liz.

"All right, all right!" Liz paused, then leaned forward and put her manicured hand on Brandy's pudgy knee. "I'm only trying to help, love. I'm sorry about what Ron did to you, even if you did leave Bobby on his own, which could've killed him. But I didn't want you to run off."

Brandy swallowed and looked at Liz's hand until she pulled it away. "What happened to him that night, then?" she asked.

"I found him on the steps of a house down the road crying in his pajamas. He'd walked all the way there by himself."

Brandy said nothing so Liz changed the subject. "Mum's no better, I s'pose?"

"Nah. She's the same old bag. She spends half her life in the bath and the other half in the pub. But she hasn't been too bad, really. More pathetic than anything."

Liz was surprised to hear Brandy talk kindly of their mother. It made her indignant. "Yeah, maybe, but mothers aren't sup-posed to be pathetic, are they? She always was a sniveling old bag. It's all right for you, you didn't have to look after her when you were only a kid, but I think it's disgusting."

"Well, maybe you didn't have to, either, Liz. You just like looking after people. She can manage on her own, y'know, she isn't that hopeless. She gets to work, collects her pay and all. She's even got a man."

"A man!" Liz laughed. "What kind of bloke would want an old bag like that? Jesus, he must be a right sight."

"Well, he is a bit old," Brandy said, and they both tittered. "He lives upstairs. George Balfrey. Remember him?"

"That old bleeder! Christ, I'm surprised he can even pull on his trousers in the morning! Imagine him fooling around on his wife!" Liz pulled a face. "It's revolting, really, when you think about it."

"Well, it keeps 'em busy. Who cares anyroad?" Brandy slumped back into her scowl, fed up with the effort of making conversation. What did Liz want of her anyway, except to bother her about something or other? Brandy already knew she'd botched everything; she didn't need her sister lording it over her to remind her of that. She felt a sudden yearning for Molly, or Reardon, someone she didn't have to pretend with, someone who'd understand. She just wanted to be left alone.

Liz watched Brandy for a while, feeling sad. She didn't like to see Brandy so bitter, not when she could remember her as a laughing little girl. She thought of her sister's perpetually grubby three-year-old face and the wide-eyed belief with which she'd always listened to her stories, and felt a real affection for Brandy— not just the sisterly sense of ownership she'd always had, but a genuine concern. Brandy was nothing but a foul-mouthed tart when she was in one of her black moods, but when she was laughing or happy with Bobby there was something about her that really pulled at Liz. It hurt Liz to see her so defeated.

"Brandy?" she said at last. "Is there anything I can do to help out?"

Brandy glanced at her with surprise. What was this? Her sister was looking at her, seriousness all over her pointed face. Brandy felt a lump grow in her throat, but she resisted the urge to reach out to touch Liz, to let go at last. She knew she couldn't go that far.

"Well?" Liz said. "Is there?"

Brandy shook her head. "Nah, Liz, there's nothing you can do for me. You know that." She attempted a smile. "You can buy me a ticket to America, if you want. Or find me a millionaire." Brandy paused. "Look, Liz, I'm sorry for what I did in Brighton, if that's what you're here for. It was daft, I know. I just wasn't thinking right. I love Bobby. I wouldn't harm him for the world." Brandy looked over at her, her green eyes pleading. "All right?"

Liz was surprised at how much this moved her. "Oh, Brandy"—she sighed—"that's not what I came for." She shook her head. "I wish . . ." She paused, searching for what she wished. "God, Brandy, I wish we were different."

9

Mary sat in the corner of the pub, humming to herself, her face in its fresh evening makeup as bright as a toucan's. Her friends had just left in a rush of laughter and jokes, but she had chosen to stay on and savor her last swallow of whiskey alone. She liked this pub, with its cozy leather seats, the voices that gently washed over her, and the cheerful warmth of her old mates—it was a cradle to her, a soft and twinkling embrace. Leaning back in her seat, she closed her eyes and let herself drift into pleasant oblivion.

"Glasses please, ladies and gents!" the bartender shouted, startling her. She sat up quickly, looking around with her characteristic birdlike movements.

"Dozing off a bit, were you, darlin'?" chuckled an old woman sitting nearby.

Mary finished her drink and, standing unsteadily, pulled on a red overcoat that billowed around her like a parachute. "Tra,"

125

she said to the bartender, and stumbled out of the door into the unwelcome cool of the night.

On the bus she quickly fell back into her half-doze. She'd had a difficult time of it lately with Brandy skulking about the flat, morose and silent, picking on her and nagging her for money, and that night she felt unusually tired and sodden by the drink. Every day, all day long since the girl had arrived, Mary had been racking her brains for a way to help her, but she'd come up with nothing. Brandy was as immovable as the Town Hall. All she ever did was go out for a few hours every evening, then come back more morose than ever. It got on Mary's nerves. "You can't help people as won't help themselves," she kept saying to Brandy, but it did no good. Sometimes the only thing that kept Mary from turning her daughter out was the dread of Brandy getting into trouble again. God, it took a long time for your children to grow up.

At her stop Mary got off the bus and plodded slowly towards the flat, looking about her warily. Just last week some girl had been gang-banged behind a building, and one old geezer or another was always getting knocked over and robbed. Sighing, she pushed open the front door, jabbing herself on the broken coat hangers, and staggered in, surprised at how wobbly she felt. Two people were waiting for the lift, a West Indian man from upstairs and one of the pack of skinny boys who always hung about looking like starved rats. They both nodded at her, eyeing her blurry face, and said, "Good evening," but she ignored them. She had better things to do than talk to people like that. All she wanted was the peace and quiet of her solitary bed—not even George would be welcome tonight. She got off the lift, unlocked her door, and stumbled into the flat.

"Surprise!" Brandy called. "Look who's here, Mum."

Mary stared at the girl on the sofa, skinny and bright in a yellow outfit and matching earrings. Her first impression was of hard, red lips and a grim expression. "Liz?" she said shakily. "Is it you?"

Liz looked up with an uneasy grin. "Yup, it's me."

"Jesus." Mary pushed the door shut and fell against it. "Where the hell did you come from?"

"Mars, didn't you know?" Brandy giggled.

"I came for a visit, Mother," Liz said primly, looking Mary up and down with distaste. The woman was so drunk that even her lipstick was crooked. "I brought Bobby, too."

"Bobby?" Mary glanced from one daughter to another. She had the sense that they were making fun of her. For a moment the two of them seemed like twins, sitting there so secretively with those suspicious glares and heavy jaws. They both looked full of spite.

"Bobby's your grandson, Mother," Liz said.

"I know that. Where is he?" Mary's words were slurred. She reminded Liz of certain types of women who frequent Brighton pubs, the kind with blue eyeliner leaking down their cheeks and too much rouge.

"He's asleep in Brandy's room," Liz said in her salon accent. "You'll see him in the morning."

"Oh. Well that'll be nice." Mary was impressed at how neat and sophisticated Liz looked. She couldn't help being glad to see her, even if the girl was acting the snob—after all, it had been, what, five years? And Mary had missed her so. She wobbled over to a chair and sat down carefully, trying to disguise her drunkenness. She didn't want Liz to be ashamed of her. "Well," she said brightly, "how long are you staying for?"

"Just the weekend."

"Is that all? There'll hardly be enough time to get to know you again."

"I do have a job to get back to, y'know," Liz said, but she caught herself and made an effort to sound pleasant. "How have you been keeping then, Mum?"

Mary nestled into her chair. "Oh, it's dreadful getting old, Liz," she moaned, her words slurring again. "Me rheumatism's acting up—I think it's from having me hands in water all the time—and me back's killing me. And it gets so lonely living here all by meself. No one to talk to. No visits from me daughters or me grandson for years and years. How old is Bobby now?"

"I told you in the letter, Mum, he's three."

"What's his real name, Richard?"

"Robert. Robert James Dunbar."

"I'll call him Jimmy then. I don't like Robert."

"Well no one asked you, did they?"

"No they didn't, and that's the trouble!" Mary struggled forward in her chair, burping. "Why didn't you invite me to his christening like other daughters do? You did have him christened, didn't you?"

"Course we did. What d'you think I am, a bloody heathen?"

"Well, why didn't you invite me, then?" Mary's eyes filled with easy tears. "What kind of daughter are you, not even telling me about me own grandson till he's three years old!"

Liz pressed her lips together. "Don't start, Mum. We're here now, aren't we?"

"Huh! And about time!" Mary fell back in her chair and sulked, her eyes glazing over. It was so strange to see her two daughters in the sitting room after so long, right there on the sofa, just like in the old days before Willy left . . . Mary jerked her thoughts away from that and gazed at Liz. The girl reminded her of herself at that age: slim and quick. Why, the lads Mary'd had running after her when she was young! The whole village had been jealous! Even when she was first married to Willy she'd attracted stares—he had been so proud. Mary looked down at her hands, puffy and red now with ammonia and age, and at the wedding ring embedded in her swollen flesh. She'd always had strong hands, but there had been a time when they'd still looked delicate. She glanced at Liz's hands, pulling at each other in her lap. Liz's were scrawny and nervous, with knobby fingers. No, Mary had been prettier than Liz, softer around the edges. Liz looked as if you'd cut yourself if you touched her.

"Mum, are you listening?" Liz longed to yank her mother up in the chair, tuck her pathetic wisps of hair back in place, and straighten the slash of lipstick that lay lopsided over her mouth.

Mary blinked. "So why did you take so long to visit me, eh? Five years you've stayed away, you have. Or is it six? I can't even count it's been so long."

Liz sighed. "Look, Mum, I didn't come all this way to listen to your nagging."

Mary's mouth crumpled, and she continued as if Liz hadn't spoken. "Never mind that I've been working me arse off all this time without so much as a peep from you, eh? Never mind that I've got one daughter in Borstal and murderers down the hall and rapists in the lift: My one and only decent daughter is too busy to see her own mum." Her voice changed from a whine to accusation. "So what did you come crawling back for, eh? You planning to leave your lug of a husband, is that it? Come crawling to me for money and a roof like your layabout sister? Is that it, eh?" Her words stumbled over each other, sliding around loosely on her tongue.

"Jesus, Mum!" Liz said, too disgusted even to be angry. "What's got into you? You've been here five minutes and you're already trying to start a row. And you're pissed as a newt, as well. You haven't changed a bit, have you?"

Mary's face reddened. "Is that the way you're going to speak to me after all these years?"

"Oh, gawd, here we go again."

"Don't you bloody well dare, my girl! You're such a saucy bitch, you are, putting on all those airs. Who d'you think you are, anyway?"

"I'm a respectable woman living a decent life, that's who I am, no thanks to you!"

"Ooh, you're a nasty bint!" Mary swung into the old routine easily. "Up and left you did, leaving me stranded without so much as a by-your-leave. And after all I sacrificed for you! You never did have a heart inside that skinny chest of yours."

"We have got vicious in our old age, haven't we?" Liz said. "The best thing I ever did was leave this place. It's disgusting here, it is. You keep it like a pigsty! Gawd, I thought you might have sorted yourself out a bit by now, but here you are living like a tramp in a flophouse!"

"Don't you dare!" Mary's voice rose to a sloppy wail. "Coming up here all high and mighty! You should be apologizing to me, you should, running off like that without a word. You call that being decent . . ."

Ever since Liz and Mary had begun bickering, Brandy had felt paralyzed. She hated it when they fought; it made her feel like a brittle rubber band stretched between them, yet at the same time shunted aside and forgotten. All during her childhood she'd been haunted by their fights—even in Borstal she'd had nightmares about them. As Liz and Mary kept at it, raking over old resentments, Brandy looked at her mother's face, red, jowly, and sweating along the brow, and at her sister, cold as an icepick, and felt as if she didn't know them—as if they'd turned into hostile strangers with screaming mouths, swallowing up all the air around her. She dropped her eyes to her lap and tore at her fingers. The cacophony of their voices reminded her of the midnight shouts in Borstal, only shriller and more chaotic. She put her hands over her ears to shut out the noise but her mother and sister didn't stop, didn't even notice. She began muttering "Shut up, shut up, shut up," but just as in her nightmares they didn't hear her. She said it louder. Soon she was shouting, trying to drown out their hateful squabbling. "Shut up! Shut up!" Then, above it all, above the shrill and bitter whine of the Botley family's existence came another shriek, and Liz called, "Bobby!" and ran out of the room.

Mary and Brandy stared at the floor until Liz came back in, carrying her frightened and trembling son. He was clinging to her neck, crying. Liz sat down, patting him. "It's all right, love, it's all right. It's only me and Gran having a row." His crying subsided a little but he wouldn't look around.

Brandy gazed at him with relief—the one spot of purity in the room. "Hey, Bobby," she said, and pushed past Mary to crouch beside him. "It'll be all right, love. There's no need to cry."

Bobby clung tighter to his mother, so Brandy lowered her voice. "Did your mum tell you about the Indians, how they took me off in a canoe?" He reined in his sobs and turned his tearful face to her. "Yeah," Brandy went on, her voice full of mystery. "They came in the night, tied me up in a pillow case, and carried me off!" He smiled, the tears still sliding down his cheeks. "They did, Bobby. It was terrible, I'll tell you. I wasn't half scared! They was going to cook me in a big pot!" Bobby giggled, still half crying. "Don't you believe me?" He shook his head. "It's true, y'know. I would've been somebody's supper by now if your mum hadn't rescued me. Know what she did? She lassoed them all and dumped them into the sea!"

Bobby laughed. "Nah, Mum isn't a cowboy. She's a girl. You've got it wrong."

"I have, have I?"

"Yeah." Bobby was serious now, lecturing her. "Indians don't eat people. Only cadibals do."

Brandy smiled and patted his back. "You are a clever little bugger, aren't you? I didn't know half that much at your age!"

Through all this Mary was staring at Bobby. So this was her grandson, this skinny mite of a thing. She looked at the bony knees sticking out beneath his pajamas, at his stringy arms and pale, pointed face. The boy was certainly no beauty. He had Liz's hair, blond and thick in a nice tousle on his head, but he looked so underfed with that sharp little chin, like a bleached weasel. A child shouldn't look so wise. "Don't you feed him?" she said, speaking her thoughts aloud.

"Course I do!" Liz snapped.

"He looks half-starved, poor thing. I can see his ribs sticking out."

"Leave off, Mum, will you?"

Mary ignored her and lurched forward to poke Bobby in the

back. "See? You can feel them right there, sticking out like twigs. What do you feed him, Liz?"

Bobby wriggled away from Mary's sharp touch. Liz cradled him protectively. "He eats perfectly well, thank you. We don't fatten up our kids like suet puddings anymore, y'know. The doctor says he's very healthy."

"I don't need no doctor to tell me what I can see with me own eyes."

"Will you leave him alone?" Brandy said suddenly. "Jesus fucking Christ, Mum, all you do is pick, pick, pick!"

"All right, all right!" Mary spluttered, reddening again. "You two are like a couple of devils, you are. I've never seen such tempers. You must have got it from your father."

Bobby whimpered again, clinging to his mother. "I don't like it here, Mum," he said. "I don't like her." He pointed at Mary.

"Now see what you've done!" Liz said. "So much for the sweet old Gran I was telling him about."

Mary's eyes watered. "I can just imagine what you've been telling him, you snotty bitch. You with your 'actuallys' and your 'well, Mothers.' You never gave me a chance, Liz, even when you was little. Complain, complain, that's all you ever did. You never understood what I had to put up with. You've got no sympathy in you. A charming mother you must be!" She subsided into her swollen jowls, glaring at her daughters out of small, black eyes.

" 'Mother'! " Liz snorted. "You don't even know the meaning of the word. Come on, Bobby, let's get out of here. I can't stand this old cow one minute longer!" She stood up, heaved Bobby onto her hip with a wince, and stalked into the bedroom, slamming the door behind her.

Brandy watched Liz leave, badly wanting to follow her, to side with her once and for all against their mother, forever. But Liz had her own private world with Bobby and Brandy wasn't sure she'd be welcome, so she slumped back on the sofa and picked at a cigarette burn on it.

Mary sat unmoving for some time, mumbling to herself. "If only someone would listen to me for a change." Not even old George upstairs was interested in her family troubles—all he ever wanted was a back massage and a quick poke. She squinted at Brandy, wondering if she could get some sympathy from her. She just wanted to tell someone that she loved Liz, had always loved her, and that Liz's hate hurt her so much she could hardly breathe. She just wanted to tell someone she was lonely. "What's so terrible about me, Amanda?" she finally said in a small, whining voice.

Brandy looked up from her thoughts. "What?"

"What's Liz hate me so much for, eh? What did I ever do to her?"

"Gawd, Mum, don't you know?"

"Nah, I don't. I don't get it at all, Amanda. Do you know what a lot of mothers would've done in my position? They would've gone out on the streets, they would, or put you two in a home."

"Yeah, well, you did, in case you forgot."

"That was your own fault—you could've stayed here if you'd behaved yourself. But I'm not talking about you. I mean Liz. I looked after her properly, I did. I was a good mother to her. I don't understand her at all."

"You don't understand anything, Mum," Brandy said wearily.

"Well, I can't bear it! You two are breaking my heart, you are, and neither of you gives a damn. What am I supposed to do with you, eh? Are you going to hang about here all your life, poncing off me?"

Brandy blinked. "Oh, so we're picking on me now, are we?"

"Yeah, well, o'course. Liz may be an icy bitch, but at least she's fixed herself up a decent life. But you! You're a bleeding waste, you are."

"You're one to talk, spending your life drinking and cleaning up rubbish all day."

"How dare you talk to me like that!" Mary said, her cheeks flaming. "You can't even keep yourself out of trouble, never mind support a family! I've always worked for you, remember, and for Liz!"

"Like fuck you did! You spent every penny you made on booze, and you know it."

"That's a lie! Where d'you think your food came from, eh? And your clothes?"

Brandy leaned forward, her face tightening. "Liz, that's where! She's the one paid for me things, not you. It was all she could do to keep you on your fucking feet, you were so pissed most of the time!"

"Liar!" Mary struggled to her feet, swaying. All her hurt and anger had a focus now. "I slaved away for years for you two! And look how you've repaid me, eh? You're nothing but a barmy Borstal girl! And ugly to boot! You should be locked up where you can't do any more mischief!"

"You fucking old bag!" Brandy shouted.

Mary raised her arm, the fat on it wobbling. "Get out!"

"I will!" Brandy leapt up. "I can't fucking wait to see the last of you, you bitch!"

"Just get out, you ugly little tart!" Mary's anger was cutting through the drink now, making everything clear and fierce. "No wonder no man wants you—you're just an ugly, stinking criminal! Get out of my home!"

Brandy inhaled, paling. "Don't."

"You are!" Mary shouted, ignoring her. She was dizzy with fury, almost high from it. "You're nothing but a miserable thief! That Jeff probably took one look at you and laughed!"

"You cunt!"

At that Mary lunged forward and slapped Brandy hard on the cheek. Brandy staggered for a moment, dizzy, then leapt at her mother, knocking her over easily with one push. With half her mind blazing and the other half coldly detached, she fell on Mary, grabbed her pudgy neck, and squeezed. "Don't you fucking dare!" she sobbed. "You're a cruel, fucking bitch! I hate you, I hate you . . ." Mary spluttered and gurgled, trying to heave Brandy off, but Brandy didn't budge. Her wiry hands bore down on Mary's throat, deep, determined, and strong.

10

Jeff lay with his nose buried in Nora's breast. She was asleep on her back, breathing noisily, and the bed was still hot and moist from their lovemaking. He liked to nuzzle her while she slept, to feel her flesh as tender as powder beneath him. He rubbed his cheek over her nipple, one eye surveying the room. Everything looked so bright and clear when he was stoned—the shadows crisp, the torn shade over the window solid, the very furniture alive in its depth—as if the room bore a message that only he could understand. He closed his eyes and breathed in, inhaling Nora's smell of booze, sex, and perfume, souring in the night like a rotting rose. This is the life, he thought: a bird in his bed, dope in his drawer, a wad of fivers in his pocket; he had people's respect now. All he needed to do was lie low for a few weeks, keep Nora happy, and they'd be in the clear. Then, who knows—Blackpool, Jersey, Brighton? He'd take her somewhere for the time of her life.

A banging came from the front door and Jeff leapt up

quickly, scrambling for his trousers lying on a chair. Nora moaned and turned over but didn't awake. The banging started again, louder. Jeff lunged across the room in a panic and snatched the hashish out of the dresser drawer, looking frantically for somewhere to hide it, then thought of the fivers in his pocket and grabbed them, too. He went to the window and peered through a tear in the shade. No flashing lights, no police cars. He stood in the dark room, confused.

"Jeff!" he heard. "Jeff!" It was a girl's voice, gruff and hoarse. He relaxed, shoved the money and dope back into his pockets, and, naked except for his tight black jeans, tiptoed down the hall to the front door. Three heads were silhouetted against the glass panel and he stopped, frightened again. "Jeff!" the voice shouted. Recognizing it at last, he walked to the door and opened it.

"Who the hell are you with?" he hissed.

"It's all right, let us in."

"D'you know what fucking time it is?"

"Please, Jeff. You've got to let us in."

"All right, all right. Bloody hell." He opened the door wider and stood back, watching in astonishment as Brandy and a skinny woman carrying a small child traipsed into his secret hideout. He closed the door and turned to them, scratching the hair that was tangled and spiking out of his head like a hedgehog's. "What the fuck is going on?"

"Sorry, Jeff, I couldn't think of where else to come." Brandy put down a load of bags and looked up at him pleadingly. He glanced at the other woman, a bitter-looking bird, and her kid, who was leaning against her shoulder with a drawn, exhausted expression on his face.

"Who's the circus?" he said.

"This is me sister, Liz. Look, can we stay tonight?"

"Why? What happened?"

Brandy grinned in a lopsided, peculiar fashion. "I murdered me mum."

"You wha—?"

"No she didn't," Liz said quickly.

Jeff looked alarmed. "Is the fuzz after you? 'Cause if they are you can't stay here."

"Don't worry. There won't be any coppers," Liz said. "Brandy attacked our mum a bit, that's all. We just had to get out, right, Brandy?"

"You attacked your mum 'a bit'?" Jeff turned to Brandy.

"What did you do, leave her on the kitchen floor with a knife in her chest?"

Brandy grinned again, more ghoulishly than ever. "Not exactly. She was breathing last time we looked."

"Christ, you're a fucking maniac."

"Look, Jeff, we'll be gone in the morning. It's just too late to take a train, that's all. And the kid's exhausted. Can't we stay, just for tonight?"

Jeff glanced at Bobby, who had his eyes closed. "All right, I s'pose, but this isn't a bleeding nursery, y'know. You can stay in the sitting room. There's the sofa and . . ."

"Jeff?" It was Nora. "What's going on out there?"

"Nothing, go back to sleep." He looked uneasily at Brandy. "Come along, then. I'll find you some extra blankets."

He led them down the winding hall to the sitting room and turned on the light. At night the place was even more depressing than before, its pea-green walls murky under the bare light bulb, its sofa and chairs faded and stained. Liz glanced around but didn't let herself react. She was just relieved to have somewhere to rest after what they'd been through: throwing their things into their bags in a panic, hauling Bobby through the streets at all hours of the night until they'd found a taxi. Now her money was gone, Bobby was beside himself with fear and confusion, and on top of everything Mary was wheezing on the floor, half strangled. Liz staggered over to the sofa, her back clenching once more in pain, and laid Bobby down, covering him as best she could with a small, ragged blanket she found on a chair. Bobby whimpered and reached out for her hand, clinging to it with unusual strength, and Liz sat on the floor next to him, resting her head on the sofa. "There, there, love, it's all right now. I'll stay right here." If she could just see him through this, she thought, get them all through it, that'd be enough.

After Jeff handed them some sheets and went back to his room, Brandy made up beds for herself and Liz out of a few cushions on the floor. Her head was still reeling from her fury and the sudden flight and she felt confused, as if she had just walked away from a car crash. Glancing over at Liz, she noticed that her sister looked unusually vulnerable crouched there beside the sofa, her skinny back bent over, her hair a mess, her white hand clutched in Bobby's pink one, and all of a sudden Brandy felt a splash of gratitude towards her. After Liz had yanked her off Mary, shaken and slapped her until she'd calmed down, she hadn't even scolded Brandy. She'd just taken one look at their mother, lying there gasping and red, and said, "We better get you out of here." It was like being rescued, Brandy thought, like that *Bonnie and Clyde* film she'd once watched at the Saturday flick—outlaws on the run. She went over to her sister and touched her. "Thanks, Liz," she whispered. Liz grunted. Her eyes were shut and she looked almost unconscious with fatigue.

Brandy left the room to ask Jeff for more bedding. Through his open door, she saw a dark-headed girl lying naked on his bed, so she looked away. It didn't even make her angry anymore, Jeff and his woman, it just added to the hurt that was already scraping inside her chest like a rough stone. "Jeff?" she said, keeping her eyes on the floor.

"Yeah?" He looked up. He was sitting on the bed trying to explain things to Nora.

"You got a pillow and a blanket to spare?"

"Yeah, hold on a sec." Jeff pulled a pillow out from under Nora's head. She objected but he ignored her. He took a spare blanket off a chair and handed the bedding to Brandy, who remained outside the door, looking at the ground. "You all right?" he said softly. She seemed so small all of a sudden, lost in the blackness of the hallway. Brandy shrugged and held the pillow in her arms, hugging it to her and still not looking up. Jeff pulled the bedroom door shut, blocking Nora's view. "D'you want to talk?" he whispered. His voice was so kind that it hurt Brandy even more. No one but Jeff had ever used that voice with her, but what was the use with that girl lying there reminding him of what a real woman was? "Do you?" he asked again.

Without warning, Brandy felt the tears coming. They came silently, flowing down her cheeks and dropping to the pillow. She felt a wound open inside her, cracking along that old crack that always threatened to give, but instead of shouting or hitting or screaming as she usually did when it opened she only felt her hopes crumble into it. She'd screwed up for good now, and she knew it. Jeff put his arms around her, the pillow sandwiched between them, and held her tight, rocking her as if she were a child. She kept her head bowed, ashamed yet unable to resist his sympathy. She cried until her whole body shook, until her mind seemed to be leaking out with her tears. Jeff led her to the stairs, lowered her down, and sat beside her, holding her against his shoulder.

"All right, all right, love. Just cry, it'll do you good," he crooned, squeezing her gently. "Poor kid, what a lot you've been through, eh?" Brandy nodded, awash in tears, feeling as if her insides were smeared out for all to see. She knew Jeff probably thought she was crying about her mother, maybe the Borstal, the beating she'd got, but that wasn't all of it. She was crying about that crack in her that never mended. She was crying about the way she always, always fucked up. She was crying about him.

At last Brandy's sobs subsided. First she became aware of her crying, then of herself listening to her crying, then of Jeff's wiry arm around her and the sour smell of his armpit. She put her hand on his lean bare stomach. It was so hard compared to a girl's and covered with soft, fuzzy hair. She stroked it, feeling soothed by the hair tickling her palm. A girl always had some pudge on her stomach, something to sink your hand into, but Jeff had nothing but the slightest fold of skin. She could feel his ribs hard and sharp, the stomach muscles taut. His bony shoulder stuck into her cheek.

"Oy, what're you doing?" he said, a chuckle in his voice. "That tickles."

Brandy snuggled closer, dropping the tear-soaked pillow from her lap, and went on stroking his belly. "You feel nice," she whispered, her voice still shaking from the tears.

Jeff lifted her chin with his hand. "You're a funny bird," he said, and kissed her. It was a nice kiss, long and soft, and Brandy felt herself dropping back under him, swooning a little as he lowered her towards the stairs. She slipped her hands around his hips and turned him over on top of her—his hips were as slight as a greyhound's. She wanted to pull him into her, to feel his strength and assurance all the way inside, as if he could fill in her wounds. He eased her thighs apart with his, pressing against her, fitting right in.

"What the fuck is going on?" It was Nora, standing in the bedroom doorway with a sheet around her. Jeff jumped to his feet, leaving Brandy to struggle up on her own.

"It's all right," he said. "I was just helping . . . I mean, y'know."

Nora squinted through the darkness. "So I see. You better come back in here right fucking now!"

"Yeah, okay," Jeff said, and shuffled after her without looking back at Brandy once.

*   *   *

Early the next morning Liz shook Brandy awake in the sitting room. "Get up," she whispered. "We've got a train to catch."

Brandy opened her eyes and stared at her sister for a moment before she remembered all that had happened. "Oh, Jesus," she said.

"I know. A bloody mess, innit?"

Brandy sat up, wincing, and put her head in her hands. For a moment she stayed like that, afraid to look up. "Is Bobby awake yet?" she mumbled.

"No, poor love. I'm letting him sleep a bit longer. He pissed all over the sofa, though. Think what's-his-name will mind?"

"Who, Larry?"

"Larry?"

"Yeah, this is his flat." Brandy paused. "Oh, you mean Jeff. Nah. Who cares if he minds, anyroad?"

"Well, we've got to get some money off him, Brandy, remember? I spent it all on the taxi last night. There isn't enough for your ticket back."

"Back where?" Brandy raised her head.

"To Brighton, of course." Liz sat down on the floor, hugging her knees to her chest.

"Brighton? You mean you're taking me home, Liz?"

"Yeah, course I am, love. I can't leave you here, can I? If Mum finds you gawd knows what you'll do to each other next. I'll have a coupla corpses on me hands!" Liz grinned.

"Liz!" Brandy wrapped her arms around her sister. "You're an angel, you really are! I swear I'll never leave Bobby like that again, I swear to God I won't." She hugged Liz, hard, and let go. "But Liz, what're you going to do about Ron?"

Liz shrugged, frowning. "I dunno. We'll just have to take that as it comes. He knows I came up here to find you—it'll work out." She didn't look as sure as she sounded but Brandy was satisfied.

"All right. I'll ask Jeff to lend us a few quid, then. When d'you want to get back?"

"I told Ron tomorrow, but we better go today. I mean, we can't stay here." Liz looked around. The sun was gleaming through the windows, casting pale squares of light on the floor, and thick dust swirled in the sunbeams. "This place is a tip."

"Yeah, you're right. I'll go put on some tea." Brandy stood up and straightened the denim skirt and white blouse she'd slept in. She looked at Liz again. "D'you think she'll be all right?"

"Who, Mum?"

"Yeah."

Liz shrugged. "I think so. The old bag was so pickled she probably didn't even feel it." She paused, searching for a way of reprimanding Brandy that wouldn't start a fight. "Still, you better keep away from her from now on, know what I mean?"

Brandy nodded.

In the kitchen Brandy found Larry sitting at the table spooning egg and toast into his mouth and reading *News of the World*. He looked up when she came in and gaped. "Fucking hell, it's the bleeding maniac. What're you doing here?"

"You mean you slept through all that?" Brandy put on the kettle. "Close your gob. Your toast's falling out."

"I didn't expect to see you again in a hurry. Nora know you're here?"

"Nora who."

"What about Jeff?"

"Course Jeff knows we're here. He let us in."

"Who's us?"

"Me sister and her kid. Got any more mugs?"

"Top right-hand cupboard. Kid?"

" 'Morning!" Liz came in looking fresh and combed and nodded at Larry. He stared again. "Are you Larry?" she said in her most cheerful tone.

"Uh, yeah. 'Morning." He watched while Liz prepared more eggs and toast. When she bent over to take out a frying pan from under the stove, he eyed her bum appreciatively. "Who would have thought nutter Brandy had a gorgeous sister like you?" he said. Liz stood up blushing.

After breakfast Brandy washed the dishes while Liz went in to wake Bobby. He was groggy and ill-tempered so she had to move slowly, allowing him time to get used to the unfamiliar surroundings. She peeled off his wet clothes, led him to the bathroom, which looked even dirtier than her mother's, and washed him down with warm water. He whimpered, still sleepy, and leaned against her. "I wanna go home," he said while she rubbed his little pink bottom dry.

"I know, love. We're going home today, don't worry."

"Are we going on the train again?"

"Yeah, back to see your dad." She shivered and pushed Bobby's limbs into clean clothes.

"I miss Dad."

"I know, sweetie. Come on, let's get you some food."

The kitchen was now crowded with people. Jeff was on a chair with Nora in his lap, still in her dressing gown and looking sleepy and cross, and Larry and Brandy were leaning against the sink with cups of tea in their hands. At the sight of these rumpled grown-ups Bobby whimpered again and hid behind his mother. Liz led him to the table, pulled him onto her lap, and gave him a glass of milk and a plate of toast and egg. He ignored the egg but ate the toast. Liz noticed that Brandy was keeping her eyes on the floor.

"Quite a little party we've got here," Larry said cheerily. He seemed in a bright mood and Liz found herself liking him. She smiled, noticing the suntanned biceps bulging out of his T-shirt. "Why the sudden visit, eh?" he added.

Liz looked to Brandy to answer but her sister's eyes remained fixed to the ground. She seemed withdrawn and sullen and Liz wondered if she was thinking about their mother again.

"They had a bit of trouble with their mum," Jeff said, "didn't you, girls?" Liz didn't like the condescension in his voice. "They're on their way home this morning though, right?"

"Well, I don't see why they have to be in such a hurry." Larry turned to Liz. "Why not stay a bit?"

She smiled again. "Thanks, but we really do have to go, don't we, Brandy?"

Brandy shrugged, still refusing to look up. Liz turned and glared at Jeff—how could he be so insensitive? At least he could have the consideration to keep that tart off his lap, she thought. Nora was a voluptuous girl with big thighs and was such a bulk sitting on Jeff that she made him look like a broomstick. She yawned and stretched, squirming around in his lap. "I hope they don't stay long," she said. "There isn't room for all of them here."

"Course there is," Larry said, winking at Liz. "We could get a little booze at the pub and have a party, eh?"

Liz found herself blushing again. No one had flirted with her like this for years. She patted her hair self-consciously and shifted Bobby on her knees. Maybe they could stay a bit longer, she thought. She wasn't looking forward to confronting Ron with Brandy again, and he wasn't expecting her back yet anyway . . . She leaned down to Bobby, who was concentrating on biting his toast into a perfect circle. "What d'you think, love? Want to stay for a bit and have some more adventures? We could still catch the afternoon train home."

Bobby shook his head. "I wanna go now."

"There's a playground over the way, y'know," Larry said, leaning towards him. "Got a smashing set of swings. I'll take you there if you want."

"Not if Mum don't come."

"Course I'll come. You want to go? It'll be nice for you to get some exercise before we get on the train again."

"All right." Bobby tried to jump up but Liz caught him. Larry laughed.

"Not yet, lovey. Finish your breakfast first." Liz glanced over at Brandy, expecting her to smile at Bobby, too, but Brandy was frowning and tearing at her fingers. Liz felt guilty for a moment but then shrugged it off. After all she was doing for the girl, at least Brandy couldn't object to her having a bit of fun.

Yawning noisily, Nora put down her empty teacup and slid off Jeff's lap. "I'm going to read the papers," she announced to no one in particular. "Who's got *News of the Screws?*"

"Here." Larry handed her his newspaper and everyone watched her slink out of the room. The girl exuded sex, Liz thought. Poor Brandy. Once Nora was gone, though, Brandy at last lifted her head. Her face was drawn and serious.

"Is it all right, Jeff?" she said. "D'you mind if we stay?"

Jeff looked confused. "I dunno. I s'pose, if you want." He glanced out of the kitchen after Nora. "Just for a bit, though. Sorry but . . . you know."

"Yeah." Brandy looked down again. Liz decided that she was in the way so she lifted Bobby off her lap and ushered him out. Larry followed her.

Brandy and Jeff stared down at the grimy kitchen floor in silence. It was covered with blue linoleum that hadn't been washed in so long it looked gray, with torn patches scattered over it like spills. "Sorry to ask, Jeff," Brandy said at last, "but d'you think you could lend us a few quid for the ticket home?"

Jeff looked up at her from his chair. He was dressed as he'd been the night before, bare-chested but in tight jeans. "Are you skint, then?"

"Yeah. We need about ten quid. I'll send it back to you when I can, honest."

"All right, love." He reached into his pocket and pulled out the most enormous wad of fivers Brandy had ever seen. Her eyes widened. He counted out three and put the rest back. "Fifteen do you?"

"Yeah, thanks." Brandy took the money. "D'you want us to leave now, Jeff? We will if you want."

"Oh, Jesus, I dunno. That was a near thing last night . . ." He glanced at Brandy, whose mouth was tightening. "Look, love, I'm sorry about that. It's just that Nora and me, well . . ."

"What's she got on you?" Brandy pinned her gaze on him. She was genuinely curious.

"Nothing! Well . . ."

"Well what?"

Jeff glanced out the kitchen door. "She's got connections, Brandy. The kind that's good if you're on the right side, but if you're not . . . know what I mean?"

"You scared of her, then?"

He dropped back in his chair. "Jesus, you do ask the questions."

Brandy looked at him, hard. "You do still like me, don't you, Jeff?" Her voice trembled and her mouth grew even tighter. The stone revolved again in her chest.

"Course I do, love. Can't you tell? But it's no go. Just can't do it, babe."

Brandy nodded, turned to the sink, and began washing up frantically. Jeff watched her back, square and stolid yet as wounded as a child's. "You can stay for a bit if you want," he said gently. "Your sister's a nice bird and the kid's all right. I don't mind."

"What about Nora?"

He sighed. "I'll explain."

Liz and Larry walked down the street to the playground, chatting about their wild pasts while Bobby skipped alongside them, excited now and enjoying the warmth in the air. It was a gray day but bright and hot, making them all squint a little, and Liz was grateful for the change of clothes she'd brought: the sleeveless blouse and new tight jeans that showed off her slim hips. She saw Larry looking her over and it made her feel gorgeous.

The playground was in surprisingly good shape and empty but for three other children and their mothers. Bobby squealed when he saw the slide and raced over to it, while Liz and Larry sat on the roundabout, chatting. Everything Larry said seemed to make her laugh. She looked at Bobby's yellow head sailing down the slide, at his cheeks bunched in delight, at Larry performing for her, and decided that this, at last, was pleasure.

143

"Are you married, then?" Larry asked later, while he was pushing Bobby on the swings.

"Yeah." Liz sat on a swing next to them.

"D'you work?"

"Oh, yes. I'm a hairstylist." She always used that phrase when she wanted to sound sophisticated. "I work in a salon called Hairline. It's quite fancy."

"You must be good then. What d'you think of my hair?" Larry said this teasingly.

Liz studied him. "Nice. It makes you look like Rod Stewart."

"Thanks. It cost a bleeding fortune."

"It is a bit long in the back, though. I'd get it trimmed if I were you."

Larry shrugged and went back to watching Bobby. There was a moment's awkwardness and Liz longed suddenly for a drink. She looked at her watch. "Are there any pubs 'round here? I'm getting thirsty." Larry frowned. Jeff had warned him not to show his face around yet because the police were still looking for them after they'd robbed that off-license the week before. "It'd have to be one with a garden 'cause of Bobby," Liz continued. "I'd love a shandy. It's hot out here."

"Yeah, good idea," Larry said, remembering a family pub a few streets away. The fuzz wouldn't look for him there—it was full of shopkeepers and their wives. "It's a bit of a walk but I'll carry the kid if you want."

"That's all right," Liz said, hopping off the swing. "Bobby, fancy some Coke and crisps?"

The pub was crowded, it being Sunday lunchtime, but they found seats out in the garden on wobbly metal chairs, and Bobby was soon playing with a group of older boys. While Larry went in to buy the drinks, Liz freshened her lipstick in her pocket mirror and watched her son happily. She was proud of him, his tough little face, his fearlessness, the way he could leap right into play with perfect strangers. She smiled. After yesterday's dramas, whoever would have thought this would turn into such a nice holiday?

Larry came back with a pint of bitter, Liz's shandy, and Bobby's Coke balanced in his hands, and three packets of crisps in his teeth. Liz reached up to take them from his mouth, blushing at the intimacy of the gesture. "Ta," she said, and helped him put down the drinks. She was about to call Bobby over but decided against it. "If a child's happy, leave him alone," a friend had once said, and a better piece of advice she had never heard.

Larry raised his glass. "Cheers." They both drank deeply, thirsty from the hot, still day.

"It's nice here," Liz said, looking around. The pub was a modern blob of a building in dull brown brick, but the large garden was done up prettily, with umbrellas over the round, white tables and the grass thick and green. "I've never seen anything this nice in Birmingham before."

"Yeah, well, Brum isn't all concrete and bulldozers, y'know." Larry smacked his lips over his beer. "What's Brighton like, then? I've never been there."

"Haven't you? Ooh, it's lovely. I like it best in the off-season when the tourists aren't there. The sea gets all choppy and gray, and when the fair things close down it seems sort of haunted. I love it then."

Larry was leaning towards her, the tip of his knee touching hers under the table, and Liz talked on excitedly. The image of her mother gasping under Brandy's hands, which had been searing her mind all morning, began at last to fade. She drained her drink quickly.

"Want another?" Larry nodded at her empty glass.

"It's my round." Liz felt for her bag then suddenly remembered that she didn't have a penny left. "Oh," she said, embarrassed, "I just thought . . . I left me cash at the house. Sorry."

"That's all right, I got plenty." Larry reached into his pocket and drew out a thick pad of notes. Liz gazed in astonishment as he ostentatiously extracted a tenner out of at least a hundred others. She'd never seen so much money outside of a bank, not even in Jenny's till. "Half a shandy, right?" he said, standing up. She nodded.

By the time Liz and Larry had got through several rounds, Bobby was tired. One of the bigger boys had hit him, then he fell and scraped his knee—the hiatus of Sunday lunch was coming to an end. Eventually, to stave off a full-scale tantrum, Liz suggested they leave. "I'll just take Bobby to the loo first," she said, and left Larry waiting.

In the toilet, a small cubicle of white tile and septic smells, she and Bobby peed and cleaned up. She washed his hands as best she could and sponged her own face, which was sweating from the sun and beer, her body tense with excitement. "Liz me girl, calm down," she told herself. "A little flirt's all right, but for Christ's sake leave it at that." If Ron ever found out she'd been with another man, Liz knew, it would be the end of everything. She looked down at Bobby, who was ineffectually trying to dry his hands on a paper towel, and stroked his hair. He needed her and Ron the way he needed air. She couldn't risk it.

Back at the house, Liz found everything much the same. Jeff and Nora were still in bed with the papers and cups of tea—Liz had never seen people so lazy—and Brandy was alone in the sitting room watching television. Liz sat down beside her and pulled Bobby onto her lap. Larry went into the kitchen.

"Everything all right?" Liz said. Brandy was watching a football game but her mind didn't seem to be on it. She didn't reply. "It's a nice day, y'know," Liz added. "You should go out."

"You been to the pub?" Brandy could smell the beer on Liz's breath.

"Yeah. And the playground. Bobby had a good time, didn't you, love?"

"D'you know what fucking time it is?"

Liz glanced at her watch. "Shit! I forgot!"

"I bet you did. What're we going to do now, eh?"

"I'm sorry, all right?" Liz looked down at Bobby, who was sucking his thumb, his interrupted night catching up with him. "There's only the late trains now, I suppose."

"Right."

"I don't really want to take him back that late, Brandy, he's too knackered. Will they mind if we stay another night?"

"I know one person who won't."

Liz blushed. "D'you think I could have a bath?" she asked to change the subject.

"I'm not going to stop you. I'll watch Bobby if you like."

"No, it's all right, he needs one too." Liz pushed him off her lap and stood up. Brandy was still scowling. "I didn't do it on purpose, Brandy. I know you're dying to get out of here."

"Fucking right I am."

"Would you mind asking Jeff if we can stay, then?"

Brandy shook her head. "You ask. I've had enough of them lot."

Liz loved having baths with Bobby. She loved the way his body grew pink from the heat and his belly stuck out, as smooth and tight as a balloon, and the way his limbs felt underwater when

146

he rubbed against her, all soft and firm. She looked at his wet hair, curling up in ringlets, and at his normally pale face turned rosy, and marveled at his beauty. "You're a darling little thing, you are," she said while she soaped him up, then leaned back to let him play. As he torpedoed her toes with the soap she watched his little penis, thin and pointed, floating about in the water as innocently as a bit of string, and thought about what he'd be like when he grew up, how he'd become hairy and rough and private. It made her sad to know that she wouldn't see his body anymore then, that the smoothness and pinkness would be gone forever. Ron was right really, they should have another baby. She looked down at her own body, whiter than ever under the water, and examined the wrinkles on her thin stomach that had come with pregnancy. Her breasts looked flat and tiny when she lay down like that, her stomach old, and her pubic hair wiry and coarse. She always felt grotesque when she was naked with Bobby.

At suppertime that night Larry and Jeff cooked up a huge pot of spaghetti and tinned meat sauce. The kitchen was full of activity: Liz and Brandy setting the table, Bobby waving a raw piece of spaghetti in the air as if it were a sword, Jeff and Larry clowning over the cooking, and Nora slicing up bread and garlic. They broke into the wine early and all but Liz smoked joints, so soon everyone was high; even sullen Nora was laughing and cracking the odd coarse joke. Brandy was the only one who was quiet, setting the knives and forks down carefully but keeping her head lowered and her mouth shut. Liz looked over at her once in a while, when she remembered to, and saw that Brandy was trying to join in, but it was clearly an effort. With a pang Liz thought again of how Brandy must be feeling after the previous night, but then Bobby poked her with the spaghetti and she forgot her sister again. She hadn't had this much fun since she was . . . well, perhaps ever.

When the meal was ready Larry brought out a candle in an old wine bottle, lit it, and turned out the lights. They all pulled up their chairs and dug in, knocking back the strong red wine eagerly. Liz felt her head getting light and giddy and her excitement seemed to splash the room. She even let Bobby have a few swallows.

Jeff and Larry soon turned the conversation to tales of their squat days. This brightened up Brandy a little, and she began to reminisce about the time the place caught fire and all the ingenious ways they'd avoided the police. Liz knew nothing about this time in Brandy's past and was fascinated. She had never realized how much a part of Brandy's life Jeff had once been.

"Remember that time the building inspector came 'round, Jeff?" Brandy was saying. "She was a stiff old bird all dressed up in black like a fucking crow, remember?" Brandy turned to the table at large. "She came to look over the place and we all hid, watching her through a crack in the wall while she jotted down all sortsa stuff in this notebook of hers. And then, when she came 'round the side, Jeff dumped a pail of water all over her!" Brandy and Jeff laughed.

"Yeah," Jeff said, "then the fuzz came 'round, but they couldn't do nothing to us 'cause we had the door padlocked and we hid inside like a bunch of mice, all silent—they couldn't even tell we was there! And after they left, we all went 'round squeaking." He turned to Brandy. "You was the best squeaker of the lot. Can you still do it?"

She shook her head. "Nah, I ruined me voice in Borstal." She stopped, aware that her mention of the place had cast a gloom over the table. "Well"—she shrugged—"we had good times in that squat while it lasted. At least till you got nicked, Jeff." She looked over at Larry, shooting him a contemptuous glance. Liz followed her look, puzzled.

Larry cleared his throat and got up from the table. "Well, them days are over," he said abruptly. "They knocked the bloody building down and good riddance, that's what I say. Living like that's okay for kids, but . . ." He shrugged and began stacking the dishes. "Let's get this muck out of the way and move up to my room. I got a gramophone up there. We could put on some music."

Larry lived in the attic, and his ceiling sloped down on one side of the room to only three feet above the floor. A double mattress lay in the corner, covered in a faded purple Indian bedspread, more of the same cloth was tacked over the window, and a dusty red rug lay rumpled on the floor. Along the sides of the room were fat, foam-filled cushions on which Liz, Brandy, and Bobby settled themselves. Nora and Jeff took the bed.

"What d'you want to hear?" Larry asked Liz, handing her a bottle of wine.

She took a swig and passed it to Brandy. "What've you got? I don't care, you choose."

Bobby pulled at her sleeve. "I want the Bay City Rollers," he said shyly.

Larry laughed and chucked him under the chin. "You're right up to date, aren't you? Like a tiny teenager." He crouched by the gramophone, an old blue box standing on an orange crate in the corner, and put on the record, afterwards sitting next to Liz and rolling another joint. This time she took a toke, noticing him watching her with approval. Bobby got up to dance.

For a while everyone sat and watched Bobby. They passed the wine around, finished it and opened another bottle, the joint following closely, while Liz leaned back against the wall and indulged in sentimental pride of her son. She hadn't smoked hashish since her days on the estate because Ron disapproved and she'd never liked it that much anyway, but tonight it just seemed to blend in pleasantly with the general sense of warmth and dizziness that was slowly pressing her to the ground. She wondered briefly what Val would think of her, and smiled.

Bobby jumped about the room jerking his little limbs in approximate time to the music. He was relaxed with all these people now and enjoying center stage, his face flushed and grinning, his hair curling with sweat. He kept throwing himself in the air and landing with a thump on his knees or stomach, making the needle skip, but everyone merely laughed. Liz watched him, worried that he would hurt himself, but unable to keep the grin off her face. The child could really keep a rhythm, she thought—he had a natural grace, just like hers. Suddenly Nora spoke up. "Can't you stop him? He's fucking up the record."

Liz frowned, but told Bobby to stop jumping. He wiggled about a bit longer, looking crestfallen, then ran to her lap and burst into tears. He hated being reprimanded by strangers. Liz comforted him, more annoyed at Nora than ever.

"That wasn't very nice," Brandy said, looking directly at Nora for the first time.

"Fuck you," Nora replied. "I never asked for any brat to be in this house. Larry, why don't you change the music? This stinks."

"Cool down, Nor," Larry said, but he changed the record. Brandy scowled—the bloody bitch seemed to have the whole household under her thumb.

Liz's favorite song from the disco came on, "Rock You Baby," and she immediately sank into that slightly aching, nostalgic feeling that slow dance music always gave her. She stroked Bobby's head—by now he was sucking his thumb and resting against her chest—and watched the lamplight blur as her eyes slipped out of focus. Larry came to sit down next to her again but Liz didn't

149

look up, too absorbed in letting the music wash over her. In a minute, she decided, she'd have to take Bobby down to bed. Nora was making things unpleasant.

Brandy, meanwhile, was staring at the floor, furious. If this had been Bullwood Hall, she thought, she'd be tearing that Nora's hair out by now. No girl got away with speaking to her like that—she knew how to teach that type a lesson right off! She just didn't dare do it here, not with Larry and Jeff glaring at her. She glanced up at Jeff and caught him watching her again, a worried expression on his face. Nora was draped over him like a blanket, showing off her possession. He hadn't even stood up for Brandy just now—he'd probably let Nora walk all over her. Brandy looked at Larry, sitting with his leg against Liz's. Christ, she thought, that's all she needed—that wanker getting it on with her sister! God, the world was a load of crap.

The record came to an end but no one moved. Larry had snuggled even closer to Liz, Bobby was falling asleep in her arms, and Liz was staring at the ceiling, a half smile on her lips as if she were hypnotized. Suddenly Brandy couldn't stand them anymore, any of them, all smug and sensual with their booze-sodden minds. Larry clearly couldn't wait to get his paws on Liz, Nora the same with Jeff—Brandy was nothing but a spare prick at a wedding. She got up, turned the record over, and went to get Bobby. "I'll take him to bed if you want," she said sullenly.

Liz blinked and looked up at her. "Oh, would you, love? That'd be lovely. Go on, Bobby, Aunty's going to take you to bed."

Bobby whimpered but was too tired to object. Brandy lifted him, staggering under his weight, and carried him out the door and down the stairs. In the sitting room, which seemed cold and dark after Larry's cozy room, she laid him on the sofa without turning on the lights, took off his shoes, and covered him with a blanket. "I want me mum," he whined.

"Shh, it's all right lovey, I'll stay with you." Brandy squeezed onto the sofa beside him, put one arm around his warm belly, and tried to settle down. The room was murky with shadows, lit only by the occasional sweep of headlights as a car drove past on the road, and she could hear Larry's music upstairs and the drone of voices as they partied without her. "Would you like me to tell you a cowboy and Indian story?" she said.

"No. Doctor Who."

"All right. This one's about Doctor Who and the Daleks."

And as Brandy related a story she remembered from a televison episode she'd once watched in Borstal, Bobby drifted into sleep.

Upstairs, Liz was fighting a losing battle. At first they all talked some more, lazily telling jokes or commenting on the latest football results, but gradually the dope and wine got the better of them and they were content to retreat into their private worlds of intoxication. Nora and Jeff soon began kissing—long wet kisses that seemed to suck the breath out of them—and Liz watched absently, remembering the snogging parties she used to go to as a teenager and telling herself to get out of there and go down to Bobby before it was too late. Larry put his arm around her and moved closer, but she couldn't quite make herself push him away. He pointed at the bottle. "Want another swig?" he whispered.

She shook her head and the room spun. Slowly he bent down to her ear and caressed it, first with his lips, then his tongue. She shut her eyes, her resistance instantly fleeing. Her head felt heavy, as if the wine had filled and weighed it down, and she let it drop back against the wall, exposing her neck. Larry ran his tongue down to her collar bone and kissed her, moving around her as he worked his way slowly up to her lips. She liked that, the way he took his time. His soft mouth brushed hers, then moved away again. "Is this all right?" he whispered, and she nodded, turning to him eagerly. Again he nibbled her lips and moved away, playing with her. She grabbed him, feeling his back lean and solid under her hands, and strained towards him, hungry now and wanting everything he could do to her.

The music stopped and the needle began to scratch back and forth. Bothered by the noise, Jeff pushed Nora off him and got up to change the record. He saw Larry lying on top of Liz on the floor, his hand under her blouse and, grimacing, turned off the music and pulled Nora out of the room. He didn't like watching other people screw—he'd had enough of that inside.

When the door shut behind them, Larry lifted his head to look down at Liz. Her face seemed blurred, her lips swollen and eyelids heavy. She gazed back at him and moaned, sending a thrill through him. He unbuttoned her blouse, opening it slowly to reveal her breasts arching up to him. Phrases about wanting her and fucking her and how gorgeous she was kept running through his head but he didn't say any of them, afraid to break the spell. He sat up, pulled off his T-shirt, and laid his bare chest on hers, kissing her again. She writhed and strained under him, panting.

She was a ball of fire, this one. He hadn't had anyone this hot for months. He slipped his hands down to her jeans, unzipped them, and pushed them off.

Brandy lay below them, listening, her eyes wide open, as if held by pins. She heard Jeff and Nora come down the stairs, giggling, and go into their room, then she heard a thud upstairs and the beginning of rhythmic creaking. She couldn't believe it, that Liz would go for an ugly brute like Larry. How could Liz let her down like this? She wasn't behaving like a real sister anymore, not even like a mature woman. She was behaving like all the other girls Brandy knew—like Brandy would have herself! She heard a moan from Nora down the hall, and let go of Bobby to put her hands over her ears, squeezing her eyes tight as if they, too, could shut out the sounds. At least in Borstal she hadn't been left out like this. Why, Reardon had wanted her so much she'd practically made herself into a slave for Brandy. I could have done anything with that woman she was so besotted, Brandy thought, she even risked her job for me! Brandy remembered the yearning looks Reardon used to send her across the room, and the woman's big, soft hands, caressing her reverently. At least Reardon and the other girls had believed Brandy was worth something. She closed her eyes, images of Reardon and Jeff, of Ron's fists pounding into her and her hands on her mother's throat whirling around in her head like a storm. She heard a sob break out in the room and, hardly knowing it was hers, buried her face in Bobby's back.

Above her, Larry was crouched over Liz with her legs on his shoulders, taking his time. He wanted to be an expert, to make this glamorous, married bird remember him for the rest of her life. She was the first normal woman he'd ever had, the first one who wasn't a crook or a Borstal girl or some whore going with him on the side. She was a real woman, older than him, experienced, and sexy as hell. He was making her swoon with desire and he loved it, watching her moan and toss her head as he pulled in and out, hard and slow. He ran his hands over her body, her slim stomach, tight breasts, her exposed throat, and pushed her legs wider. He pulled out, on the verge of coming, and turned her over, lifting her behind up to him and spreading her legs again. She moaned louder, her face against the floor, her head swimming around in a whirl of lust and wine, and let him move her about like a doll. He put his hands on her buttocks, as round and tight as melons, and entered her again.

*   *   *

152

The only person in the house who didn't feel awful the next morning was Bobby. He woke up in a chirpy, energetic mood and was soon racing about the sitting room urging Brandy to play Daleks with him. She groaned, sat up, and clutched her head, which was pounding from the wine and lack of sleep, and glanced at the clock in the corner. It was seven-thirty in the morning—she'd been asleep for only three hours. "Pipe down, Bobby, you're giving me a headache."

"Where's Mum?" he said suddenly, looking around the room.

"She's upstairs. I'll get her. You wait here." Brandy stood, giddy for a moment, and tried to smooth down her rumpled clothes. She longed to get out of there and onto the train, to get away from Birmingham and all it stood for. She walked past Jeff's room but looked the other way, not wanting to be reminded of all the moaning and thudding she'd had to listen to until four in the morning. His door was slightly ajar and she could hear him and Nora breathing steadily with sleep. Brandy was just about to go upstairs when she changed her mind, turned around, and tiptoed into his room—neither he nor Nora moved. She picked up Jeff's trousers from the floor and felt in his pocket. Yes, there it was. She pulled it out and looked, impressed—at least two hundred quid in fivers. He and Larry must be onto something big, she thought, dealing perhaps. Spreading evil, as Reardon used to say about dope pushers. She counted out a hundred, stuck it in her skirt pocket, and put the rest back, slowly replacing the trousers on the floor. Even Reardon would agree Jeff deserved that. She left the room and walked softly up the stairs.

At Larry's door she knocked and waited. There was no answer. She knocked again, calling "Liz? You awake?" All was silent so she opened the door and walked in. Liz and Larry were asleep naked on the bed, the bedspread barely covering them. Larry's penis lay pink and swollen over his thigh. It seemed to glow in the dark.

"Liz!" Brandy hissed. She didn't give a damn if they were embarrassed. Her sister was sprawled across Larry's chest with her bottom in the air. She had a nice bottom, Brandy mused, and nudged it gently with one foot. Liz opened her eyes and blinked. "Wake up, will you," Brandy said, "we've got a train to catch." Liz rolled over and looked around her, shocked. When she saw Brandy she yanked at the bedspread, trying to cover herself. "Come on," Brandy said again, "Bobby's going to be up here looking for you in a minute."

That got Liz moving. "Sod it," she muttered, and tried to get out of bed. "Uh." She clutched her temples. "My God, me head. Where are me clothes?" She seemed utterly disoriented so Brandy collected them off the floor and gave them to her. Liz dressed slowly, moving as if in pain.

"Mum! Mum!" Bobby's voice floated up, sounding frightened. They heard him begin to climb the stairs.

"Shit, keep him out of here!" Liz pushed herself to her feet. Snickering, Brandy walked out the door.

"She's coming, Bobby, don't worry." Brandy went down the stairs and caught him by the hand, trying to turn him around towards the kitchen. "Let's go get you some grub."

"I want me mum!"

"Shh, you'll wake everyone up. Come on, I'll be a Dalek. Beep, beep!"

"Nah!" Bobby tried to twist out of Brandy's hand and go on up the stairs.

"Here I am, sweets, it's all right." Liz came to the landing, looking pale and disheveled, her mascara smudged over her face. She staggered down, gripping the banisters to steady herself, and Bobby grabbed her legs, almost toppling them both. "Watch it!" Liz cried, clutching him.

"What happened to your eyes, Mum?"

Liz raised a hand to her face. "Oh, it's just makeup. You go into the kitchen with Aunty and I'll wash up." She winced as she spoke, every word knocking against her head like a fist. She made her way slowly down the rest of the stairs, stumbled into the bathroom, holding on to the walls as she went, and took four aspirin out of a bottle in the medicine cabinet. She swallowed them with water from the tap and washed her face, unsure whether she'd even be able to hold the aspirin down, she felt so sick. She laid her forehead against the mirror and closed her eyes.

In the kitchen Brandy had the kettle on and some toast made. She was moving quickly and efficiently, getting everything done as fast as possible: the tea brewed, the milk poured, the toast buttered. "What're you in such a sodding hurry for?" Liz said when she came in. Brandy just looked at her until Liz blushed. Imagine letting Brandy find me like that, sprawled starkers across a strange man, Liz scolded herself. What kind of example was that to set her wayward sister?

"I want to get out of here before they wake up," Brandy said. "And the train leaves at nine, remember."

"Why before they wake up?"

Brandy scowled. In her pocket she had her pathetic revenge. "I don't like good-byes."

"Are we packed then?"

"Yeah. I did it last night while you were making all that racket up there."

Liz glanced at Bobby, who was unconsciously tucking into his toast and jam, and shook her head at her sister, frowning.

Before they'd finished drinking their tea, however, Larry staggered in. He'd pulled on his trousers but his brown chest was still bare, and Liz admired the muscle and patch of black hairs all over again. He rubbed his hand over his head and looked at her sleepily. "What's going on?" he said, his voice thick. "Fucking hell, I feel like a dead rat."

"We're leaving," Brandy said crisply. She wiped Bobby's face.

"Oh yeah?" Larry turned to Liz. "Already?"

She nodded. "We have to catch the nine o'clock train." She couldn't look at Larry this morning; she felt shy and exposed.

"Any of that for me?" he asked, pointing to the tea.

"In the pot," said Brandy.

Larry poured himself a cup and leaned against the sink. "Weren't you even going to say good-bye?"

Brandy heaved a sigh and stood up. "Here we go again. Come on, Bobby, let's get your shoes on." She hauled him out of the room, muttering.

Liz watched them go. All of a sudden this was too much for her, the freedom and the sex and the emotions. She wanted to get back to normal.

"Well?" Larry pressed.

"Well what?" she said irritably.

He ignored this and pulled up a chair next to her. "Can I have a kiss from the sexiest bird this side of London?" He put his arm around her shoulders. Liz gave him a peck on the mouth but she wasn't in the mood now that she was sober. "Am I going to see you again, then?" he persisted. "Maybe in Brighton some time?"

Liz darted a look at him. "I dunno," she said. "I am married, remember."

"Yeah, course I remember, but wouldn't you like another night like that? Wasn't it the best?"

Liz frowned. Larry seemed young and stupid to her all of a sudden, a barnyard cock crowing about himself. "Yeah, it was lovely." She stood up, letting his arm drop off her. "But I've got to go now. Sorry."

Larry's face fell but he tried to shrug it off. "All right." He stood up, too. "Maybe I'll drop down there one day, you never know. What's the name of that salon you work in?"

"Hairline." Liz hurried out of the room.

But when they were all on the train, Brandy and Bobby exclaiming at the view out of the window, their bags on the floor between them, the night with Larry began to revisit Liz. They had made love four times—she'd never done it so much in one go—and the memory of it, still so fresh she could smell him on her, thrilled her all over again. Things he had said, the way he'd stroked her thighs and touched her between the legs, the way he'd pushed her into all kinds of positions. A thrill of lust shot through her and she squirmed in her seat, almost moaning aloud. She leaned her head against the window, regretting that she'd been so short with him in the morning. She might never see him again, might never have another night like that—Liz felt the gloom settle over her like dust. The excitement was over. It was back to Ron and motherhood now.

Brandy was watching her sister. Even though Liz looked exhausted as she leaned against the window, those puffy lips and heavy-lidded eyes were a dead giveaway—any sod could tell she'd had the life fucked out of her the night before. Brandy curled her lip. How could she have gone off with that wanker, she thought, with his monkey face and smooth, vicious words? Jesus, Liz was naïve. She didn't know a bastard when he spat in her face.

"Liz?" she said, wanting to wake her sister out of her disgusting reverie. "What're you going to tell Ron?"

"What?" She seemed half asleep.

"Ron. What're you going to tell him?"

Liz blushed. "Nothing. What he doesn't know isn't going to hurt him. It's over now, anyway. One little night. It's not as if he hasn't done the same, y'know, Brandy."

"I'm not talking about that fucker Larry. I'm talking about me. What're you going to tell him about me?"

"Oh." Liz frowned and looked out of the window again. It was raining, the mugginess of the day before broken at last, and the countryside looked dull and drenched. "I dunno. I haven't thought it out yet."

"No, I bet you haven't. You haven't had a lot of time to think."

"What's that supposed to mean?"

"Liz, why that bloke of all people? D'you know what he did, d'you know what kind of sodding creep he is?"

"What d'you mean?"

"He's the one got Jeff caught, Liz—he fucking ran away on him. He's a bleeding coward. And that's not even half of it."

Liz grew paler and her mouth tightened. "What d'you mean?" she said again.

"He treated me like shit, Liz, after Jeff was gone. Like a bit of meat he found in a gutter somewhere. He made me—"

"Shut up!" Liz put her hands over her ears in a gesture that reminded Brandy of Bobby, it looked so childish. But then she lowered them again. "Have you screwed him?"

"You must be joking. I wouldn't touch him with a barge pole. But he made me—" Brandy glanced at Bobby, who was looking from his mother's face to hers with his mouth open. "I'll tell you later if you really want to know. But you've got fucking terrible taste in men, I can tell you that."

"You're one to talk!" Liz said, her hangover throbbing sharper than ever. "That Jeff bloke looks like death on legs—I've never seen anyone so bony! Anyway, what a bloke's like all depends on how much he respects you, any woman can tell you that, and men respect me, Brandy. They respect me a lot."

Brandy glared at her. "And they don't me, is that what you're saying?"

"Well . . ." Liz lifted her hands, palms up. "Isn't it . . ." She broke off, remembering Brandy and their mother and the pickle they were in. She let her hands fall. "Oh, Christ, let's not start a row. It doesn't matter anyway, I'm not going to see him again. We've got other things to worry about now."

"Not going to see who?" Bobby said anxiously.

"Come here, love." Liz leaned over and lifted him off Brandy's seat and onto her lap. "Never mind, it doesn't matter. We're going home now, aren't you glad?"

"Are we going to see Dad again?"

"Course we are, lovey. That's not what I was talking about, don't worry."

"But why're you and Aunty fighting?"

"We're not fighting, sweetie. Look, see how those raindrops are racing down the window?"

"You are fighting! Is Aunty being bad?"

"No, no, it's all right. We're friends now, right, Brandy?"

Brandy scowled. "Yeah," she grunted and looked away. "We're friends."

11

Brandy stood fidgeting on the doorstep while Liz searched through her bag for her keys. The thought that Ron might be waiting behind the door, his fat fists dangling, made Brandy so nervous that she found herself edging behind Bobby as if he were a shield. Glancing over at Liz, she could see that her sister felt much the same: her jaw was clenched and her thin mouth grim, ready for battle.

Liz found her keys at last and swung open the door. "Ron?" she called timidly. "Ron, we're back!" There was no answer. She went into the dim hall, turned on a light, and looked into the bedroom. "Ron?" Her voice thudded gently against the wall. "You might as well come in," she said to Brandy. "He's not back from work yet."

"Dad?" Bobby shouted, shooting off towards the kitchen the instant Brandy let go of him. "Dad, where are you?"

"He's not home, lovey," Liz said, bending to scoop him up.

"He must have gone down to the pub. It's time for your tea now—you'll see him later."

Bobby's face crumpled. "I want me dad."

"Shh, I know. Come along, let's see what we can find to eat." Liz carried Bobby to the kitchen and turned on the light. The room was surprisingly tidy; food put away, counters wiped, table clean. She set Bobby down and opened the refrigerator but he immediately leapt up and ran into his room to rediscover his toys.

Liz fixed Bobby some bread and Marmite, rehearsing again what she would say to Ron. She wondered what he had been doing for the last three days, where he'd been, but was glad he wasn't home yet; it gave her more time to get back to normal. Bending over to take the butter out of the refrigerator, she caught a whiff of sex on herself. "Brandy!" she called, straightening up.

"Yeah?" Brandy was in Bobby's room, putting away her clothes.

"Will you give Bobby his tea? I've got to have a bath."

"All right," Brandy said. "When's it going to be my sodding turn around here?" she muttered. "Come on, Bobsy boy, it's time for tea."

Ron still hadn't shown up by the time supper was eaten and Bobby put to bed, so Liz and Brandy lay on the bed together to watch an American documentary on television about a boxing champion. Brandy didn't like the film—the swinging fists increased her fear of Ron's return and the sweating, muscular men filled her with a vague disgust. When the program was over, she glanced at Liz, who was leaning back on the pillows, smoking furiously, and said, "What d'you think the point of all that is? I mean, y'know, once he made the money, why'd he keep doing it?"

"'Cause he wanted to be famous, I s'pose." Liz stubbed out a cigarette and immediately lit another. She kept jumping at every sound, expecting it to be Ron.

"Yeah but . . . I thought the whole point of being rich was so you didn't have to keep getting knocked about all the time. I mean, you'd have thought he'd had enough of it by then." Brandy laughed. "Can you imagine choosing to keep on living like this if we got rich? We'd be right daft, wouldn't we?"

Liz squinted at her through the cigarette smoke. "Living like what?"

"Well, you know—the way you have to work all the time and

cook and clean and stuff. Look after Bobby and Ron. You wouldn't have to do all that crap if you was rich, would you?"

"Course I would! Well, maybe I wouldn't cook and stuff but I'd still look after me baby, wouldn't I? And be with me husband, as well. What's the point of being alive otherwise?"

"Wouldn't you want to see the world? Travel and such? Buy clothes and go to fancy discos. Own a hair salon maybe?"

"Own a salon?" Liz looked at her in astonishment. "What would I want to do that for? It's nothing but headaches. Nah, people who do that sort of thing are just wasting their lives, if you ask me. What good can they do anyone, all dressed up and flouncing themselves about, eh? Those nobs make me sick with their pointed noses stuck up in the air. Just read the papers and you'll see—their lives are a mess! Always getting divorced, the kids offing themselves from neglect. Nah, I wouldn't want to live like that."

"Gawd, Liz, you aren't half strange. Christ, if I had money like that . . . I'd be a different person. No Borstal, none of that fuck-up with Jeff and Mum. I'd go to one of those beauty farm places, y'know, get meself made over all slim and gorgeous-like. Then off to America. Parties, booze . . . whew, it'd be fantastic."

Liz lit another cigarette and ran her skinny fingers through her hair. She'd curled up at the head of the bed and Brandy was next to her, lying on her side, propped up on one elbow. They both had the habit of rubbing their stockinged feet together as they talked. "Money wouldn't make you different, Brandy."

"Course it would! What else could do it?"

Liz sighed, not sure she wanted to get into that now. She was so tense about Ron that her fingers were trembling.

"What d'you think would make me different, then?" Brandy urged.

"I dunno. Love, maybe. Money wouldn't solve your problems, anyway."

"What problems?" Brandy got to her knees.

"Well . . ." Liz waved her hand. "Y'know, that stuff with Mum. Attacking people like that. I know she'd drive a saint mad, but still, Brandy, it isn't the way a girl's supposed to behave, is it? You get so sodding furious all the time! Supposing you'd murdered her?"

Brandy looked away, scowling. "Good riddance."

"Nah, I'm serious, Brandy. You could've killed her, y'know."

"Bollocks! She's as strong as a bleeding horse, that old cow.

You said so yourself, Liz. Anyroad, hasn't she been killing me all these years?" Brandy glared at her but Liz thought she saw something uncertain in her eyes.

"Well, that isn't the only thing, Brandy. You've got other problems, too, and you know it."

"Like what?" Brandy shouted.

"Calm down, you'll wake Bobby." Liz watched her sister slump back to the bed. "I mean, well, with men like."

"Men?"

"Yeah. I can't understand how you can fancy that Jeff bloke. I mean, he's not a man, Brandy, he's a piece of wet string. He's like a . . . he's like a little boy."

"Not in bed he isn't." Brandy flashed a grin, but then suddenly dropped it. Her mouth sagged. "He's me best friend, Liz, that's all. Or he was. He likes me. He cares."

"Well, I do, too, y'know. You don't need him."

Brandy smiled at that and looked down. She stared at the cigarette cupped in the palm of her hand, watching the smoke curl out from under her thumb. "What're you trying to say, Liz? About men, I mean."

Liz shifted on the bed uneasily, remembering Brandy's reaction when she'd scolded her about that Yank in the salon. "Well, maybe Jeff's all right, then. But I mean—well, you don't seem that interested in blokes, really. I mean . . ." She stopped because Brandy was looking at her with a smirk. "What are you grinning at?"

"You mean me and girls, don't you?" Brandy said, enjoying Liz's embarrassment.

"Yeah." Liz blushed.

"I'm not ashamed of liking girls, y'know," Brandy said, turning serious. "Everyone does it inside, even the screws. And some of us do it on the outside, too, that's all. But I like men, too, Liz. I am going to get married one day when I find the right bloke."

"But it's not normal, Brandy, it's like you're trying to be a man!" Liz looked at her curiously. "Don't you see it's not healthy?"

Brandy narrowed her eyes. "You're one to preach! D'you think screwing Larry is healthy? You didn't even stop to find out what he's like, did you? You didn't even ask me about him first! D'you know what that bloke did to me after Jeff was nabbed?" Brandy was determined to shock her sister out of her smugness. "He made me screw three of his friends. He sold me to them for some dope. Like a packet of fags he sold me, Liz."

161

Liz drew back. "What d'you mean?"

"What I said. He threatened to beat me up if I didn't do it. I was like a slave with them, Liz. I had to do whatever they told me. Like a piece of sodding bubble gum—chew her up and spit her out! That's what it was like till I got meself nicked."

"I don't believe you."

Brandy sat back on her heels and shrugged. "You can believe what you like, but it's true. That bloke doesn't have a decent bone in his body. He's evil, Liz."

"Does Jeff know about this?"

"Nah, course not."

"Why didn't you tell him then, if it's so true?" Liz tried to sound mocking but her voice trembled. She found herself shrinking back against the pillows, trying to get away from the horrors that were bursting out of her sister.

"I was going to but . . . I didn't see the point, I s'pose." Brandy turned away, staring at the floor. "It wouldn't make no difference now, anyroad. Jeff and Larry are in thick together. It's too late."

"Is that why you shoved over that old lady?"

"Yeah. It seemed like the only way I could get away from them, the fucking bastards." Brandy fell silent, the fight suddenly gone out of her. She watched her cigarette burn down to its butt, the hot ash falling into her hand, but didn't flinch. Liz stared at her, her mind assaulted by pictures of Brandy being forcibly pressed to the floor by man after man.

"Did they rape you?"

Brandy snorted. "What d'you think it was, a sodding party?" She got off the bed and dumped the ash in a saucer, stubbing out her cigarette angrily. For a moment the sisters were silent, Liz still staring at Brandy. Finally Brandy sighed and looked up. She didn't really want to dwell on all that anymore. She didn't even want to fight with her sister. There was no point. "What the hell, Liz, eh?" she said at last. "Things are going to be better now, aren't they? Now that I'm here again with you and Bobby. Right?"

Liz blinked, then forced a smile. "Right, Brandy," she said.

After Brandy went to bed, Liz changed into her nightdress and lay back smoking. She stared at the ceiling, watching the smoke curl up to it, and tried to sort herself out. The memories of Larry flipping her over, pushing apart her buttocks, which had thrilled her so on the train, were rapidly turning ugly. At one moment she'd feel a pang of longing, at the next a sudden revulsion as if she herself had been raped. Her body was utterly confused, not knowing how to interpret the memories. Larry had been nothing but a passionate lover to her last night, even something of a gentleman with an edge of roughness she liked in sex. Liz couldn't understand how he could have done such a thing to Brandy. Jesus, she thought, had he watched while she was raped? Was he that bad? She closed her eyes against the smoke, feeling her hangover sloshing around in her like old wine. No, last night had been great. He had been great. Liz firmly believed that sex was the closest thing in life to truth. When people made love, she believed, they became utterly honest, their pretenses stripped away by passion. Sex made people want only to please and be pleased, like children. There was nothing wrong with Larry. Brandy must have lied.

She heard a rattling in the hall and the bedroom door swung open. Startled, she sat up just as Ron lumbered into the room. His face was red and Liz could tell immediately that he'd been drinking. He glared at her. "So, the queen bee returns, eh?" he said.

"Yeah, we're back." Liz tried to sound bright and ordinary, but her hands were shaking.

"Gawd, I can hardly breathe in here. What did you do, smoke a whole carton?" He walked across the room and threw open the window, letting in a gust of cold night air. Shivering, Liz pulled the quilt up around her shoulders. Ron sat on the bed and struggled to get his shoes off while Liz gazed at his fat back, waiting to find out if she'd feel revulsion or relief. "Bobby all right, then?" he muttered.

"Oh yeah, he had a great time. We stopped in London to look at the shops for a few hours between trains, and he loved it."

"Hm." Ron sat still, with his back to her.

Liz lit another cigarette. He looked so tubby compared to Larry. "Did you get on all right, then?"

"Course. Val and Dave came 'round and she cooked me some suppers."

"Oh, that was nice."

Ron picked up her packet of cigarettes, shook one out and lit up. Liz decided to get it over with.

"Brandy's here."

He whipped around to face her. "What?"

"I brought her with me. It'll be all right, Ron, if you don't bully her. Leave her be and it'll be fine. She's a good girl at heart."

"Good girl! Don't make me fucking laugh."

"Don't start, Ron. We've been through this."

"I'm not having her here." He sounded grim. "I'm not having her, understand?"

"She's here, Ron." Liz spoke deliberately. "She has no place else to go. I want her here. She's me sister."

Ron grabbed her by the shoulders. "Don't you fucking talk to me like that! Putting on those high-and-mighty airs like I'm an idiot! First you run off without so much as a by-your-leave, then you come back talking like a fucking nun—who do you think you are, eh?" He shook her and glared into her face.

"Don't shove me around, you wanker!" Liz shouted, struggling and waving her cigarette dangerously near his eyes until he winced and let go. She fell back and kicked out at him with a bare foot. "Talk about high and mighty! Trying to tell me what to do with me own family! I had me family 'way before I had you, and I know what's right. All I want to do is make a little good 'round here for a change, help me own sister, and you act like I'm some sort of criminal! You're so stupid sometimes, Ron, I can't believe it."

Ron stood up, took a deep breath, and roared. "I wouldn't be surprised if you did start nicking things next! You're as bad as your sister, you are! A family of bleeding nutters!"

"So what are you, perfect?" Liz clambered to her feet on the bed. "I know what you were doing those nights you didn't come home! Don't play the saint with me, Ron. You're a sodding hypocrite and you know it!" Ron stared at her in surprise, and Liz knew she had him now. "I'm not daft, y'know," she continued, folding her arms and sneering at him. "Late-night poker games indeed—what d'you think I am, a bloody schoolgirl?"

Ron tried to look shocked. "Bollocks! You're imagining things!"

"Oh yeah? Why else would you come creeping in here near dawn and taking a bath, eh? To wash off the smell of the cards?"

Ron frowned, but then he pulled himself together. "You're getting off the point, Liz. It's not me and you we're talking about here, and you know it. I don't want Brandy in this house, that's all. It's too small, she's a bad lot, and I like me life with you and Bobby the way it was before."

"Well, what am I supposed to do?" Liz yelled again. "Kick her out on the street now, in the middle of the night?"

Ron scowled and stamped around the room. "All right, all right," he said at last, "you can keep her for the night. But she'll have to go tomorrow, Liz, I mean it."

"I can't do that, Ron, don't you see?" Liz made an effort to soften her voice. "She's got nowhere to go. Can't you try to understand? She's me baby sister, Ron. I am not going to shove her out this time." She paused, watching Ron for the effect of her words. "It'll be all right with Brandy here, you'll see. She's learned her lesson by now. And Bobby does love her, y'know. Please, Ron!"

"Why can't she just stay at your mother's?"

Liz looked away. "They don't get on," she mumbled. "She'd do better here, honest."

Ron stared at her, undecided. Liz noticed that his red face had paled and that he looked exhausted. She, too, felt suddenly tired.

"All right." He sighed. "All fucking right. I'll give it a go, for a bit, anyroad, but only as long as she doesn't fuck up. And don't expect me to love it." He paused. "Can't we talk about it in the morning, for God's sake? I'm too bloody knackered for all this rowing." She nodded, smiling slightly, and he stepped up to the bed, put his arms around her waist, and pressed his face into her belly. She looked down on his thinning hair and stroked it. "And don't run off with Bobby again like that, Liz, all right?" he said into her stomach. "I can't stand it."

Liz hugged him and kissed his curls. "I won't," she said, "I won't." She knelt down on the bed and bent forward to kiss him. He felt whiskery and tasted of beer, but his bulk was reassuring in its familiarity. She stretched her arms around him, feeling the muscles hard and solid under her hands. He wasn't so bad really, old Ron. She liked the way he smelled, the way he always squashed her a bit with his heavy build. He rubbed his big head on her shoulder, nuzzling up to her and kissing her neck, and much to her surprise, Liz found herself aroused.

"Dad!" Bobby burst into the room. "Dad, Dad!"

Brandy came in after him, hanging back in the doorway. "Sorry. I tried to keep him out but the noise woke him and I couldn't."

Ignoring her, Ron turned around to pick up Bobby. "Hello, me little lad," he said, giving him a hug, "missed your dad, did you?"

Bobby put his arms around Ron's neck and squeezed. "Yeah." He wriggled against his father's chest. "Did you miss me, Dad?"

"Course I did." Ron glanced over at Liz. "I missed you both."

12

"Don't bother to talk if it hurts," old George said, patting Mary on the hand. "You need a rest." Mary closed her eyes gratefully and lay back on the bed, the bruises around her neck preventing her from nodding. "I'll do the explaining, love. We'll get it all on record that way."

She frowned, not yet sure what was happening around her. She remembered George clucking over her, his grizzly face puckered with concern, the bustle of nurses when he'd taken her to the hospital and the discomfort of the journey home again, but she was far from clear on the rest. She opened her mouth and, with an effort, croaked out a question. "Can't you just tell them I fell?"

George guffawed. "Don't be daft, woman, no one'll believe that! Not with all them bruises 'round you. The nurse said you was lucky your vocal cords weren't crushed. It's as plain as day you were attacked, and the police'll be wanting to know if you're going to press charges."

"I don't want them meddling in this. Leave them out of it, George. I can't stand all this fuss."

"All right, all right. You've got to relax, dear, the doctor said so. You've had a bit of a shock, y'know. I'll come downstairs to see you again tomorrow morning and we can talk about it then."

Mary moaned. "Where's Liz?" she said, her voice still a sore rattle in her throat.

"She's not here, Mary. The two of them took off, the little bints."

At that a tear welled up in Mary's eye. "She's mad, that Amanda. She ought to be in a looney bin. How could she do it, George? Her own mother!"

"Shh, there, there." George patted Mary's hand, then stroked her hair, its orange frizz turning gray in the evening light. When Mary shut her eyes again, he studied her with affectionate pity: a plump, sorrowful woman with shadows under her eyes and bruises around her neck, her aging face sagging against the pillow, grooved by all her trials. Mary had always been good to him, soft and easy, ready with her large breasts and ample belly to pull him into her. He couldn't understand the lean viciousness of her daughters, of any of the young people these days for that matter. They seemed so full of fight, so full of themselves. He felt indignant on Mary's behalf, being childless himself. He would be her hero, have those girls punished.

"You get some sleep, love," he said at last. "You've been through a lot since last night. Just leave it to me."

"Don't tell the police," Mary whispered. "I'd be so ashamed, George. Please."

"I know, Mary, but you need to think it over more. If we don't do summat, what's to stop her doing it again, eh? She might come back anytime, and God knows what she'd do to you next, love."

Mary whimpered. "You think so, George? You think she might come back?"

"Well, what's stopping her? She's got to learn her lesson, Mary."

"But I don't want to talk to the police."

"Yeah, yeah. We'll talk about it tomorrow, when you feel better. Go to sleep now, love."

"I'm frightened, George."

"Shh. Go to sleep."

13

Brandy studied Ron over the kitchen table, amused that after a week he was still treating her with sullen resentment. She had tried to thaw him out with her usual repertoire of winks and Borstal jokes, but he had been resisting her with the stubbornness of a rusted door. She turned her attention to Bobby and wiped a dribble off his chin. At least she had a trump up her sleeve, she thought. All she had to do was picture Liz tangled up in bed with Larry to feel a sense of power over Ron as secretive and delicious as a cherry in a chocolate.

"Pass the beans," Ron said with a grunt, and Brandy complied, watching his face for the chance to catch him out with one of her cocky smiles. She'd flash it at him, the way she'd learned inside, as if to say "Nothing wrong with me, mate, how about you?" and he would never fail to look disconcerted.

After supper, the family went into the bedroom to watch television. Liz dropped into a chair, Ron turned on the news, and

Brandy dumped Bobby on the bed and tickled him into helpless laughter.

"Do you have to do that here?" Ron grumbled. "I can't hear a bloody thing."

Brandy sat up, her face flushed, and Bobby leapt onto her back, putting his sharp little fingers around her neck and clambering onto her head. "Is there summat important going on, then?" she said seriously.

Ron looked at her, sitting there all polite and earnest with Bobby draped over her head like a hat, and a laugh cracked out of him, loud and abrupt. Bobby reached around and squeezed Brandy's nose.

Ron laughed again, realizing they were clowning for him. "Come on, Bobby," he said, "get off your poor aunty. You're squashing her." He lifted Bobby up and carried him back to his lap. "She's not an apple tree, y'know." Brandy caught Liz's eye and winked.

The next afternoon, as Liz was doing a shampoo in the back of the shop, she thought about Ron and Brandy. She wished Ron would ease up on the girl, for Brandy really was trying her best. She had started a job sweeping up for friends of Liz in a salon down the road, she was helping with all the shopping and cleaning—Liz was even ready to trust her to mind Bobby again soon. If only Ron would let it go, she thought as she ran her fingers through the customer's hair. She turned on the tap, and began rinsing out the suds. At least Bobby held them all together, she mused: the one bit of joy in the house.

"Liz?" Jenny said, breaking into her thoughts. "You've got a visitor outside."

"Oh, all right." Liz finished off the rinse quickly and hurried out of the shop. She stood in the entranceway, looking over the street for Brandy.

"About time."

She whirled around. Larry was leaning against the wall, looking at her.

"What're you doing here?" Liz exclaimed, turning bright red.

"You ought to know." He moved closer.

"What d'you mean?" She rubbed her hands nervously on her smock.

He didn't answer.

"Look, Larry, I don't know why you bothered to come all the

169

way down here. I told you it's no good." She began to walk away but he whipped around in front of her, putting one arm on either side of her shoulders and pinning her against the wall. "Get off!" she cried, surprised, raising her hand to push him away, but then she stopped herself, remembering all that Brandy had told her about him.

"I'm not here for that and you know it," he said, his voice low. "Give it back."

"Give what back?"

"Don't give me any of that crap, just give it back. I don't care how you get it—go into that fancy salon of yours and take it out of the till for all I care—but give it back."

"I don't know what you're talking about."

"Stop playing games, you silly bitch."

"Don't you call me that!" Liz pulled away from the wall and gave him a shove. Somehow, even after all Brandy had told her about him, having screwed Larry helped her not to feel afraid of him.

Larry stepped back a minute, confused, but quickly recovered himself. He grabbed her arm and slammed her against the wall. "Look, you cunt, you and that barmy sister of yours nicked a hundred quid from us and I'm down here to get it. Now."

"A hundred quid?"

"Now!" Larry squeezed her arm. "Else you'll regret it."

"I don't know anything about it!" She tried to pull away.

"Where's that other cunt then? I've got a personal message for her from Jeff." He sneered.

"She doesn't work here." Liz looked at him a moment, his words sinking in. So that's where Brandy had got all that money she'd been flashing about. "Can't Jeff do his own errands?" she said mockingly.

Larry scowled. "Course he can! He's just got to lie low for a bit, so I thought I'd do him a favor." He dropped his voice. "And I wanted to come down and give you a piece of my mind. A right pair of tarts you two are, sponging off us like that and then nicking our cash into the bargain! And you so hoity-toity with your 'I'm married,' and 'I'm a hairstylist.' You're no better than your nutter sister."

"I didn't have anything to do with it!" Liz snapped, but she was shamed.

"I don't give a shit. Get me the money or I'll break your fucking arm!"

"Simmer down for Christ's sake!" Liz glanced around, frightened that someone might hear them. "All right, I'll get you the money—just get away from me and stay out of sight."

Larry ran his eyes over her. "I'm coming in with you. No tricks."

"You come in and I'll call the frigging police."

"You wouldn't dare—they'd have your sister locked up in a wink!"

"You and Jeff are the ones they're after, Larry, remember? I saw all that cash in your pocket, and you're not going to tell me you got that with an honest day's work. It's not my sister they want." Liz looked at him coolly.

"All right," he muttered, "I'll wait here."

Turning on her heels, Liz went back into the shop, her heart thudding. She walked to the cloakroom, took out her purse, and counted the money in it. She still had thirty pounds from Ron's last pay packet, but that didn't solve much. She put the money in her pocket, trying to work out what to do, but her mind was in a whirl. The Larry out there was an entirely different person from the one she'd met in Birmingham. He was cruel, just as Brandy had said. Gawd, Liz thought, perhaps the girl had been telling the truth—he was just a bastard. A rapist bastard. She looked around the cloakroom in a panic, trying to think of who she could borrow the money from. Jenny? Definitely not. The bank? She and Ron were already overdrawn—they'd never let her have it. Finally she thought of Val.

She was just about to go back out and take Larry to Val, who worked as a receptionist in a nearby office, when she realized how humiliating that would be, too. "Here's me lover, Val. Can you lend us seventy quid?" Christ, Val would think she was buying men! Liz sank to the bench under the coats and put her head in her hands. God damn you, Brandy, she thought, why'd you have to get me into this? She glanced at her watch. Larry would come storming in at any moment. She caught sight of a customer's bag hanging on a coat peg, looked around quickly, opened it, and counted the money inside. Only sixteen pounds. She put it back and took the wallet out of another bag sitting on the bench. That one had fifty in it! Acting quickly, Liz shoved the wallet in her pocket and put both bags in their original positions. With luck— with a lot of luck—the wallet's owner would think she'd been robbed outside the shop.

Liz went into the toilet behind the cloakroom and flushed it, then hurried out the back door and around the building. Larry was pacing up and down, eyeing the shop's entrance. He jumped when she came up on him from behind. "Here," she said, handing him the cash. "Now bugger off."

He took the money and counted it. "You've only got eighty here," he said.

"That's all you're getting from me, mate." Liz looked him in the eye. "You better get out of here before I call the coppers."

He gazed at her for a moment, hesitating. Liz kept her eyes fixed on his. Finally he smiled a crooked, nasty grin. "You are a tough little bird, aren't you? Just like your sister!" Grabbing her, he gave her a bruising kiss on the lips. When he let her go she almost fell down. As he walked off she rubbed her mouth in disgust.

Liz hurried away from the salon and threw the wallet into a rubbish bin, covering it with paper, then ran around the corner and into the back entrance. She quickly replenished her lipstick and, face still burning, went back to work. The sweat gathered under her arms and trickled down her sides as she watched the customers getting ready to pay. She'd never stolen before, at least not more than a Mars Bar or two when she was a child, and she felt soiled, as if her hands had been dipped in sewage. She glanced around at the customers, women in various fashions, and was relieved to see that at least they all looked moneyed.

The showdown didn't happen for over an hour. The customer she'd robbed turned out to be one of the older ones, who'd come in for a rinse and set rather than a fashionable cut. Liz had washed her hair, listening to her chat in a posh voice about her teenage daughter and all the trouble she was—they'd had a nice motherly complain together. When the customer reached into her bag to pay Jenny, Liz watched uneasily. She saw the woman peer into it and turn red.

"Oh!" she said. "Where's my purse?" She stood still, frowning, and Liz prayed that she'd think she'd left it somewhere. At last the woman got upset. "I know I had it with me. I went to the bank yesterday and I'm sure that I had at least sixty pounds in it." She looked around the shop. "I've been robbed!"

Jenny didn't believe her. "Are you certain, madum?"

"Of course I'm certain! Do you think I wouldn't notice losing that amount of money?"

"I wouldn't know." Jenny was annoyed at the woman's tone.

"I'm very sorry. Perhaps it happened on the seafront. But we must insist on payment here."

"On the seafront?" The woman frowned again. "Are you . . ." She stopped herself and looked around, embarrassed, clearly too timid to go as far as accusing anyone. "Well, perhaps you're right. I did take a walk earlier and I hear Brighton is full of pickpockets. Will you take a check?" Jenny said she would and as the woman wrote it out, Liz couldn't help admiring her victim's dignity.

That evening at home, however, she still felt shaken. It wasn't so much her conscience, she had to admit, as fear of being found out. The thought of being exposed as a thief, of looking no better than her Borstal girl of a sister, as that wanker Larry had said, was so abhorrent to her that it made her stomach turn. She watched Brandy, who was reading a magazine on the bedroom armchair, twirling her hair in one finger and chewing gum, and tried to decide whether to tell her about what had happened. She didn't blame her for taking that money, really—Jeff deserved it—but still . . . Liz opened her mouth to reprimand her but then the memory of Brandy's face in Jeff's kitchen came back to her. She had looked so defeated, her fire of rebellion utterly quenched. She had looked so hurt. Liz shut her mouth and turned away.

Yet later that night, when Ron was out with friends and the sisters were watching television, Liz still felt the need to talk about Larry. The way he had treated her that afternoon had utterly ruined her memory of the night in Birmingham. Now she wanted to scrub her flesh until it smarted, to go to church and swear on a Bible never to be unfaithful again. The thought of what she had let him do to her made her flesh tighten with horror. But it also made her more curious about Brandy. If what the girl said was true, men had been treating her like that for years. Liz gazed at her sister with new respect, as if the fact that she could sit there watching the telly like any old person was a miracle. No wonder the girl lost control sometimes, Liz thought—anyone who's been treated like that should be raving and sticking knives into people! Yet most of the time there she was, ordinary.

"Brandy?"

"Hmm?"

"What was it like in Bullwood Hall? You never told me."

Brandy looked over. "That's a funny question outta the blue."

"I know, but I've been wondering ever since you told me all that stuff about Larry and such. I just thought, y'know, that you never speak about it much but you were in there for, what, two years or something?"

"Fucking forever. Twenty-seven months counting both times."

"Was it awful the whole time?"

Brandy stretched in her chair, shooting her legs out in front of her and her arms above her head. She yawned noisily. "Nah, it wasn't so awful. You make friends, girlfriends, that sorta thing, then it isn't so bad. The worst is the first few days, getting used to being in a cell all the time. That first night you hear them lock it, that's the hardest for everyone. Makes you want to scream, it does. It's like a coffin going bang down over your head."

Liz shuddered. "Does it . . . but what does it feel like, being locked up for so long?"

Brandy folded her arms and looked at Liz with amusement. "Feel? You think anyone lets themselves feel in there? Don't make me laugh. You start feeling and you're doomed. Imagine looking up every morning and seeing those bars marching down your eyes, eh? Or seeing that spyhole lifting and some fat nose poking in at you—think you want to feel? Nah, the only way to cope in there, Liz, is to act simple. You grin a lot, sneak around, and laugh for all you're fucking worth till they let you out."

Liz looked at her, frowning. "D'you ever miss anyone in there, though? Any of those friends you made?"

"Funny you should ask, Liz. I was just thinking about that. There was one girl in there, Molly, who'd always fancied me but I never knew it. Then I met her in Brum and . . ."

"I don't mean that kind of friend, Brandy. I mean normal friends."

"Normal? And what's normal, I'd like to know?"

"You know. A girl you can talk to, confide in. Not someone to stick your hands up."

"Ooh, aren't we coarse today? You should try it, Liz. I could introduce you to some girls I know would fancy you like mad. You might even like it." Brandy winked.

"Ugh, shurrup!" But Liz was curious. "D'you know girls like that here in Brighton, then?"

"A few."

"How?"

"There's this pub down by the seafront. One of me mates inside told me about it. Fancy going down there with me some night?"

"Not on your life!" Liz pulled a disgusted face and Brandy chuckled. "Is that where you've been going on your nights out, then?" Liz said.

"Only once. I didn't fancy it much, to tell the truth. It's too . . . it's desperate, sort of. Inside you can take your time over these things, get to know a girl first, decide if she likes you. Time is one thing you've got plenty of in there. But outside it's all hustle and grab before someone else gets in first. I don't go for that."

"Does it get serious ever? With the girls inside, I mean?"

"What d'you mean, serious?"

"Y'know, love and all that."

Brandy smiled and scratched her head, swiveling around in the chair towards Liz. She was looking better these days, a little thinner, with a tan and a new softness over her hard, flat face. She looked more alive than Liz had seen her in weeks. "Yeah, it does get serious, Liz—you'd be surprised. Girls are always falling in love in there. It gets all romantic and intense-like, just like in the flicks. But I'm not like that. I always thought it was a bit too soppy for me." She snickered. "I was saving me heart for Jeff. That'll teach me, won't it?"

"Ah, Brandy."

She waved a hand. "Don't bother yourself about it, Liz. I'm almost over it now. I shoulda known it wouldn't last all that time. You forget things like that inside, y'know. You forget life goes on without you—you get to thinking it just stays still, waiting for you to get out. Pathetic, really."

"Was it lonely inside, though? I mean if you weren't being in love and such?"

"Lonely? When isn't it lonely?" Brandy's mouth twisted. "Nah, if anything it's lonelier out here. You never know where you stand here, what'll happen, who'll kick you out." Liz winced at the allusion. "But inside it's always the same. Course that gets stifling at times, but at least you know where you are. And then I was always a bit special, Liz. You think I'm just a fat girl with bad habits out here, don't you? But in there they like me. I had lots of them hot for me, I did." Brandy chuckled. "I could tell you things that'd knock your knickers off!"

"Like what?" Liz's eyes were large. She was always amazed by what Brandy told her until she remembered how easily the girl lied.

"You know who I had stuck on me?"

"Who?"

"A warder!"

"A warder?"

"Yeah. There was this warder there called Roanna Reardon—funny name, innit? A big woman with long hair. Built like a mountain, she was."

Liz tried to control the laugh she felt curling over her face. "And did you like her, too?"

Brandy shrugged. "Nah, not much. But there was summat about her, I must admit. Like some kind of warrior queen she was on her good days—well, at least with the little things. You know what she did once?" Brandy laughed. "I was having a fight with this Jamaican girl one night. I'm a good match for most people in a fight, but this bird was built like a sodding refrigerator—I'd bang into her and off I'd bounce, like a tennis ball. Boing! Anyroad, she had me by the hair and I thought she was going to twist me fucking head right off when in comes Reardon, roaring like a bull, picks up the bird, tucks her under her arm like she weighed no more than a teddy bear, and swings off down the wing with her!" Brandy threw back her head and cackled, forgetting Liz's presence for a moment. "Like the bloody Lone Ranger, she was. You could almost see the sunset!" Sobering up, she looked back at Liz, wanting to laugh again at her sister's astonished face. "It was funny, Liz, she was really head-over-heels for me. I couldn't do a thing wrong in her eyes. She thought I was a fucking god."

"Why?" Liz couldn't keep the amazement out of her voice.

Brandy didn't take offense. "Gawd knows. I think she was a bit of a nutter, if you ask me. One of those religious maniacs. But they say virgins always fall for the first lover, right? Maybe that was it."

"You were her first?" Liz wrinkled her nose. The idea of Brandy seducing a prison officer was so grotesque it was comic.

Brandy nodded, smirking. "Romeo, that's me."

14

The next day was Brandy's eighteenth birthday and it was sunny and hot, one of the last gasps of summer before it plunged into autumn. Liz took her shopping for a present and Brandy chose a pair of red platform shoes with thick soles and high, skinny heels, which she insisted on wearing even though they caught in the slats of the pier as she, Liz, and Bobby headed towards the penny arcade. The shoes made her look unnaturally tall, like a dwarf on stilts, but she was convinced that she looked willowy and elegant in them. "I'm almost up to your height, Liz," she said, and beamed.

The Palace Pier, an elaborate white structure fussily decorated with ornate booths and curlicue ironwork, was packed with the last of the season's holiday makers. The sisters enjoyed being part of the crowd, watching the families licking ice cream, the boys leering at them from the railing, the children running about with peeling cheeks and noses. "Y'know, I never would have thought there was a place like this in England," Brandy said. "It's like being somewhere really exotic, like Greece or summat." She and Liz were wearing bikini tops and tight, white shorts. Bobby was in a red T-shirt and swimming trunks.

"Yeah, I know," Liz said proudly. "But it gets really different here in the winter. Wait till you see it, Brandy. All the tourists leave and it gets dead depressing. Gray and damp." She remembered trying to impress Larry by telling him that Brighton was beautiful in the winter, and grimaced.

They squeezed through a crowd of people watching a fisherman expertly scale and gut his catch, and walked on past the booths selling candy floss, souvenir mugs, and rude postcards. Liz stopped to buy Bobby a stick of Brighton rock, a pink column of hard peppermint with the word "Brighton" threaded in red sugar all the way through it, and Brandy inhaled the smells of fish, seagulls, and suntan oil, giddy with the pleasure they brought her. This was the life, she thought: the sun so hot they didn't need shirts, her brain pleasantly clouded by lunchtime shandies, the comfort of her self-assured sister beside her. She had the sense of having become unbelievably lucky, as if suddenly, for no reason, a fairy godmother had waved a wand and made everything all right. She grinned to herself. Whoever would have guessed you'd get so lucky, you old sod? she thought. Gawd knows you don't deserve it.

At the penny arcade they had to pay an entrance fee, which Liz thought exorbitant, and trade in their little 1p pieces for the old pennies that would work the exhibits. Bobby squealed with excitement when he saw the tiny theaters and puppets, encased in dusty glass boxes and waiting to be set into action. After Liz had made him throw away his unfinished rock and wipe his sticky hands on a tissue, Brandy heaved him up with a grunt to see the first one, a doll's house set up as a tableau of a murder mystery. She let him drop the penny into the slot and they watched as the machine clunked, whirred, and started to play old, creaky music. Each tiny room lit up and the six-inch-high puppets moved jerkily, carrying out a quick who-done-it. Bobby was fascinated but it gave Brandy a spooky feeling, as if she were watching tiny corpses brought to life.

Bobby's favorite display was the laughing sailor, a bigger-than-life dummy with a red nose, drink-dulled eyes, and an apoplectic grin painted onto his shiny wooden face. They stood watching him rock back and forth in a repetitive sequence of movements, his arms pumping up and down in mock hilarity as

178

a recording hooted with laughter, and Bobby laughed so hard with him that his eyes teared. Brandy crouched down behind Bobby and held him to her, feeling his delicate stomach muscles clenching under her hands and smiling with him, even though she found the sailor grotesque. By the third round, however, Bobby caught on that there is something chilling about a man who can't stop laughing and grew serious, watching with big eyes as the sailor continued to rock, over and over again, as if he were having a fit. Finally, Bobby shrank back and reached out to Brandy for comfort.

"Remind you of anyone?" Liz said, looking at the sailor.

Brandy looked him over. "Mum, you mean?"

Liz nodded and laughed. "Poor fella," she said, shaking her head. "Can you imagine being trapped like that? To and fro, to and fro, never being able to stop?"

Brandy shuddered and stood up. "Come on, Bobby," she said, "let's go look at summat else."

In another glass box they found a small puppet wearing a feathered cap and riding a horse. When Brandy put a penny in it played "Yankee Doodle Dandy." She and Bobby watched, puzzled, while the horse bobbed up and down. "What's a yankee doodle?" Bobby asked.

"I dunno, love. I think this one's broken."

After they had rolled some pennies down the penny-racing track and unsuccessfully tried to work the claw machine to get Bobby some sweets, Liz suggested they go back outside. "This place gives me the willies," she said, glancing around at the dead wooden eyes of the puppets. Brandy agreed.

As soon as they were back out in the sun, Bobby declared that he wanted to go on the ghost train at the end of the pier, so Liz took him on that while Brandy lounged against the railing, watching the crowds. There were a lot of youths her age, boys in sleeveless shirts showing off their tanned muscles, girls in halter tops and hot pants, and they shouted and squealed and chased one another around the pier while Brandy watched. They made her feel dumpy and old, like some middle-aged matron who'd been through a lot. She glanced down at her pudgy legs, still white and bruised looking, at the fold of stomach protruding between her bikini top and shorts, and was disgusted with herself. Watching the Brighton lads and lasses reawakened a feeling she'd often had outside of Borstal, that sense of being a different and unwelcome species. She turned her back on the crowds, leaned on the white ironwork railing, and looked out over the sea.

The stone beach went on for miles, scalloping in gentle curves all the way to the horizon. It was light brown and dotted with hundreds of people who, in their glaring skin and clothes, looked like so much scattered litter. All along the beach stretched the front, a row of ornate white houses underlined by the road. The view gave Brandy a dizzying sense of possibilities: All those people, all that space, all that sea and blue sky extending out until it turned white in a blur of distant mist and clouds. It enabled her to imagine herself, for a moment, as one of the people below. She was walking along a street, somewhere in Brighton, the sun shining down, humming. In one hand she had a bag of groceries—some sausage rolls, perhaps, a pint of milk, a loaf of Hovis. In the other hand she had her child. That was all she'd ever wanted. It was the only thing, she could admit to herself now, that she would ever work to get.

She looked down at the people directly beneath her, able to make out their ages and shapes if not their faces. One boy in black bathing trunks crouched comically, taking a photograph of a girl poised in a white dress, her feet lapped by the waves. A baby sat examining stones while her father stood over her, his hands on his hips. A fat woman lifted her skirts and opened her mouth as the water splashed her knees. Brandy shut her eyes, feeling the sun beat down on her head, and for a moment saw herself melting like butter over the railing and into the sea, floating away forever.

That evening at home, after the family had finished tea, Liz announced a surprise. She left the kitchen with a secretive smile and Ron followed her after pouring them all some more beer, turning off the lights, and telling Bobby to sit still. Bobby climbed into Brandy's lap, frightened a little by the dark, and she nuzzled his salty hair while they waited. She saw a glimmer of lights down the hall but pretended not to notice.

"Happy birthday to you, happy birthday to you. Happy birthday dear Bra-andy, happy birthday to you!" Liz and Ron sang loudly and out of tune as they paraded into the kitchen, holding a chocolate cake ablaze with candles.

"Squashed tomatoes and stew!" Bobby chimed in, laughing, and he scrambled to his knees on Brandy's lap, poking her with his sharp bones. "Can I blow it out, Aunty, can I?"

"No love," said Liz, "it's her birthday. She has to blow them out. Go on, Brandy, make a wish."

Brandy held onto Bobby to stop him plunging face first into the candles and shut her eyes, smiling. No one had done this for her since she was small, and even her memories of those occasions were fuzzy, as if they might have been only the memories of longings, not of events. "Come on, Aunty!" Bobby said.

"All right, hold on, you little bugger." Brandy kept her eyes shut, trying to concentrate. I wish . . . what do I wish? she thought, distracted again by Bobby bouncing on her lap, by the pleasure she felt and the knowledge that Ron and Liz were watching her. I wish . . . Images of the Palace Pier and boys and clothes wafted through her mind, of Liz smiling at her, of Bobby with his tangled, sea-sticky hair, of her dream on the beach. I wish I could be like Liz. She nuzzled the back of Bobby's thin, down-covered neck and opened her eyes. "Come on, Bobby, help me blow." They leaned forward and blew out all eighteen candles.

Less than a week after Brandy's birthday, Dave and Val came to supper. The six of them sat squeezed around the kitchen table, telling jokes, while Brandy helped Liz serve. She felt nervous, knowing this was a test, but Liz winked at her so reassuringly that she even managed to ladle out the stew without spilling.

"What do Brummies do for a big event on a Saturday night?" Dave asked.

"Clean their ears!" Ron shouted.

"Sort their socks," Liz offered.

"Pick their noses," said Val.

"No, no," Dave said with a grin. "Change the channel!"

Brandy smiled, musing that she'd never even had a television set to cut the boredom with when she lived at home.

"There's a Catholic priest, a Protestant minister, and a rabbi." It was Ron's turn. "They're discussing how to decide how much of the collection to keep. The Catholic says he draws a circle on the ground, throws the money up to heaven, and whatever falls inside the circle is God's, the rest is his."

"Oh, gawd, not that one again," Liz interrupted.

"Shut up, Liz. The Protestant says he draws a line on the ground, throws up the money, and whatever falls on the left is God's, the money on the right is his. The rabbi says he throws the money up"—Ron paused for effect, his red face flushed—"and he says, 'God can take what he wants when it's up there, the rest is mine.' "

After the laughter died down, Brandy said shyly, "I've got

one." She was standing at the end of the table, the ladle poised in her hand like a baton.

"All right, what?" Ron said.

"There's three women in a train. One from Dublin, one from Glasgow, and one from Brum. The train goes into a tunnel and all the lights go out. The Dublin one screams, 'Be-Jesus, it's Judgment Day!' and starts saying her prayers. The Glasgow one opens her purse and counts her money. And the Brummy one looks around and says—" Just then the doorbell rang.

"Who could that be?" Liz said, getting up. "It's a funny time to be visiting."

"I'll get it," Ron said. He had been more willing to help around the house again since he'd grown used to Brandy's presence. "Hold the punchline, Brandy, it sounds good."

Disconcerted, Brandy sat down in her chair and pulled Bobby onto her lap. She dipped some bread in the stew and gave it to him, aware of Val watching her curiously. They heard some talking down the hall, then suddenly Ron shouted, "You can't come in!" Liz stood up, alarmed, and Brandy heard another voice, a male one, but she couldn't make out the words. She stiffened, her chest tightening, and put her arms around Bobby.

"She's not here, I tell you. You've got no right—" Ron shouted again. Brandy's eyes widened and she looked at Liz, who glanced back at her, frightened. Brandy clutched at Bobby, pulling him right to her chest. She knew already, in a way.

Suddenly they were all in the room at once: three policemen and Ron. Brandy shrank back in her chair. Bobby stopped chewing and looked up at the police, his mouth hanging open and his eyes wide. Val and Dave flattened themselves against the walls.

"Which one of you is Amanda Botley?" the policeman said, looking around at the women.

Brandy's face became very still. She focused on the policeman's top button, as she'd learned to do long ago, and stared.

"I have a warrant for your arrest here, girl. You better answer."

"You can't!" Liz shrieked, squeezing her slight body between the mass of blue uniforms and her sister hunched on the chair. "What's she done? She hasn't done anything!"

"Grievous assault, miss, that's the charge. We believe you know what it's about. Are you Elizabeth Botley?"

"Mrs. Ronald Dunbar," Liz said fiercely.

The policeman shrugged. "Well, you're the other sister, right?

We're going to need you to come along to the station later for questioning." He put both hands on Liz's shoulders, moving her aside as if she were a lamp, and pushed his way past Dave and Val until he stood over Brandy. "Now, let's not have any trouble here. Your sister can bring your things later. Come along."

Brandy squeezed Bobby tighter but didn't take her eyes off the button. The policeman bent down and took her arm.

"Get away from my boy!" Ron shouted, elbowing the officer aside. He tore Bobby off Brandy's lap and glared at the policeman. "Show me the warrant. That's the law."

The officer nodded to one of his colleagues but kept hold of Brandy's arm. She felt herself rise in his grip. The second officer took a slip of paper out of his notebook, unfolded it, and held it out to Ron.

Ron read it, his face paling. "What's this all about, Liz?" he said.

"Come along now," the other officer said to Brandy. He pulled her into the hall.

"Aunty!" Bobby cried, leaning out of Ron's arms.

Ron handed Bobby to Liz and they all stumbled after the policemen, their mouths in astonished O's.

Outside a Black Maria was waiting, its sides glistening like wet ink, and two more officers were standing by the open doors at the back. When Brandy saw the Maria, she moaned and tried to collapse out of the policeman's arms. The neighbors gathered on the pavement to watch.

"She's a right little wild one," said the officer, gasping. He put his hands under her armpits and yanked her to her feet, twisting both arms behind her back.

"Stop, don't do that!" Ron shouted, staggering forward.

One of the policemen pushed him back gently. "Best keep out of the way, sir," he said. "The less fuss you make the less you'll frighten the boy." He gave Bobby a gooey smile.

Bobby stared at him, turning his head back and forth between the policeman smiling at him and the sight of his aunty being bundled into that horrible black machine. "Aunty!" he wailed, trying to struggle out of his mother's arms. "Aunty!"

"It'll be all right, Bobby," Brandy called, as she finally let them heave her into the back of the van. She desperately wanted to reassure him, but he was crying so loudly by now she didn't think he could hear her. "I'll be all right, don't worry!" They tossed her in and slammed the doors, locking them quickly.

Brandy grabbed the bars on the window and pushed her eyes up to the light. She saw Liz and Ron standing there ashen-faced and bewildered, surrounded by people, with Bobby sobbing in Liz's arms. "I'll be back soon, Bobby! I will!" she shouted, but Bobby kept screaming as she was driven away, his crying face getting paler and smaller until it disappeared.

15

Reardon squeezed into the reserved pew with the other officers. The service had already started and she was late, but she didn't care. Yawning loudly, she surveyed the rows of pudgy backs in front of her, their bra lines showing and their shirts untucked, and poked a couple of whispering girls in the ribs. As the only officer who took the service seriously, it was her duty to see that the girls behaved.

There had been a time when the Sunday service was the high point of Reardon's week, when the beauty of the priest's gilded robes and words had replenished her soul for its work. But gradually, as the months inside turned gray and monotonous, those words lost their power. Instead of drinking them in eagerly, as she had in the early days, she found her mind wandering now to daydreams of love or escape, even to thoughts of home. She seemed to spend more time dozing or disciplining these days than attending to whatever was left of her soul.

The priest finished the prayer, fussed for a moment with his robe (Reardon had heard the girls call him Missy Prissy), and announced the hymn, William Whiting's "Eternal Father, Strong to Save." She noticed that his complexion was unusually red, as if he'd been fortifying himself on the communion wine, and that he never once looked up to face the congregation. Some people have no strength, she thought, and forced herself to concentrate on the hymn.

> Eternal Father, strong to save,
> Whose arm doth bind the restless wave,
> Who bidst the mighty ocean deep
> Its own appointed limits keep:
> O hear us when we cry to thee
> For those in peril on the sea.

She glanced over to the one window in the Borstal chapel, barred like all the others, and thought about how far the sea was from there, how even if she were right on the sea she would barely know it, shut away as she was from natural light and air; how far not only the sea but the Eternal Father Himself seemed from that place. She remembered believing that God had sent her to the Borstal, and sighed, for He seemed to have forgotten her now. Were any sailors anywhere singing for the likes of her and these girls? There wasn't much difference, she thought, between floating lost on the sea and being here. Not much difference at all.

An inmate in front of her burped loudly and a group of girls began singing obscene words to the hymn. Reardon sighed and strained to hear them, but she could only pick up "O hear us when we cry to thee / For those in peril when we pee." She clucked her tongue but in truth she had long passed beyond being shocked by the girls' irreverence. Even when one of them made slurping noises as the priest sipped Christ's blood from the communion goblet, she only shrugged. She glanced at him, wondering if he had heard, but he plowed on regardless. Did he still feel he was saving souls? Shutting her eyes, she tried not to count the minutes.

Back in the wing, the girls started to give Reardon trouble the minute she entered. Sundays tended to be like that, everyone antsy, looking for a row. "What's got up your arse, miss?" one shouted, noticing the scowl on Reardon's face. "Lover-boy stood you up last night, did he?"

"Mind your tongue or I'll snip it off." Reardon banged the

gate shut, sending echoes up and down the walls, and locked it with a loud jangle of keys.

"Miss, me bucket's got no soap," another complained. They were on weekend muck-out, down on their knees scrubbing the cell floors. Weekends were always hard, the girls remembering that outside people were finding men, going out, living life without them. The place reeked of Sunday gloom and stale sleep.

"Wash the bloody floor with spit then." Reardon pulled a chair out of the staff room and sat down against the wall. She folded her arms and frowned into space.

"You on induction tomorrow?" an officer asked, strolling up to her. She was a weak-willed Manchester woman named Clarkson, who had started working at Bullwood Hall only three months earlier. She drove Reardon potty with her relentless cheerfulness. Reardon scowled at her.

"Nah, I get Mondays off. I never do induction if I can help it."

"Lucky sod, I can't stand it, either." Induction meant a new influx of girls, some fresh, some returned. At the mention of it Reardon felt a familiar flicker of hope, like a dull flame in her chest.

Reardon hadn't always avoided induction. She used to enjoy the busyness and break from routine—the new girls arriving, the staff having to separate them into appropriate wings, to sort out their pathetic belongings in boxes, to strip them and delouse them and search them for drugs. But after a time induction came to depress her. She didn't like seeing the first-timers' fear turn into numbness, or the bitterness of the recidivists harden like rust. She preferred to lie on her bed, she found, safely alone, wondering how many girls had arrived and how many she already knew.

On some days the new inmates came in clusters, gathered from various courts and holding cells around the country, but lately there had tended to be only one or two at a time. Reardon had heard rumors that the government was talking about closing down Bullwood Hall, there not being enough criminal girls in Britain to fill it, but that only made her laugh. She knew as well as anyone that the law had nowhere else to put all the runaways and child prostitutes and mental cripples it sent her way. Why, the place was full of fourteen-year-olds who were officially too young to be there. And who else was going to look after the poor sods? Reardon asked herself. Who else would take in a girl like that Suzy on her wing, who was eighteen but looked twelve and had never had a home in her life? Who else would cope with that crazy Margot up in Martyn House, who had been raped by her father and uncle and all her brothers and spent each night screaming at them out of her cell window? No decent citizen would do it, Reardon knew that. She'd seen the attitude out there, the people who tutted and wrote a small check, then went to the theater. Nah, she knew the only people daft enough to care for these human cast-offs were women like her, stupid and slow and good for nothing else. Women who fall in love with girls and couldn't fit into the real world if they wanted to. Women whose faith disappears with the ease of melting sugar.

Clarkson shifted up nearer to Reardon and leaned against the wall, her eyes bright for conversation. "Did you see *Kojak* last night?"

Reardon glanced at her irritably. "Nah, can't stand him. He looks like a giant thumb."

"Ooh, I think he's dead sexy. I love that voice of his. D'you think all the men in America are like that?"

"Like thumbs, you mean?"

Clarkson tittered. "You aren't half in a sour mood these days, Roanna. Maybe you should transfer or something."

Reardon unconsciously raised a hand to her chest and massaged. "Where to? It'd be the same anywhere, I reckon. Adult women would be worse than this lot, probably." She shook her head and yawned. "I dunno, I'm thinking of chucking the whole thing in. I've had enough of living with these tarts." She eyed the girls as they packed away their scrubbing tools. "You watch it, Smith! I can see you!"

"What d'you think you'd do instead, Roanna?"

"I dunno. You got any suggestions?"

"Why don't you join the police? That's what a mate of mine did."

"What, me? Imagine what I'd look like in one of them daft little hats. And all of them coppers groping me all the time? No thanks."

Clarkson thought it unlikely that any man, copper or not, would grope Reardon, but she only said, "Yeah, I see what you mean. I don't know what else you could do though. If I did, don't you think I'd be doing it meself?"

That was the kind of conversation that filled Reardon's life.

The next day, Monday, Reardon spent the morning lazing in her room. It was autumn now, the early, uncertain part of the season when the days swing from hot to cold, and all week Reardon had gazed out of the Borstal windows, longing to be under the leaves, watching them fall and catch in her hair. Now that she had the chance, however, her longing was fast submerging in apathy and fatigue. Often, lately, she hadn't the energy to do anything on her days off but lie on her bed, staring at the white ceiling and drifting. Her life was in limbo, waiting for something to begin or end.

Eventually she got up, yawning, and went to the staff room to look for the post. Nodding in response to the jokes of the other officers, she leafed absently through the pile of letters and cards. What a laugh, hoping she'd get a letter, she told herself. Who would write to her? Her father had refused to have anything to do with her since she'd gone in for prison work, her sisters were too busy chasing fancy men, and her mother . . . her poor mother could barely hold a pen these days, her hands were so stiff from the jam factory. The only sort of letter Reardon could expect to get was bad news: a death, or one of her sisters ending up in the nick, like her, only on the wrong side.

"Oy, Roanna." It was Murdock. Warming up to take the piss again, no doubt, Reardon thought.

"What?" Reardon went on shifting the mail about.

"You heard the news?"

Some of the other officers tittered, and Reardon looked up suspiciously. "What news?"

Murdock nudged Clarkson, who blinked her stupid small eyes and grinned. Reardon looked from one to the other.

"Someone you might be interested in arrived today."

Reardon felt her heart speed up with a lurch. What was Clarkson grinning about? She didn't know anything. "Oh yeah?" Reardon said, trying to sound indifferent.

"A certain little birdy." Murdock laughed, sat down, and put her feet up on the desk where Reardon was sorting the letters. Her feet were thick and fat, and in their beige stockings and black shoes they looked like sledgehammers. Reardon glanced at Murdock's face, its prickly moustache, its brown teeth grinning. She never had understood why the woman was so popular with the girls. She was the devil incarnate to work with.

"What are you talking about, Murdock?" Reardon pitched her voice low, hoping to sound bored.

"Got any cake to spare, miss?" Murdock parroted in a perfect Birmingham accent.

Reardon rushed out of the room.

The induction unit was quiet by the time Reardon reached it, the shower turned off, the boxes put away, the disinfectant bottles back on their shelves, for the processing was already finished and the new girls tucked away in their various wings. Reardon peered in to see if anyone was there and, finding no one, unlocked the storage room and slipped in, closing the door behind her. She turned on the light and stood in the middle of the room, her heart beating so hard she thought it would knock her over. She ran her eyes over the shelves, praying, wishing, dreading. At first she didn't see it, too jumpy to concentrate. Perhaps Murdock had been having her on. Perhaps it was just another of the woman's idiotic tricks. But then she caught sight of it, up on the top shelf with all the other cartons where the girls' things were stored until they could be catalogued and given back. BOTLEY. She lunged at it and pulled it down, a small box with no lid and a scribbled label. Trembling, she looked inside. What she saw almost broke her heart. A red toothbrush, pathetically pale in the dim room. A few sticks of makeup. A pair of jeans, some absurdly high red platform shoes, and—at this Reardon almost sobbed for joy—the old cough drop tin. Reardon reached in and picked it up, smearing it with the sweat of her palms. She opened it reverently, her only chance to see it before it was returned to Brandy. Inside she found one roll-up, some sprinkles of tobacco, and beside it, wrinkled and a little curled at the corners, a photograph of a baby boy.

Hearing a noise, Reardon quickly put the box back, locked the room behind her, and made her way to the front desk. She opened the roster and looked up Brandy's name. Brandy was in House Two this time, and Reardon's hopes sank. She could try to get transferred to that wing, she supposed, but it would look so obvious. She glanced at the clock and ran upstairs, smelling the stink of anxiety thicken around her like a mist.

Outside House Two, just as Reardon had her hand on the gate, she stopped herself and backed away. Murdock was on that House. There would be talk, it would be intolerable. Reardon leaned against the wall and put her hands over her face. God, woman, she told herself, what are you doing? The girl doesn't care. She doesn't need you. Wake up! But the reasoning only drove her away for a moment. The most she could do was make herself wait until night.

Reardon didn't know how she passed the afternoon. She only

knew that it crawled. She tried staying in her room, but the walls pressed down on her so hard she thought they were stopping time. She tried walking around the grounds, staring at the grass or the leaves, copper and dull red, but that only made her cold with nerves. She tried making cups of tea, but they felt like acid going down. She told herself to put her mind on other things, to go shopping or see a flick, to act normal. Instead she sat with her head in her hands, and squeezed.

At last, somehow, it was night. Murdock would be safely out of the wing by now, the coast relatively clear. With her mind pulling her one way and her body the other, Reardon got up and stood in front of the mirror. Slowly, moving as if in a trance, she unpinned her hair, watching it tumble, imagining Brandy's fingers combing through it, lifting it, dropping it—her curtain of beads. She began to brush it, running the bristles through and through until the brown hairs caught amber and glowed and the electricity crackled around her head like a halo. Her hair fell in thick strands over her uniform, covering the ugly, sharp shoulders and buttons like a fur. She didn't notice how her hair contrasted with her face, how its gentle femininity clashed with the heaviness of her jaw and brow. She felt beautiful.

On the fourteenth brush stroke, she glanced at the clock and panicked. "My God, I'm going to miss her." Without looking back, she threw down the brush and ran out of the room, stumbling along the carpeted hallways, heedless of whom she might run into. She ran across the courtyard, through the shadows, her heavy shoes crashing, her hair flying, her keys clattering madly at her sides. And finally she stood, panting, outside Brandy's wing, her heart pounding like a thief's.

Inside the wing it was dark, except for a few lights shining from beneath the cell doors. Reardon shrank back into the shadows. Her hair fell over her face and her eyes glistened behind it as she searched for the officer on duty. She heard footsteps above and looked up to see the bottom of a warder's feet pacing the balcony, shoes creaking, the metal ringing under her steps, her nails scraping along the banisters. "Come on, you bitch," Reardon whispered between clenched teeth. She looked around the room, wondering which cell was Brandy's.

When the warder reached the opposite end of the wing, Reardon slid through the shadows to the cell doors hidden under the balcony and began to lift the spyhole flaps, peering through them like a pervert at a peepshow. The girls swiveled their heads at the sound, looking like the mechanical dolls at a penny arcade, but none of them was Brandy.

Reardon pressed herself to the wall and slid around to the other side of the wing. Above her the warder was still pacing, and now Reardon was in full view if the woman chose to turn and look down. Reardon stood frozen next to a cell door, barely hidden by the shadows, but the warder seemed preoccupied and just stared at her feet as she paced. Reardon turned to lift another spyhole. The girl inside looked up, her eyes streaming with tears under the harsh cell light, and Reardon almost stumbled in shock.

"What d'you fucking want?" Brandy hissed, her voice catching. "Can't you leave me alone?"

"Shh." Reardon pushed her lips up to the hole. "It's me, Roanna." She pulled away again so that she could look at Brandy now that the girl was flesh and blood, so that she could watch her actually move and talk.

Brandy stood up. She was dressed in new tight clothes from home that Reardon had never seen, and Reardon was surprised at how much thinner she'd become. Her hair was bright yellow all over now, and cut so that it lay smoothly on her head. Her face was tan, and her green eyes seemed to shine right out like the marbles children get from bubble gum dispensers. She looked so different that Reardon didn't know what to say. Brandy walked closer to the spyhole and stared at it. "What d'you want?" she said flatly.

"I . . ." Reardon wavered, ashamed, and glanced over her shoulder at the warder above. "I heard you were back today," she whispered. "I just came to see if you're all right."

"Well, you can see for yourself."

"D'you need anything?"

"Yeah, the key." Brandy looked at her, eyes flashing.

"I'm just trying to help, love. I do care, y'know." Reardon swallowed, wondering where she was getting the courage for such words.

Brandy's face softened a little, but her voice was still guarded. She stepped nearer the door. "Aren't you coming in, then?" she said at last. "I can't see you at all through that fucking rathole."

Reardon shook her head, then, realizing that Brandy couldn't even see that, whispered, "I can't. I don't have the cell keys to this wing." She glanced up. The warder above her seemed to have disappeared, which puzzled Reardon for a moment until she thought, Good God, the woman must have a girl, too. Reardon

192

was glad Brandy couldn't see her. That way she could hide the joy that was splashing through her like a purge. "What happened, love?" she whispered. "What're you doing back here so soon?" Brandy was looking down at her fingers, tearing at them in her old way.

Brandy shrugged. "What do you fucking think?"

Reardon reached out to touch her, forgetting where she was for a moment, and hit her hand against the thick wall. "Bad out there, was it?" she said.

Brandy shook her head, Reardon's kind voice triggering the tears again. "No . . ." Her throat caught. Reardon watched her struggle with herself. "That wasn't it," she croaked at last. "It was great. I was doing it, Roanna, I really was. I was making it out there!" Suddenly her mouth screwed up and her face went red. "Oh, God, I don't want to be back!" The last word came out a wail and she started crying again.

"Shh, love, shhh." Reardon glanced around uneasily, pressing her body against the wall as if her warmth could somehow penetrate it. "Come over here."

Brandy stumbled forward and put her fingers through the spyhole, needing comfort. Reardon took hold of them gently, resisting the impulse to kiss them.

"There, there, love, I'll look after you." She stroked Brandy's knuckles.

"I had a family out there," Brandy said with a sob. "It was working out." She let her fingers rest in Reardon's.

"You'll be all right," Reardon whispered. "You will, I know it."

Brandy shook her head, although Reardon couldn't see her, and pressed her forehead to the wall. "How long d'you think they'll keep me here, Roanna?"

"What did they do you for?"

"GBH." Pulling her hand away, Brandy stepped back so that Reardon could see her. "I tried to choke me mother."

Reardon gazed at Brandy's tough face, amazed. There the girl stood, her jaw set and her eyes shining like some Crusader's on the march, not even aware of what she'd said. She had confessed! She'd just up and blurted out the truth the way Borstal girls never did, the way even Reardon never had. Reardon blinked, thinking of her own cowardice, of the harm she'd done Brandy, the secret that was a burning shame inside her. "She's all right now though, your mum, isn't she?" Reardon said.

Brandy shrugged. "Yeah, I s'pose." She looked at Reardon pleadingly. "I didn't mean . . ."

"I know, love, I know."

"So how long do you think they'll keep me?"

Reardon paused, considering. It wasn't the first time she'd heard of such a thing. Those mothers who never came to visit, the ones who never wrote. "I dunno, love . . . it could be worse. We'll get you out of here soon, you'll see. I'll do what I can."

"Will you?" Brandy stared at Reardon through the hole, trying to make out the woman's sincerity from the segment of eye and nose she could see. "I'll be as good as fucking gold if I have to, Roanna," Brandy said fiercely. "I did it before, didn't I? I would've got out early if that cake thing hadn't bollixed me up, wouldn't I?"

Reardon blushed in the dark. "Course you would, love. You can do it again, I know you can." She thought of the hymn the day before, of those in peril, of the need to save, and the last verse came back to her:

From rock and tempest, fire and foe,
Protect them wheresoe'er they go.

She really would try to help Brandy this time, she decided. She wouldn't do it for sex—Brandy was worth more than that. She would do it for faith. And for forgiveness. Maybe this was the mission she'd been seeking, she thought, maybe this was the way she could get back to God.

Brandy drifted away from the hole and sat on the bed, off again in her own thoughts. Reardon watched her. The girl seemed so solid, even framed as she was by the narrow spyhole. Her shoulders were square and firm, her head up and free of secrets. Reardon pressed closer to the wall, her longing and goodwill rushing together in a surge of faith, and put her lips up to the hole.

"Brandy?" she whispered. "Don't worry love, we'll find a way."

Brandy swiveled her head and looked at her from across the cell.